THE LAST RESORT

A WANDERLUST MYSTERY

THE LAST RESORT

APRIL STAR

FIVE STAR
A part of Gale, Cengage Learning

GALE
CENGAGE Learning

Detroit • New York • San Francisco • New Haven, Conn • Waterville, Maine • London

GALE
CENGAGE Learning

Set in 11 pt. Plantin.
Printed on permanent paper.

LIBRARY OF CONGRESS CATALOGING-IN-PUBLICATION DATA

Star, April.
    The last resort : a wanderlust mystery / by April Star. — 1st ed.
        p. cm.
    ISBN-13: 978-1-59414-768-5 (hardcover : alk. paper)
    ISBN-10: 1-59414-768-X (hardcover : alk. paper)
    1. Ocean bottles—Fiction. 2. Private Investigators—Fiction. 3. Murder—Investigation—Fiction. 4. Saint Augustine (Fla.)—Fiction. I. Title.
    PS3619.T37L37 2009
    813'.6—dc22   2009005242

First Edition. First Printing: June 2009.
Published in 2009 in conjunction with Tekno Books and Ed Gorman.

Printed in the United States of America
1 2 3 4 5 6 7 13 12 11 10 09

DEDICATION

Dedicated to my husband and best friend, Jerry. You made this possible by standing beside me, always glowing with an ever-shining light, even in the darkest of nights. Always there when needed and without fail, not just for me, but you shine a light upon others to help them sail as well. Like a shining beacon amid the pounding surf, your love and support has always cast a light upon the most uncertain things. Thank you. I love you with all my heart and till the end of all time. You are my forever inspiration.

ACKNOWLEDGEMENTS

I believe every good story is a gift of divine inspiration. Thank you, St. Jude, for all your help.

As always, to my parents, Curtis and Magdalen Stahl, my most loving and encouraging supporters. Thank you. When God was handing out parents, I was truly blessed. I love you both.

My thanks to D. P. Lyle, MD, for sharing your expertise on forensics. Your thorough explanation of how a medical examiner would uncover secrets from a charred body helped in moving my story forward with authenticity and factual creativity.

A special thanks to the staff of Anastasia State Park in St. Augustine, Florida, for your warm hospitality and chilling explanations as to why certain areas of your park would make for a good place to "dump a body"! My fictional Harbor Lights RV Resort was inspired by your beautiful park.

Finally, to you, the reader. Your enthusiasm and impatience for this second title in my series gave me all the motivation and determination I needed to continue the journey with great joy and anticipation. Thank you. Without you there would be no true purpose for authors.

PROLOGUE

The cloaking fog appeared strangely protective. There were areas along Anastasia Island's coastline where no one could hear you scream. And it was in such an area that the bottle was launched, spinning through the air and landing with a splash. It bobbed and weaved quietly eight feet above the sandy bottom before deciding on a direction. It seemed to be floating a quarter mile off the northerly point of St. Augustine Harbor.

As the day progressed, feeling the pull of the tide, the bottle moved imperceptibly westward before making a gradual circuit around the jetty outward along Salt Run inlet starting its journey into the path of the sunlight. Glinting through the sparkling Atlantic, the bottle reflected blue, gold, and pink.

Three days later it had cleared the inlet area and was moving north by northwest, about two hundred feet offshore, in fifteen feet of water along the Ancient Sand Dunes.

The rolling waves of the Atlantic and gentle westerly breeze blew across the tropics. Despite the westerly wind, the bottle continued to float west. St. Augustine, Florida, has over four and a half miles of beach that stretch along the northeastern tip of Anastasia Island. It is situated right in the middle of modern Florida—a mere forty miles from the glassy skyscrapers of downtown Jacksonville, one hundred miles from the rocket ships of Kennedy Space Center, and one hundred miles from the fantasy theme parks of Orlando—but its nearly four and a half centuries of history make it seem worlds away. The bottle had floated aimlessly for over two hundred miles and seven days before drifting into an offshore basin where the water circulated in a counterclockwise motion. The bottle was in the extreme south of this basin. The circulation moved the bottle westward, back toward home.

For two days, the bottle washed back and forth against the rock and wooden structure of the south end of the jetty, as if it were uncertain whether to go inside, toward St. Augustine, or outside back into the Atlantic.

The romantic symbolism of bottles containing proclamations of love and being tossed out to sea has intrigued people for as long as there have been bottles. Oceanographers have charted these romantic journeys; Hollywood has made blockbuster movies centered on the tenderness of the notion.

The bottle that had been hurled out into the Atlantic on a balmy spring day from St. Augustine Harbor contained no messages of undying love and passion. Nor did it contain charts or maps of shipwrecks. What it did contain were secrets, lies, betrayals, and the most unspeakable of crimes: murder. And just as the journey of the bottle itself, its contents would alter the course and direction of many lives, beginning with the life of whomever discovered this message in a bottle.

ONE

"Gone forever!"

"Murdered!"

"Dead!"

"How could this have happened? How could her mother be dead, when less than a week ago she was alive and well? Poor Gracie."

Campers and staff spoke in hushed whispers, condolences mingling with mixed emotions of anger, shock, and disbelief. Men quietly touched Gracie's shoulder; women embraced her and murmured their offers of help; everyone asked if there was anything they could do, any way they could further assist the authorities. Mourners, not sunbathers, covered the St. Augustine beach.

In spite of the intense heat, Gracie Schaffer shivered with a sudden sense of foreboding, as if a shadow had blocked the sun. Her breath caught in her throat. She stopped short, ambushed by an unexpected wave of torment, but the sensation of imminent disaster passed as quickly as it had arrived.

She had to get out of here, away from these people. She headed back toward the resort. Humidity engulfed her like wet cotton batting and dispersed the remnants of her sudden chill.

Gracie fought her way through the endlessly long days of memories, the painfully heart-wrenching moments when she could not resist looking at the happy, smiling face of Patricia

Marsh, her mother, in framed photographs throughout her home.

She spent a few nights in her mother's modest, comfortable art studio just behind the house, recalling her childhood, how her parents had never seemed to want her around. Growing up, Gracie knew the feeling of isolation and loneliness.

Gracie recalled her mother's insistence that she go to a private boarding school, to which her father had initially objected. But it had been the right decision, all the more so because of the frequent outbursts between her parents—and her father's violent temper.

With a fond smile, she remembered the way her mother disliked flaunting her considerable wealth, instead preferring the simple and quiet pleasures of life. Once the divorce was final, it was only months before Cory swept Gracie's mother off her feet.

The thought that such a giving, caring individual could have been murdered only made the tragic loss of her mother more distressing. What kind of person killed like that? Gracie wondered over and over. Whoever had killed her mother had to be found, stopped, dealt with.

After a few days of being alone with these tortured thoughts, Gracie resumed her duties as the now new manager of Harbor Lights RV Resort. Her position there kept her busy meeting daily needs of the campers, but she often found herself distracted by painful emotions. Unbidden images of her mother's murder interrupted her concentration.

All the staff, a group of incredibly compassionate people, seemed to try to understand. But in the frantic pace of a seasonal resort, anyone who failed to move quickly and attentively toward the ultimate goal of placing the "happy" in the "happy campers" could create complications.

Gracie returned many times to her mother's bedroom and

studio, gathering up the small treasures she wished to keep for herself. After the will had been read, she knew she could not live in the house where so many, many loving memories would haunt her constantly. Cory. She wondered what he was feeling now. What memories were going through his mind? Was he thinking of her as she was him? Should she go to him? Comfort him? She was tormented by the undeniable passion they had for one another, increased now by the guilt of her mother's demise.

Gracie felt the acute responsibility of having to settle all matters regarding her mother's estate. At the reading of the will, she'd not been surprised by the size of the trust fund left to her.

Cory leaned back in the chair in his office, studying Gracie over his glasses, and said, "You don't have to work this hard. We could spare you a few days, you know."

Cory Marsh, at forty-five, was twenty-five years her senior; but he was an invitingly handsome forty-five. Suave, sexy, and debonair. Strong, well-muscled shoulders filled out his shirt above a trim waist. When Gracie looked into his face she found herself gazing again at the most gorgeous gray eyes she had ever seen. A tickly sensation in her belly made her look away with a shiver. She focused instead on his left hand, which still bore the ring on that all-important finger.

She smiled, shook her head. "I need to work, keep myself busy instead of brooding. But . . ."

"But what?" he asked.

"It's just that I keep wondering why the authorities haven't found out what exactly happened to Mom."

He sighed, rubbing his eyes. "Who knows? Didn't they question you, and then explain about why there were no suspects?"

"Yes, an investigator I saw there . . ." She swallowed hard, unable to avoid the painful memory of having to identify her mother's belongings in a morgue. No one could identify the body, charred to ashes beyond recognition.

"Gracie, darling, are you sure you don't need some time away from here, a vacation or something?"

She shrugged. "Maybe."

"How about the crime victims' meetings?"

"I've been attending, but I feel like I need to do more, try and find out something else about the murder . . ."

"You are a fine woman, and the investigative pieces you've done in your journalism classes were good work, but you're too personally involved in this situation. Besides, my dear, that's what investigators are for, to find these savage criminals. You could get killed yourself if you did somehow locate the murderer before the police did."

She bit her lip, knowing Cory was right, but that didn't stop her from saying, "I need to get out of here for a bit. I'm going to take a walk on the beach."

"I'd warn you to be careful, but . . . well, knowing how impulsive and persistent you can be, I'd be wasting my breath." He grinned. "Yes, go for a walk. Get some air and clear your mind. But I want to stress I consider this time to deal with your grief, not go chasing after a killer."

"Thanks. And I will try to be cautious," she said, knowing he couldn't very well condone her conduct, but that, as a former reporter himself, he did understand. She went back to her desk, where she turned off her computer, grabbed her purse, and left the building.

Once outside, she stopped at the sound of a familiar voice. Mom?

But a deathly silence was the only response.

TWO

The drive from Big Pine Key to St. Augustine took David and Laura a little over twelve hours. There were a number of reasons the 438-mile drive, normally made in eight hours tops, took them so long. One was the fact that David had never before driven a motor home, and the Featherlite Vantare Platinum Plus with a Saturn SKY Roadster in tow became quite the challenge. He was given the middle-finger salute so many times that he concluded it had most likely originated when the first motor home driver entered the first highway. Another factor was Laura acting upon her passions and desires along Interstate 95 as David swerved in and out of the traffic in Daytona. David was pleased, but he wasn't keen on crashing.

She also insisted they name their home on wheels. David finally gave up his argument of, "But, my dear, you don't name motor homes—only boats!" Somewhere on the Florida Turnpike, between Ft. Lauderdale and Ft. Pierce, in one of many stops at a service plaza, their mansion on wheels became properly christened *Passion's Palace*.

Now, after a relatively restful night in their new home, David and Laura took an early morning stroll along Anastasia Beach, located directly adjacent to the Harbor Lights RV Resort.

Laura dug her toes into the deep sand as she looked out at the vast Atlantic, the gentle breeze blowing through her hair. She lifted her head for a moment, savoring the trailing ocean spray washing over her. She felt her blood surging at the touch of David's lips on her neck. As they proceeded to walk away, hand-in-hand, her toes touched upon a bottle. Her foot jerked back with thoughts of poisonous jellyfish.

"What? What's the matter?" David asked. Startled from her sudden jerk.

"I stepped on something. I don't know what." Her eyes followed David's hand as he bent down to retrieve the object.

"It's just a bottle," he said, handing it to her in proof.

Laura held the clear triangular-shaped bottle to the sunlight. "A bottle with sand in it. That's strange. I wonder where it came from."

"The ocean."

"I know the ocean. But look . . ." She handed it back to David, pointing at its contents. "That sand or whatever didn't get in there by itself. I've heard of people tossing messages out to sea in bottles—but sand?"

David tipped the bottle from side to side. "It doesn't look like any sand around here. Not white and powdery like this beach. Almost looks like ashes." Upon more careful inspection, he noticed fragments of some unidentifiable matter.

There wasn't a cloud in the sky; it was as clear and blue as the ocean itself. They'd only been in St. Augustine half a day, but Laura had already fallen in love with the quaint and historic city. After the departure of the others on the beach, she'd had the feeling of being on a deserted tropical island with the man she loved with every fiber of her being.

The waves continued to roll up steadily on the shore, and Laura was beginning to see that bottle as an intrusion.

"You're staring at that thing as if you expect a genie to pop out of it." She received no reply and she smiled as she watched David tilt the bottle in one direction and his head in the other as he gently shook the bottle. "Helllloooo . . ." She waved her hand between the bottle and his face.

"Sorry." He let out a long, frustrated sigh. "I think we've stumbled upon something here. I just can't figure out what."

"I stumbled upon it, and that something is just a bottle. Some little child building sand castles somewhere probably filled it with sand and tossed it out in the ocean. No big mystery, David." She took his arm and, with the bottle still firmly grasped in his free hand, they headed back toward the campground. She'd felt a twinge of curiosity herself over the bottle but wasn't about to let David know. After all, she was the logical-minded one in this marriage. He was the analytical one. She could see a whole new investigation about to begin. It was their combined logic and analyzing that'd helped them close in on Slippery, the stalker back in Big Pine Key, and she'd no doubt it would be those same traits that would eventually uncover what that bottle was all about.

Even though it was the end of March and the end of the tourist season was fast approaching, Highway A1A, which ran north to south along the coast, was still bumper-to-bumper as they waited to cross the highway to the resort. Travelers along this route could see unobstructed shoreline views and quaint beachside communities.

"Looks familiar," Laura said as she pointed at a group of about a dozen campers perched on a picnic table around a Bounder motor home. "What is it about camping resorts that seems to bring out the gossipmonger in all of us?"

"What else do they have to do? They're retired and bored." David seemed especially interested in one of the members of the group. A pretty little blonde in her twenties. "She certainly looks out of place," he commented.

Laura raised her eyes to inspect the blonde, keeping her head down so as not to look conspicuous. "Doesn't look too happy, either."

As they passed the group toward their campsite, a woman's

voice startled them.

"Excuse me, you two."

Laura turned to see the blonde coming toward them.

"Pardon. You speaking to us?" Laura replied.

"Yes." She extended her hand. "I'm Gracie Schaffer, manager of Harbor Lights." Her eyes and attention seemed to be more focused on David, almost ignoring Laura completely.

David sensed her curiosity. He released his hand from Laura's and extended it to Gracie. "Nice to meet you. This is my lovely bride, Laura."

"Beautiful place you have here," Laura said without her smile and in a formal tone of voice.

"Thank you. What's that?" Gracie asked, nodding at the object in David's hand.

He looked at the bottle, then at Gracie. Shaking it up and down he replied, "Oh, this? Interesting, don't you think? Just washed ashore and ended up right at our feet. Strangest thing— seems to be filled with sand from some origin other than around here." He passed it over to Gracie. "Want to take a look?"

"Someone's always polluting the ocean with something." She took a step back. "How long are you here for?"

"A month," Laura answered. *So get those saucer-sized blue eyes off my man. Now.* "Then we're heading to Alabama for the NASCAR races."

"Well, I hope you enjoy your stay. If there's anything we can do, just give a yell." Gracie turned and headed toward a rustic-looking building with a sign marked OFFICE.

"Bye," David called out.

"Prissy little thing," Laura said, watching Gracie disappear inside the building. "And don't you think she's kind of young to be managing a resort?"

"I don't know," David said. "Let's go introduce ourselves to the neighbors." Knowing exactly what he'd better do, he took her hand, kissed it, and they headed toward the group where Gracie had been.

Laura gave his arm a jerk. "Wait," she whispered. "Listen." They hesitated behind a huge oak tree that sprawled over the Bounder motor home and the group in front of it."

"What exactly happened?" They heard an older woman ask. She was dressed in a royal blue t-shirt and khaki shorts. "I understand an autopsy was performed. Anyone hear anything of the results?"

"There was no autopsy cuz there was no body to slice and dice," an old, skinny, unshaven man answered.

"I dunno anything about an autopsy, but I heard the cops found something on the beach," another woman chimed in.

"I heard that, too," said another. "Same area that just happened to be Patricia's favorite spot."

The group became silent.

"Let's go," David whispered as he pulled Laura out from behind the tree.

Her foot had gone to sleep. "Ouch!" she yelled.

Startled, the skinny little man hopped off the picnic table and called out, "Someone there?"

"Hi," David answered. He helped Laura as she hopped behind him. "I'm David Jennings and this is my wife Laura. She stubbed her toe." He looked at Laura, who picked up on his cue and started rubbing her foot.

"You okay?" the man asked.

He looked like a nice man. Nicer than he sounded, Laura thought. "I'm fine, thank you."

"You new to Harbor Lights? I don't believe I've seen you around here. I'm Ethel Carter." Ethel Carter extended her hand first to David and then to Laura.

"Just checked in last night," David said. He turned his head and nodded in the direction of their motor home. "Parked in site four-twenty-three."

"Ohhhh, the big bus?" Ethel was craning her neck to see if she could spot the two-point-five-million-dollar mansion from where she stood.

"We saw that roll in last night."

"That's our humble abode," David replied.

The boney man looked suspiciously at the couple. "Don't look so humble to me."

Laura ignored the comment, already feeling somewhat embarrassed by the extravagance of their home. She was still trying to get used to the fact that she was a multimillionaire's wife. "We were just returning from a day at the beach. It's lovely here. And the beach is absolutely gorgeous. All that white sand. Looks like someone dumped a truckload of salt on the island."

"We come here every year," Ethel answered. She took Laura's hand. "Come, dear . . . sit down."

"I'm Stanley Parsons," the scrawny elderly man announced. He eyed the bottle in David's hand. "You gonna toss that in the ocean or something?"

"This?" David lifted the bottle up. "No. Apparently someone already did that. Washed up to shore and we thought it'd be a unique souvenir."

"We just met Gracie," Laura said. "She seems awfully young to be managing such a big resort."

"She don't just manage it," Stanley said. "Now that her mama's dead, she and her stepdaddy own the place."

"Humph!" Ethel grumbled. "Stepdaddy! There's more hanky-panky going on around here than meets the eye."

"Regular little Peyton Place," another woman, who'd been fiddling with her crocheting, remarked. She looked up and gave an introductory nod toward Laura and David. "I'm Mildred Wright."

"Pleased, I'm sure," Laura said.

Mildred went back to pulling her needle in and around the skein of yellow yarn. "Patricia Marsh, Gracie's mother, God rest her soul. Now *she* knew how to make campers happy." She shoved the crochet needle into the yarn with force and nodded toward the office building.

"Them other two," she continued, "Gracie and Cory—they just use us seniors. I'm no teenager. You can see that yourself. I'll be eighty-five next month, although everyone tells me I don't look a day over seventy-five."

"Yeah," Stanley said. "Take today for instance. We're sitting here playing euchre and Gracie comes up to tell us she'd like us to organize a weenie roast for next weekend." He folded his hands together and then pushed them outward to crack his knuckles. "Guess they assume we're bored and would like nothin' better than to run their place."

"Laura here understands and can appreciate your beefs," David said. "She used to manage a camping resort that belongs to her family. Down in the Keys." He brushed his fingernails across his lapel. "But I swept her off her feet and rode her off into the sunset."

Laura gave David a sultry look. He had her leg up on his lap and was giving her foot one of his famous massages.

"I married him for his therapeutic touch," she said. She pulled her foot free from David's hands and stood, taking David's hand. "We really should be going," she said. "We want to change and see some of the sights."

"If you go just over the Vilano Causeway you'll be at the Castillo de San Marcos, the fort that guards this fine city," Stanley said. He reached down and picked up the bottle. "Don't forget this." He handed the bottle to David.

"Nope, don't want to forget this." David gripped the bottle. "We'll be sure to visit the fort."

The two waved and headed once again toward their motor home.

"Is it me, or is there an eerie aura about this place?" Laura asked.

"It's not you, my dear," David answered. He looked at the bottle as if waiting for it to speak the secrets buried in the resort.

THREE

The next morning it was obvious by the sluggish movements of everyone in the RV camp that no one had slept well. A campground community, regardless of its size, is like a political battlefield. Within a matter of moments, everyone knows everyone else's business. And, like a political battlefield, campers soon discover, as did David and Laura, if they're in the midst of a verbal bloodbath. Had Mother Teresa been a guest at Harbor Lights RV Resort, she too would have been a murder suspect. No one was immune to the gossip, accusations, and innuendos buzzing throughout the campground.

Jeremy Myers, a tough old retired forensic anthropologist, and Katie Green, his alluring "traveling partner," sixty-somethings, played judge and jury with the group of campers outside the campground office. "I just feel Stella might be right. It's that nasty little assistant manager," Katie said. "He runs around on his little blue golf cart, shouting and threatening we'll be outta here on the transient code if we don't all do what we're told. For chrissakes," she moaned, "what does he think we are? The Stepford Campers?"

"What's he got to do with the murder of Gracie's mother?" David asked.

Good God, Laura thought, *here we go again.* She'd thought they'd left all the mystery and mayhem behind them in Big Pine Key.

"It has everything to do with the body, Danny," replied Stella

Greenberg, a tough old broad with a beauty-shop hairdo and the metabolism of a Florida mosquito.

"David," he corrected.

"Whatever," Stella snapped. "The fact remains that charred remains were discovered on the beach . . . remains of Patricia Marsh, God rest her soul. And she was the owner of Harbor Lights. Old Sam didn't like it, Patricia being the owner of Harbor Lights, flashing all her money, so my guess is he dragged poor Patricia to the beach and read her the riot act about where a woman's place was in this world. The poor woman got so scared she probably had a heart attack. Old Sam got spooked, he killed her. Murder. Pure and simple."

Jeremy was obviously beginning to get agitated about Stella's crazy and hysterical conclusions. He clenched his jaw and cracked his knuckles. "Yes, ma'am, if you say so." He just wanted the woman to shut up.

Stella sneered and finalized the conversation. "Think what you want Mr. New York bone man. But I say Old Sam is a murderer and I hope they fry him."

"I think I know how this Stella got her groove," Laura said, taking David's hand in hers.

"That's ridiculous, Stella!" another camper argued. "I know Sam has a few screws loose and thinks because he's Cory's brother he runs the place, but I hardly think he's capable of murder."

"Everyone's capable of murder," Laura chimed in.

David gave her one of those looks—the type that says *please don't get involved.* "Who's Cory?" he asked.

Lucy Loose Lips, a member of the campground's busybody club, had kept quiet long enough. "Cory Schaffer, Patricia's husband, who soooooooo loves his stepdaughter, Gracie. And Laura's right. Hey, this is Florida. The temperature soars, the barometric pressure drops, the full moon rises, and the scum who would do anything surfaces around every corner. Know what I mean?"

"Y'all can think what you want," Margie Parker said, "but I say it's a damn pity." Better known as "the Cookie Lady," Margie was passing out Ziploc baggies of her freshly baked chocolate chip cookies as she rambled on.

"Patricia wouldn't hurt a flea, and she never said a bad word about no one." She peered in the direction of the two office clerks who were huddled on the porch. "Now, someone wants to do something like that, they oughta look at Norma Rowland. Someone needs to give her what she deserves. Yapping on all over the campground, spreading gossip about everyone, minding everyone else's business instead of her own. Hell, any one of us would have loved to have seen her shut up for good, silence her once and for all. Ms. Queen Bee of the busybody club!"

David had heard enough. What he wanted to do—no, needed to do—was get himself and Laura away from these chatty-catty campers as quickly as possible. He turned his head toward Laura and slipped his hand into hers. "Excuse us, please." He extended his hand to Jeremy. "Catch you later, Jeremy. Maybe you and Katie could join us this afternoon for some drinks."

"We'd love to," Katie answered for Jeremy. "Our place, okay?"

Laura offered Katie a wide smile as she addressed the rest of the group. "Yes, we do have to go. It's been nice meeting all of you. We'll see more of each other, I'm sure."

"About six?" Jeremy called out as the newlyweds departed.

"Great," David said. "See you guys then."

David didn't think any of the other campers heard or noticed their retreat. "Jeezus," he mumbled as they turned and headed toward their motor home. "Is this an indication of what our journey into the wild blue yonder is going to be like?"

Laura laughed. "Oh, come on. You know you love this. Mystery, murder, whodunit . . . ever since Slippery and your ingenuity in bringing him out of the shadows, you've been addicted to this sort of thing."

He shot her his famous look of innocence. "*Moi,* my darling?" He tightened his hold around her waist, pulling her to his side, and whispered in her ear, "Maybe you're right. But I did hope we'd have at least a few days of a different sort of excitement at our first stop."

Laura kissed him long and hard before pulling herself free from his hold and grabbing his hand. "Come on, I want to show you something."

"Whoa, am I ready for this?" he asked, stumbling behind her as they headed for *Passion's Palace.*

Forced to stifle the anticipation and fantasies running through his mind, David came to a complete halt, jerking Laura to a stop just in front of their motor home. "Oh-oh," he said. "The cops."

Laura turned her head, observing the way Cory had his arm wrapped around Gracie's waist. Not far from where Cory and Gracie stood, Laura watched as Stella popped out of nowhere and somehow managed to make her way to the patrol car before Cory and Gracie. Before the detective could make it out of the cruiser, the woman was tapping on his window with her walking stick.

"What are you doing in the sheriff's car? You detectives are supposed to be in unmarked cars! No wonder there's so many criminals walking the streets."

The detective looked warily at the overbearing woman as he swung his door open. "Excuse me, ma'am, I'm Detective Bradley Miles." He looked over her shoulder to where Cory and Gracie stood. "I'd like to speak with Mr. Schaffer."

Stella turned and gave Cory a distasteful and accusing stare. "Right there." She nodded toward Cory for the detective. "There's your man!" She shot Cory one more look of disgust, then stormed away, walking past David and Laura and settling at the picnic table in front of *Passion's Palace.*

"What's she plopping herself here for?" David whispered.

Laura shrugged her shoulders.

"What you guys gonna do with this bottle?" Stella called out.

"Ah-ah-ah . . . please, Stella, don't grip it like that. It'll pop loose from your hand and break!" David leaped forward and grabbed the bottle from Stella.

"David collects unusual bottles," Laura explained.

"Didn't you find this bottle on the same beach as those charred remains? I think you oughta give it to the detective there."

"Oh, Christ . . ." David mumbled. "I wonder if we can get our site changed."

Stella's little Terry travel trailer was parked directly across from David and Laura's. She'd discovered, by looking out the little window above her kitchen sink, that she had full view of both Jeremy and David and any shenanigans going on in either motor home.

"Shhhh," Laura said with a cross look. "You have to learn to just ignore campers like Stella. She's definitely one of those who have her nose into everyone's business."

"Yeah," he whispered. "Look at her sizing up Cory and Gracie." Seizing the moment of Stella's distraction, he opened the door to the motor home and placed the bottle inside. Turning to Laura, he winked as he whispered, "Maybe if we take a little walk, she'll go away."

"This is ridiculous," Laura replied. "Let's just tell her we'd like to be alone. I'm sure even she was once a newlywed and would understand."

"Don't place a wager on it, honey."

As it turned out, their problem was solved.

"Sorry, kids," Stella announced as she swung her legs over

the seat of the picnic table. "I'd love to stay and chat, but I gotta get my exercise in."

"Have a good day," Laura called out.

"Humph! Exercise. Funny how she doesn't need that walking stick now as she makes her way south to see where that detective, and Gracie and Cory, went." David watched as the woman hobbled quickly toward the resort office.

"I wonder what the detective wants with Cory," Laura said.

David walked up behind her and wrapped his arms around her midsection. "Routine," he whispered as he nibbled on her ear. "The husband is always the first suspect."

Laura brushed his mouth away with her hand. "I don't know. That detective looked pretty serious."

"I have a feeling that by tomorrow morning we'll have Stella Greenburg's full report." He kissed her neck. "Now, what was it you wanted to show me?"

"Pardon?"

David sighed. "Never mind."

FOUR

"Ready to see Saint Augustine?" David asked Laura. He bent forward and kissed her. "Burnt, just the way you like them," he said as he placed a plate of pancakes before her.

"Thanks." She gave him a sleepy-eyed look and wide smile. "I thought you said yesterday we'd just hang around here today."

"That was before detectives started showing up and people started talking about bodies being charred like burgers on the grill. Frankly, I think this is a good time to get out of here."

Laura put a forkful of pancakes into her mouth, chewed, took a sip of coffee, swallowed, and continued. "You seemed to be enjoying yourself earlier."

David resisted the urge to groan in denial. *Enjoying myself? It was a detective's nightmare! Interrogating the seventy-something members of the busybody club of Harbor Lights RV Resort.* "I enjoy being here with you. Like this. No more sleeping on your couch, protecting you from adolescent pimple-faced psycho stalkers."

Laura took her napkin and reached across the table to wipe a spot of maple syrup from David's chin. She smiled. "Yes, I fantasized about us like this so many times when I was on the other side of that door—in my bed . . ." She craned her neck to the side of her chair as her eyes traveled to David's lap. "Fantasizing about how I'd like to rip those red satin boxer shorts off of you with my teeth!"

David choked as he swallowed his mouthful of pancakes. "Pardon?"

They laughed, pushing their plates aside.

David waggled his eyebrows and nodded toward the king-sized bed.

"Don't think I'll do it, do you?" Laura made a chomping gesture with her teeth before sauntering off to the bedroom. David bolted and beat her to the bed.

Laura went to close the vertical blinds in the bedroom. From her years at Big Pine Key RV Resort, she was well aware of the number of window peepers in a campground. "What's that?" she asked, coming to a standstill. David was stretched out on the bed and propped up on his elbow with his head resting in his hand. He patted the bed. "Never mind what's that. Come here. The boxers await."

"Shush. It's that Norma woman and Detective Miles," Laura whispered. "She's got some book or something she's shoving under his nose."

David blew out an exasperated sigh and hopped off the bed. He wrapped his arms around Laura's waist and looked out over her shoulder. "Hey, we need to get us a couple of those."

"A couple of what?"

He pointed. "Those golf carts—like Norma's." He pulled her gently away from the window. "Are you gonna play *I Spy* all day or go see this fine old city? Or we could . . ." He jumped onto the bed.

Laura tossed him his cut-off shorts. "We have a lifetime for that, but only a month in Saint Augustine. Let's go."

"Guess the honeymoon's over," David grumbled.

"Pardon?"

"I said, my love for you keeps growing—over and over."

"Welcome to Saint Augustine," the trolley guide announced as she settled into the driver's seat. She pulled away from the curb and set off on a route that Laura soon realized was crisscrossing between the Old Jail, Potter's Wax Museum, and the Old Drug Store, moving back and forth, covering territory from one angle, stopping at various points to pick up more passengers, then swerving around in another direction. After initially attempting to monitor where they were headed, Laura took hold of David's hand, deciding to enjoy her honeymoon and relish the joy she felt being David Jennings' wife—being Laura Jennings.

This trolley was more of a challenge than a delight. The seats were barely twelve inches deep, the backs upright at a rigid ninety-degree angle, the leg room inadequate for anyone over the age of eight. Passengers were crammed in as tightly as possible. David and Laura shared their seat with a couple from Michigan, David on the outside, bending his knees awkwardly out the side of the trolley in a futile attempt to try to stretch his legs.

"In September 1565, Pedro Menendez, with seven hundred soldiers and colonists, landed here and founded Saint Augustine," the guide said, "making it the oldest continually occupied European settlement in North America. Menendez successfully destroyed the French Fort Caroline at the mouth of the Saint Johns River forty miles north of Saint Augustine and ended the French incursion into Florida. Saint Augustine settlers, isolated and often near starvation, lived in constant fear of attacks by pirates who roamed the coast and preyed upon Spanish commerce. Diminishing supplies and increasing hostility of the Indians made life treacherous for the early settlers. Menendez had established other military outposts, but only Saint Augustine survived."

The trolley moved down narrow roadways as the guide pointed out the Castillo de San Marcus Fort, built in 1672, the old 1791 Cathedral, and the Mission of Nombre de Dios, America's most sacred acre.

"Where's the ghosts," the female seatmate asked David in a

piercing tone.

David was momentarily taken aback. "I think they only come out at night."

Mr. Michigan harrumphed. "In the graveyards, woman, where all ghosts are."

So much for the paranormal frightseeing.

"Saint Augustine in the late 1880s had its birth as a resort community," the guide told them a moment later. "With the arrival of Standard Oil co-founder Henry M. Flagler, who built two hotels and took over another to serve as the base of his Flagler System Hotels. To your right you'll see Flagler College, which was one of the three of his former Saint Augustine hotels. The other two are now the Lightner Museum and the City Hall and the Casa Monica."

Laura pretended to lose her balance, landing in David's lap as she craned her neck and stretched forward to get a look at Flagler College.

"You can sit here, dear," he murmured, kissing her on the back of her neck and patting her behind as she rose. "We can ride out the bumps together." He thought he detected a flattering blush on his bride's cheek.

"Excuse me, sir," she joked.

The trolley had circled around, and Laura had lost track of the route they were on with the lap distraction. "We're now passing under a stone arch introducing you to Aviles Street, which is Saint Augustine's oldest and most authentic community." The guide glanced back at David and then continued. "Please keep your feet and legs inside the trolley, as the passageway here is very narrow. Dating back to 1572, this area is identified easily by the carriage-tracked brick streets, fragrant orange blossoms, and original Spanish buildings with overhanging balconies."

They approached the Old Tolomato Cemetery, dating back

to 1763. "This site," the guide said, "was occupied by the Christian Indian village of Tolomato, with its chapel and burying ground served by Franciscan missionaries."

A man rose suddenly from behind a grave and stumbled into the roadway, nearly colliding with the trolley.

"He needs to be more careful," David whispered, "or he'll be taking up permanent residence in there."

The trolley stopped on Saint George Street and the guide announced, "Here on Saint George Street you'll find eleven city blocks of pedestrian-only traffic. This area is filled with shops for every person and taste. There are also plenty of restaurants."

"Hungry, sweetie?" David asked, as he lifted Laura's hand to his lips and kissed it.

She responded with an affirmative smile.

David dropped a five-dollar bill in the guide's tip jar, and Laura thanked her for the interesting tour.

Later, back at Harbor Lights resort, David and Laura were looking forward to a relaxing happy hour with their new neighbors, Jeremy and Katie. David had told Laura at lunch that he wanted to brainstorm with the retired forensic detective and compare notes on just exactly what was going on, or, more appropriately, what had gone on, here at Harbor Lights RV Resort.

From what he'd studied and learned about law enforcement and Laura's fascination with criminal profiling, he was sure that Patricia Marsh had indeed been murdered . . . burned to death? Partially? Entirely? He didn't have any answers, only suppositions, because it seemed like everyone he and Laura had talked with so far had a different story about this place and the key players. He also wanted to get Jeremy's thoughts about his ideas on what was in that bottle he and Laura had stumbled upon on the beach.

David snatched an olive from the hors d'oeuvres tray. When he didn't get any response from Laura, he snapped his fingers in front of her. "I find you fascinating and intriguing when you're so deep in thought, my love."

Laura put down the knife and cheese she was slicing. "I was thinking about that Tolomato cemetery. Was it just me, or did you find that place seriously creepy?"

"It wasn't just you. I had shivers running up and down my spine until we were out of sight of the place."

Laura tore off a piece of tinfoil and placed it over the platter before David ate the entire tray. "Well, I certainly can't imagine anyone wanting to go at night on one of those ghost tours through the place. C'mon, let's get out of here and go get happy with Jeremy and Katie."

"Speaking of creepy," David said, "where did we put our bottle?"

Laura opened the fridge and pulled out a bottle of white zinfandel. "Right here, all nice and chilled."

David laughed. "Not *that* bottle. The bottle from the beach."

Laura walked into the bedroom and kneeled down. "Here, under the bed." She pulled the bottle out and handed it to David.

"Under the bed? We're hiding it now?"

Laura shrugged her shoulders. "It's the first place I thought of."

They exited their motor home and headed out across the shuffleboard courts to Jeremy and Katie's fifth-wheel trailer. Laura came to an abrupt stop in front of a tree bearing white flowers. "This is beautiful," she said, bending over to sniff a blossom.

"Don't get too close," David said. "That's oleander, and it's poisonous and deadly."

Laura jerked back, wiping her nose with the palm of her

hand and almost dropping the hors d'oeuvres with the other. "Oleander? Poisonous? Deadly?"

"Only if you ingest it." David laughed.

"Why would anyone want to have a deadly plant in a camping resort? Where children or anyone could get hold of it?"

"Good question," David replied.

FIVE

There were only a few seats left at the picnic table when David and Laura reached Jeremy and Katie's. *Oh, crap!* David thought. There were others invited to his neighbor's happy hour. Or, more likely than not, they invited themselves.

As he and Laura approached the group, conversations quieted and gazes drifted their way. Only the chewing continued, and David was reminded of the curious way cows looked at you when you approached the pasture fence. David nodded and waved, as he'd seen the campers so often do when trying to hide the fact that they'd been on a gossip marathon.

Laura stood fiddling with the tinfoil on the platter of hors d'oeuvres, hoping Katie would show her face, when Jeremy opened the door to their trailer and emerged with paper plates and cups.

"Just take a seat anywhere," Jeremy said. "Katie will be out in a sec."

David and Laura squeezed in between old Stanley Parsons and some gawky woman who was running her eyes up and down David and Laura as if they'd just landed from another planet.

"Good evening," Laura said to the woman. "I'm Laura Jennings and this is my husband David."

"Humph!" was the only response.

"Hey, what is it with you and that bottle?" Stanley asked. "Seems every time I see you, you got that thing with you." He stretched his neck out like a turtle to get a closer look. "What's in there anyway?"

"Can I get anyone anything to drink?" Katie asked as she exited her trailer.

Nosey old geezer, David thought. Thank goodness, Katie's timing was perfect.

"No, thanks, Katie. I just poured Laura and me a glass of zinfandel."

"Come, Stanley," the gawker ordered her companion. "I want to get back in time to watch *Wheel of Fortune.*"

"Don't leave on our account," David said. "Happy hour has just begun."

Another humph, followed by, "It's not you. We're just a wee bit out of place with you young folks and think we'll leave you to chat amongst yourselves."

"We never got your name," Laura said.

"I never gave it," the woman said. "It's Camelia Johnston. A pleasure, I'm sure."

Jeremy was bobbing his head from one to another as Katie pretended to be dishing out the appetizers. The atmosphere had become thick with tension. It finally lifted when Katie spoke. "Stay and have some snacks, Camelia. You too, Stanley."

Stanley stood up, eyes still focused on the bottle that rested beside David. "Camelia's right. We have to get back. Thanks for the drink, and we'll do it again soon."

Jeremy just nodded and waved. After all the others had finally left as well, and it was just the four of them, he spoke. "Strange people, some of these campers."

"I hope we didn't intrude," Laura said.

"Nonsense," Katie responded. "We invited you two. The others invited themselves."

"Yeah," Jeremy added. "Said they just happened to be walking by, saw us outside setting up the table, and thought they'd stop and say hello. Only problem was, after the hellos they sat themselves down and were soon followed by a posse of their peers."

David's laugh was a little louder than he'd wanted. He couldn't help but think how much Jeremy reminded him of his pal and former business partner, Eddie Cameron—tall, muscular, and built ready for action. Now that the others had left, David jumped right in with the opening Jeremy had left with his comment. "Speaking of posses and this group of campers at Harbor Lights, have you heard any more about what did happen before Laura and I got here? With Patricia Marsh? Anything from that detective who was roaming the grounds?"

Jeremy grabbed a handful of olives and popped a few in his mouth as he stretched back in his lawn chair. He nodded as he chewed, a signal, David was sure, that he had heard something. Finally, Jeremy swallowed and spoke, "Heard all kinds of things. You guys missed the fun."

"We went on the city trolley for a tour of Old Saint Augustine," Laura said. "It was okay—interesting, but I don't think David enjoyed it too much."

David was in awe at how easily Laura seemed to be able to pick up on his thoughts, feelings, and emotions, sometimes even before he did. He rubbed her neck gently with his thumb, just the way she liked it. "What can I say? She knows me better than I know myself sometimes. So, what did we miss?"

Katie was drumming her fingers on the table, apparently wanting Jeremy to get on with it. Which he did.

"Seems Detective Miles had a long chat with both Ken Schaffer and Cory. Don't know exactly what went on with those interviews, but did hear from one of the resort's most reliable busybodies, Stella, that the two of them have been told not to think about leaving town." Jeremy sat forward and placed his hands on his knees, then whispered as if there were others lurking around. Instinctively, Laura, David and Katie moved closer in toward Jeremy.

"Ken?" David whispered. "Who's Ken Schaffer?"

"Patricia's first husband. Stella said it was a big mess here a couple of years ago when she filed for divorce and married the young stud, Cory. Guess this Ken dude was abusive. Patricia didn't want her kid, Gracie, being exposed to that, so the kid grew up in boarding schools. Finally the mousy, frightened Patricia gets the balls . . ." Jeremy looked over to Laura. "Sorry."

"No problem, go on," Laura said.

"Anyway, she gets the nerve to leave this guy after twenty years of marriage, marries the stud, Cory, and lives not-so-happily-ever-after."

"What are you saying?" David asked. "That the suspicion is on the ex-husband?"

"That's not what I'm saying, it's what the majority of the campers here are filling that detective's head with."

"What's with this Norma person?" Laura asked. "She was nose-to-nose with the detective this morning. Had some book she was shoving at him."

"I don't know. Could be she thinks she's the long-lost Cagney or Lacey. Maybe she's running around getting her own info." Jeremy reached for a cracker, topped it with a slice of Monterey Jack cheese and an olive, and popped it in his mouth.

Katie poured herself another glass of chablis. "David," she said, "you look like you're dying to tell us about your bottle."

He'd been spinning it around on the table, not really conscious that he was. "Well, I did want to run it by Jeremy."

"Are we leaving the what-happened-to-Patricia topic and moving to the mystery of the bottle from sea?" Jeremy took the bottle from David and tipped it from side to side, studying it. "What's in here? Doesn't look like sand to me."

"Exactly!" David said. "It didn't to us either. That's what I wanted to ask you. What would you say it is? And aren't those fragments of some sort inside?"

Everyone was silent. Everyone watched as Jeremy's trained eyes studied the bottle's contents with intrigue. He put the bottle down, looked at it, picked it up, shook it, and then placed it back down. "Did you say you were a cop, David?"

"No. I owned and operated a karate studio. Then I ran into a little money and quit. Did some PI work."

"Ha!" Laura chuckled. "A little money? Oh, yeah, only thirty-six million."

Katie gasped. "What?"

"A five-week rollover in the Florida lottery. Believe me, you don't want to waste your money on lotto tickets. You'll have every wacko in the state on your doorstep."

"And balcony," Laura added.

"Huh?" Katie said.

"A women stalker who leaped to her death from my balcony. It's what made me go into the PI business. To help other stalking victims."

Laura smiled wide. "Like me. My hero."

"I've no idea what you guys are talking about," Jeremy said. "Sounds like something right out of Hollywood."

"Never mind," David said. "It's another whole story. Can we get back to the bottle? What do you think? About those fragments?"

"I can't be sure . . . without a more thorough examination, but offhand, I'd say they were bone fragments."

"As in human?" Laura asked.

"I think Laura still has her mind on the cemetery we visited today," David said.

"I hardly think human bone fragments would end up in a bottle at sea," Katie added.

"They appear at first sight to be human bone fragments to me," Jeremy continued. "Like I said, I'd have to pop this baby open and study them further to be sure."

"If there's such a possibility, shouldn't we be turning the bottle over to the Saint Augustine police department?" Katie said. "What if they are human bone fragments?"

"Not just yet. For now, all we know is it's a bottle that was found on the beach with some sand different from that on the beaches around here."

"A bottle that was found on the same beach everyone is clamoring about Patricia Marsh being set on fire and burned to death on," Laura said.

"Getting back to Patricia," David said. "Did you get a chance to talk to Detective Miles?"

"I did." Jeremy was still studying the bottle.

"And?"

He pushed the bottle aside and sat back with his arms folded across his chest. "And he said the autopsy showed poisoning."

"What a minute, let's back up," Laura said. "Autopsy? How does one have an autopsy if the body was set on fire? Unless . . ."

"Oh-oh," David said. "She's got that look. Watch out. There's no stopping her now."

"Unless the body that was charred and burned wasn't Patricia Marsh's," Katie said. "And if it wasn't, then whose was it and . . ." She pointed at the bottle in the center of the table. "If those are human bone fragments, whose are they? And what is going on at this resort?"

"Whoa, Katie, baby." Jeremy put his meaty arm around her neck. "You girls are getting way ahead of us guys. Let's slow down."

"Women," Laura corrected.

"Huh?" Jeremy asked.

"Women. Katie and I are women, not girls."

"Oh, yeah, okay . . . right." Jeremy rolled his eyes in David's direction.

David wasn't stupid, by any means. "And very beautiful women," he said, grinning from ear to ear.

Jeremy's brow furrowed. "So . . . do you want me to go on about the autopsy?"

"By all means," Laura said. "And getting back to those charred remains on the beach, the more I think about it, the more I believe they weren't those of Patricia Marsh. I mean, there was a funeral."

"From what everyone around here is buzzing about, it was a closed casket at the funeral parlor," David added. "Who's to say the casket had a corpse, charred or otherwise in it?"

"The autopsy, according to Miles, showed she died of some strange virus. Apparently she'd been sick for quite some time. Eventually her organs just shut down and stopped working," Jeremy said.

"Sounds a little too cut and dried to me," David said.

"When we were checking in I heard that lady with the Norma name badge gossiping to some old woman about how Patricia refused to go to the hospital. The old woman told Norma that Cory was beside himself trying to persuade Patricia to go to the emergency room."

Katie stood up and started to clear away all the plates. "I heard Gracie was at her bedside caring for her mother for weeks," she said. "Poor thing. Losing her mother under such suspicious circumstances and then having to deal with all this going on."

Jeremy rubbed his hands through his hair. "Can I finish?" he asked.

"Sorry," Katie said.

"It was too cut and dried to me, too. I asked Miles how someone—like Gracie or Cory—wouldn't notice that Patricia was getting so sick that she needed hospitalization. That's when he told me this virus thing was sort of like when your appendix suddenly bursts and poison travels through your system so fast that you don't stand a chance."

"What?" Laura said. "I never heard of such a thing, and . . ."

David draped an arm over Laura's shoulder. "And what?" he asked.

Laura met David's eyes. Continuing with her sudden flash of thought made her develop a headache that encircled her skull and squeezed at her brain. Maybe it was one of her migraines. Maybe her brain was about to explode. She spoke as she massaged her temples. "That word 'poison.' It just made me think of something David and I came across on our way over here. A poisonous plant."

"Oleander!" David blurted.

"Ohh—lee what?" Jeremy asked.

"Oleander. A poisonous plant," David said. "Growing right here in the campground."

"There's lots of poisonous plants and berries," Jeremy argued. "What's that got to do with Patricia? You saying she was nibbling on these plants?"

David chuckled. "Nope, not saying that at all. Oleander isn't just poisonous, it's deadly poisonous." David noticed the faraway look on Laura's face. It told him she wasn't here at all. She was analyzing. That's what she did for enjoyment. She took something of interest, dissected it, and came up with a logical conclusion. "Earth to Sherlock," David waved a hand in front of Laura. "Share what's going on in that beautiful mind of yours with the rest of us."

"Not tonight," Laura said. She stood up and stretched out her arms. "My brain feels like it's on overload right now."

"You're not leaving, are you?" Katie asked.

David saw that Laura had had enough for one night. He also

realized that a lot of the happenings within Harbor Lights RV Resort were most likely giving her flashbacks of her ordeal back in Big Pine Key. He didn't want that for her. He only wanted to give her happy times and warm memories. Not memories to look back on that had to do with poisons, charred bodies, and mysterious contents in a bottle washed ashore. But he also knew that Laura wouldn't permit herself to be sheltered in that sort of noble way. She faced life head-on—the good, the bad, and the ugly. And that's what he admired and loved most about her. He stood up beside Laura and wrapped his arms around her small waist. Her arms, still outstretched, dropped and wrapped around his. "We've had a long day," David said, "I think we'll call it a night."

"We'll have to do this again soon," Jeremy said. "Tomorrow is our turn to do the tourist thing. Y'all want to join us?"

"I think we're just going to laze around the resort," Laura answered. "Maybe take a walk on the beach."

"Look for more bottles?" Jeremy picked up the bottle, gave it a quick study again, then handed it to David.

"Puh-leese," Laura said.

David pushed the bottle back to Jeremy. "When you get a chance, can you look into this . . . literally, and tell me what you think?" He then turned to Katie, who was doing a balancing act with the plates and leftovers. "Thanks for the invite, Katie."

"You're welcome. You two are such a delight. Stop by any-time."

"You got it, David," Jeremy said. "I still have a lot of contact with my former colleagues. We'll get to the bottom of this." He held the bottle out and shook it.

David and Laura waved their good-byes and headed back to their motor home.

As they approached the oleander tree, something seemed to take hold of Laura. Like a weed, thoughts in her head germinated and grew. She dismissed them. They returned. Larger. Thicker. Bolder. She stopped dead in her tracks, forcing David to stop as well.

"What's the matter?" David asked.

She let go of his hand and paced back and forth, then walked around the tree, trying to untangle the urgency crowding her mind like a bramble of thorns.

Her world had always been an ordered one. Her father had insisted on consistency, and his military regimen had become habit. Everything had its place. Everything happened on schedule. Risks were kept at a minimum, and Laura was almost never caught off guard.

In the last six months, nothing had seemed real. She'd been stalked, almost lost her father, fallen in love with David, left her job as manager of her family's campground in Big Pine Key, married David, and ridden off into the sunset with him to live and love on the road. She suddenly felt it all catching up to her, like her world was spinning out of orbit, tilting on its axis. Nothing was falling back into its rightful place.

"Laura?" David repeated.

The dark, deep resonance of his voice lifted the fine hairs along her arms like no physical touch ever had.

She looked into the safety net of his whiskey-colored eyes and felt her heart thump at the realization that she had indeed found her soul mate. "I'll be okay," she assured him. She nodded toward the oleander tree. "It's just this sixth sense I have about this place. Bad vibes, or whatever you want to call them."

He gave a small but nervous chuckle, and she found herself smiling in return. His face was a vision of charm when he smiled. Like a child with chocolate, she needed another taste of this warmer place of her existence.

He wrapped his arm around her and pulled her closer to his side. "Let's go home."

As they walked past the office, Laura pointed at a shadowy figure seen through the window. "Look, David. Who do you think that is?"

"Maybe a lost ghost from the Tolomato cemetery," he joked.

"That's not funny, David Jennings."

Six

Deep in thought, Cory sat alone in his office. Fury tensed him up inside, made worse because he couldn't figure out why he was angry. Gracie seemed to be handling her mother's death better than he'd thought, and there had been no ugly scenes of blame at Patricia's funeral between her and her father, Ken Schaffer. They could now all get on with their lives.

That is, they could, if it weren't for the gossip of the campers and the finger-pointing from those who still believed he was nothing more than a gold digger who charmed the money out of his departed wife, Patricia. That wasn't it at all. He loved her. Wanted to rescue her from the abusive clutches of Ken. He did so by feeding and nurturing her deflated self-image through undying love and support of her artistic talent.

It had been Cory who'd talked her into moving away from the drab and cold environment of northern Georgia. Aware of her love for the sea, Cory took her on many vacations here, to St. Augustine, eventually persuading her to purchase the resort so she'd always have a source of inspiration for her paintings. He'd even agreed to let Gracie come live with them once she got out of boarding school. Everyone knew it was no easy task, dealing with a rebellious and angry twenty-year-old. But he did it. Loved her as his own. Never saying anything about the obvious crush she had on him which, he had to admit, he did find flattering.

The strain of the last few weeks showed in the campground.

Cory knew he had to do something fast to restore the happy in the campers. It wouldn't be easy as long as the gossip continued and that Detective Miles kept showing up. But he'd do it. Patricia would want him to. To go on.

Patricia. His thoughts drifted to some of their more precious and tender times. Before she got sick. Before Gracie came to live with them. Before he crossed that line and caved into Gracie's seductiveness. He wondered if it was anger he felt. Or was this what guilt felt like?

He brought his arm up close to his face to read his watch. "Damn," he whispered aloud, "ten-thirty! Shit, I've been sitting here in the dark for hours." He dropped his legs from the top of his desk, picked up his flashlight, and gave his office one last sweep in hopes of finding what he'd come here for. Nothing. He headed for the outer office, opened the front door, peered around, locked up, and left.

"Time to get up, my sweet," David called out as he cracked another egg into the bowl. "We've got a lot of ground to cover today."

"Ground?"

Laura's voice sounded sleepy. He turned around to look at her. Eyes the color of a Bahamian sea and sparkling with intelligence, her expressive face vivid with life and love, a love reserved just for him, etched on his brain forever. It felt like another lifetime ago when he'd sworn never to get involved with a woman of such beauty again. Laura had made him forget such vows. "As in investigative ground. The stuff we both live for."

"Oh."

Using a fork, he scrambled the eggs and poured them into a hot pan, swished them around, and removed the pan from the burner. With a spatula, he slapped the cooked eggs onto two plates. Working with brisk efficiency, he put the eggs and toast on the table and hunted for jam.

Laura was dressed in her emerald satin tap pants and matching camisole, and he watched as the flimsy material ruffled with her every movement, caressing her curves like a flow of jeweled water.

"Is something the matter?" She sat down and cut off a section of toast.

"You have got to be the most beautiful sight I have ever seen on any morning I've been alive." Pouring coffee into their mugs, he leaned into her and placed his mouth on hers. "Mmmm, strawberry kisses."

Laura carefully put her knife down, put her elbows on the table, and rested her chin on top of her folded hands. "So, my sexy and charming PI, what's your plan of attack?"

He sat down and wrapped his hands around the mug of coffee. "A little volunteer work for you in the office and a bit for me outside."

"I'm not sure I understand."

"For this to work, for us to get any kind of information about Patricia Marsh, former owner of this lovely resort, we need to get beyond campground gossip." David put his mug down and sat back, arms folded across his bare chest, waiting for her to admit his idea was ingenious.

Laura smiled at the way he looked. She knew exactly what he was waiting for her to say. "Oh, and you don't think there's more gossip in a campground office than there could ever be outside?"

That wasn't what he'd waited for her to say. "What?"

She pitched a napkin at him. "David, gossip begins in the office and spreads outward. But . . ." She reached over and put her hand on top of his. "It is a good idea. And it might even be fun."

He brought her hand to his lips and gave it a light kiss. "Good! Then I say its show time!"

As they headed toward the office, the trees on both sides formed a canopy over the path, allowing the shades of hundred-year-old oaks, the dominant tree, spread its arms over southern magnolias, smaller oaks, cedars, palms, and a bushy, thick understory of yaupon, red bay, and young trees. Overhead, the tree canopy was sculpted by the constant action of wind coming off the Atlantic, which was a few hundred yards distant, divided from the campground by Salt Run. Old dunes gave vertical variety to the campground. It was now, with spring in full swing and the sun burning hotter than ever, that the shady hardwood hammock all the campsites nestled in was appreciated by walkers and bike riders. Away from the blowing sand and salt spray of the ocean, each site was yet within walking distance of the beach, just over the campground's boardwalk. There were natural barriers between each site that allowed for privacy, and each site was equipped with a picnic table, an in-ground grill, and a fire ring.

Past the camp store on a sandy road, David and Laura came to the first loop, Coquina. It was located away from the rest of the campground and had thirty-three campsites. Laura was amazed by how large the campsites were, and she could understand why RV campers were so attracted to Harbor Lights.

David and Laura stood in front of a large rustic building. Behind them the sounds of campground fun echoed in the air. A golf cart slowly crunched along the gravel path; children were giggling. The scent of sun-screen lotion and salty sea breezes wafted. Life was continuing in its usual way. The way it apparently had gone on before the death . . . or murder . . . of Patricia Marsh.

The front door banged open and Gracie exited at lightning

speed, almost knocking Laura off balance on the steps leading to the front door.

"Someone woke up on the wrong side of the bed," David said. "You okay?" he asked Laura.

Laura turned to watch Gracie jump into a golf cart and sail down the path toward the back of the campground. "I'm fine."

Inside, the office was bustling with campers checking in and checking out, tension palpable the instant David and Laura entered. A ceiling fan paddled in lazy circles but didn't seem to stir the air. An older woman stood at the counter complaining about having to pay a guest fee for someone she just wanted to have over for lunch. Her ample curves gave her a motherly roundness. Streaks of gray painted her short, no-nonsense auburn hair. Her twisted frown of disapproval crinkled all the way to her eyes.

"This is utter and total nonsense!" the older woman declared as she swung herself around and slammed out the front door.

"Someone better remove the wind chimes from above that door," David said. "Maybe the glass window in the door, too."

Laura gave him an elbow nudge to the ribs.

"Ouch!"

Deep in thought, Laura kept her eyes glued to the chaos going on at the registration counter. Another girl with a name badge of Terrie was frantically looking at Laura, motioning for her to step forward. No longer able to resist her natural urge to intercede, Laura went behind the counter. "You want me to help?" she asked Terrie.

Terrie nodded a fast and furious affirmative.

Smiling, Laurie said, "I'll help the next in line."

Arms crossed over his chest, David shook his head. The expression on his face was full of pride and admiration. Laura looked up and smiled.

Just as David turned and headed toward the door, Stella

Greenburg put her hand on the door handle from the outside. She was dressed in her usual capri shorts and tank top. She didn't wear any makeup that David could see, and her gray-white frizzy hair was tucked up under a badly abused white painter's hat. He couldn't help but wonder when the woman had last smiled.

Certainly not since he and Laura had been at Harbor Lights.

"Excuse me, Stella," David said. "I was just heading out. They're kind of busy in there."

Stella spun around David, ignoring him, and slammed the office door.

Peeking through the glass window, David muttered to himself, "I gotta see this."

Inside, he could see Stella tapping the counter forcefully with her cherrywood walking stick. Perched on top of the slender shaft was a carved dragon's face. David couldn't help thinking how much it resembled the woman herself. He had to fight the urge to go inside and grab the stick out of her hands. Instead, he watched as Laura took control of the situation by grasping Stella's cane. Whatever she said worked. Stella, although looking a bit disgruntled, appeared to be behaving herself. "That's my girl," David said as he headed down the steps and into the campground.

Harbor Lights RV Resort was the last resort situated on Anastasia Island, surrounded by four miles of pristine beach and a tidal salt marsh. Yet from where David began his meandering, it was all wooded area as he headed through the ancient dunes shaded by hammock forests. The paths and camping sites were marked with signs like ANGEL WING, SEA URCHIN, SAND DOLLAR, and SHARK'S EYE. Heading out of the forests, he passed by the resort's Pirate's Cove snack bar, which was located next to the camp store. All the buildings were a shell-pink color and had murals of dolphins, ships, and mermaids on their sides. David stopped to read the flyers posted outside the camp store: kayak and canoe rentals, camping and fishing supplies, ocean toys and umbrellas. "Something for everyone," he mumbled.

A group of elderly women came out of the store dressed in knickered and skirted bathing suits, reminding David of what he had seen women wearing in an old movie, right down to the bathing caps. The sign in front of the store also read: WEL-COME SPRING BREAKERS, and David knew the group he'd seen walk past him were definitely not part of *that* group.

"Lost?" David heard someone ask. Assuming the question was directed at him, he turned around in the direction of the voice, and discovered Gracie sitting on top of a picnic table in front of the snack bar.

He shoved his hands deep into his denim shorts. "Not really. Just exploring."

"Where's your bride?"

"Laura?"

"You got more than one?"

"Nope, she's all the woman I can handle." David took a seat on the bottom part of the table. "She's at the office. Helping out with a rush you had with the check-ins."

Gracie tossed her long blond hair off her shoulder with a sweep of her hand. "I'm sure Terrie and Norma could have handled things."

"Didn't see anyone else there except some tall, thin girl." He started tapping the top of table with his fingertips.

"That's Terrie. She gets a bit jittery if there are more than one or two customers at a time. Norma must have had an er-rand or something." Gracie hopped off the table. There was something about David Jennings that made her feel she'd known him before. But where? She'd been at boarding schools most of her life—all girls. She convinced herself it was just her imagination. With his sexy smile and piercing bronzed eyes, he reminded her of Cory. How he must have looked twenty years ago at David's age. That was it! She relaxed and even managed a smile. "I was just going to get me a Bloody Mary at the Pirate's Cove. Care to join me?"

David swung a leg over the bench seat, sitting side saddle. "They serve those here? The breakfast drink of champions?"

Gracie laughed and tugged at his arm. "Yes, they do. Come on."

"Sure, why not? What can it hurt?" A sudden twinge of guilt ran through him. He was married. Was he nuts? Going for a drink with a woman Laura—his wife—described as a blond bombshell? Maybe he should back out now. Tell Gracie he just remembered something he had to do. *This is crazy,* he thought. *It's just a drink.*

"Coming?"

"Right behind you," David said.

The snack bar wasn't too crowded. It was nearing lunchtime and most folks were either beachcombing or home napping, depending on their ages. David's head turned from left to right as he hopped on top of one of the stools. He wasn't quite sure what it was or who it was he was in search of, but he decided to keep his face down as he talked with Gracie. "Nice place you got here."

The hint of a smile creased her cheek, deepening her dimple. "Thanks."

"It is your place, right?"

"Actually, it's Cory's." Gracie fiddled with the celery stick in her Bloody Mary, twirling it and mixing the drink around. "He and my mom purchased it after they were married. Just under a year ago."

"Where did you live before that?"

"Me? Boarding schools. Then in Georgia."

"Boarding schools? All your life?"

"Yes, sir. Since the age of five anyway. My dad was . . . well, I guess you could say he was abusive, and my mom sort of feared for my life. At least that was the story I was told later on."

"Must have been hard on you. I'm sorry." He reached across the counter and put his hand on top of hers. He was sympathetic, since he, too had felt no sense of home when he was growing up, but had always fantasized about the perfect family, which his was far from. But not anymore. He was now blessed with Laura's family. Marge Madison, Laura's mother, a woman who must have seen through to the scars of his childhood and had warmly accepted him ever since they'd met.

Gracie pulled her hand from under David's and chewed on her thumbnail. "It wasn't that bad, really. My mom was the one who had it bad. Taking so much crap from my dad. She was just so . . . so . . . um, passive, or maybe too scared to leave him. I begged her to many times. But she . . ." Gracie have realized she was talking too much again, something Cory always pointed out to her as her only real fault. She quickly changed the subject. "But it all turned out happily ever after once Mom met Cory, fell in love, got married, and moved here."

"Your mom died. That's not what I call a Cinderella happily-ever-after story."

"No, I guess not."

"Where's your dad now? Do you see him much?"

"He lives in Daytona Beach. Once Cory and my mom got married and moved here, they asked me to move in with them and be manager of Harbor Lights. My dad came around a lot at first. Mostly to start fights and get in my mom's face with all sorts of accusations. The last time I saw him was at my mom's funeral."

"Guilty?"

"Excuse me?"

"Did he show up at the funeral because he felt guilty?"

"About what?"

He shot her a pointed glance. "About how he'd treated her all those years?"

"Oh. No, I doubt it. Dad never felt guilty about anything. He showed up strictly to make a scene. Telling everyone that Mom ended up where she deserved to be. Cory was in no mood for him that day and . . . well, a fight broke out between him and my dad."

"Could he—?"

"Have hated her so much he killed her?"

David nodded.

"Given the right circumstances, anyone can kill someone, I guess."

"And the circumstances were right?"

"That's what the cops think."

"That he killed your mother?"

"Yes. Because of his past abuse. And because of the number of times my mom had him jailed."

"What about Cory?"

"What about him?"

"Word from the busybody club says he married your mom for her money."

"You're asking me if he could have killed my mother?"

"Everyone's a suspect in a situation like this, until proven otherwise."

"I can assure you, Cory did not kill my mother."

He put his hands up in surrender. "Case closed as far as I'm concerned."

"Gracie, can I talk to you?"

Gracie turned at the sound of a man's voice. Tension floated through her body. "Dad. What are you doing here?"

"Looking for you. Got a minute?"

David cleared his throat and pretended to be looking for someone beyond Ken and Gracie.

"Excuse me," Gracie said, "Dad, this is David . . . I'm sorry, I forgot your last name."

David extended a hand, "Jennings. Pleased to meet you."

"Yeah, same here. A camper?"

"Yes sir. Honeymooning at Harbor Lights."

"How nice." Ken Schaffer turned back to his daughter. "How 'bout it? In private?" he asked.

David got up and left ten dollars on the counter for the drinks and tip. "I was just leaving," he said, and walked away.

Glancing back, David watched as Ken jerked Gracie by the arm and pulled her out of sight. He blew out a long breath in an attempt to erase the brute force of the incident from his mind. Deliberately, he relaxed the muscles in his hands by unclenching his fists. As he headed back toward the resort office to check on Laura, he reminded himself that this was their honeymoon. He prayed that whatever had happened to Patricia Marsh would soon be revealed, that all this talk and gossip about murder would be forgotten, and that they could laugh about it when he and Laura were old and gray and telling their grandkids about their honeymoon travels. But he had a gnawing suspicion that the circumstances surrounding Patricia's demise would prove to be nothing to laugh at.

SEVEN

"She left about an hour ago," Terrie said.

The woman looked much more at ease and in control than the last time David had seen her. But then again, the office hadn't been empty of campers then as it was now. "Thanks." David reached across the counter and extended his hand. "Terrie, right?"

She smiled and lightly shook his hand. "Yes, how did you know?"

"Male intuition."

Terrie gave a little giggle and asked, "Are you Laura's husband?"

"Ahhhh, she couldn't stop talking about me, right?"

"She mentioned you. Said you guys were on your honeymoon. She was a tremendous help in here."

David looked at his watch. "I'd love to stay and chat, Terrie, but I promised Laura an afternoon stroll on the beach."

Terrie shrugged. "I understand. Please thank her again for me."

"Will do," David said. Just as he was leaving, two more motor homes pulled up. He turned back, gave Terrie a wink, and announced, "Incoming!"

She waved him off with a shy school-girl grin.

In less than two minutes, David was back at their campsite. He'd run all the way.

"Laura!" he called out.

No answer.

He headed to the bedroom in the back of the motor home, and stopped dead in his tracks to read a note lying on the bed:

> *An eye for an eye.*
> *You deserve to die.*
> *Sticks and stones*
> *Will break your bones*
> *And when you die,*
> *I won't cry.*
> *Remember me, my foe and friend,*
> *I'll smile at your deadly end.*

David stared, mouth open. He looked away, then back at the verse in his hand. "What the hell?" he said aloud.

"Pardon?"

Startled, David jumped, turned, and had one leg raised in an instinctive karate stance before blowing out a deep breath and dropping himself backward on the bed. "Damn, Laura! You scared the crap out of me."

She laughed, and he fell backward onto the bed.

Stretched across the bed with one hand resting over his chest, David said, "It's not funny." He raised himself up and held out the hand with the piece of paper now crumpled inside. "This wasn't funny either."

Laura straightened the paper and read. "No, it isn't." She looked at David. His eyebrows furrowed together, his shoulders slumped forward, his eyes narrowed. She sat beside him. "David. You don't think I wrote this, do you?"

"It was on our bed. In our motor home. What was I supposed to think?"

She stood and yanked him up with one quick pull on both his hands. "I might have seen you and Goldilocks at the snack bar on my way home, and might have thought about how I'd kill you when I saw you alone, but I assure you, I much prefer to jump your bones than break them."

Oh-oh, David thought. *She saw us.* "Well, where did the note come from?"

"The office."

"The office? Norm—"

"No, Norman the Slippery Stalker did not get loose from the Monroe County jail and follow us to Saint Augustine." She walked into the kitchen and laid the note on the table as she smoothed it out. "We ran out of registration forms, and Terrie, the girl in the office, told me where to find more. I was rummaging through the supply closet and this note fell from a top shelf."

Picking the note up from the table, David arched an eyebrow. His expression remained otherwise neutral. He read the verse again, then let it fall from his grip back to the table. "It may not be the handiwork of Norman Bateman," he said. "But whoever wrote this is just as crazy."

"Is there a way to find out who wrote it?" Laura asked.

"The paper is your average copy store stock. The ink, even with the bloodlike 'Chiller' font, looks like a common color-printer type. If this person has even more than an ounce of brains, he'd know to wear gloves to handle the paper. Not that that would matter. Who knows how many fingerprints are on it by now?"

"Like mine," Laura said.

He saw her shudder. He embraced her, held her close, and kissed away her frown. "Don't worry, my dear. You could never be implicated as a suspect of such prose."

Her eyes were deep and now darkened with determination. And confidence. In him. Her face shone with passion. "So what do we do? Everyone in this campground, campers as well as staff, probably have computers and printers."

"We'll discover who the author is." He looked at her, certainty and excitement brimming in his eyes. "One at a time, anyone we talk to, we need to let them think we've figured out their secret and see if someone takes the bait. If someone does, we set up a trap and catch them."

She kissed him. "Sounds like a plan to me, Mr. Jennings."

"We can start in the morning. Right after our kayaking."

Laura pulled herself free from his embrace. "After our what?"

"Our kayaking. Remember? We signed up for the early-morning kayak ride." He reminded her.

"I was hoping you'd forget."

"Well, I didn't. It'll be fun."

"You know I don't care that much for the water. That's why I never learned to swim." Laura massaged her temples, feeling the onset of a migraine.

David took her by the hand and led her to the sofa. "Come here." Sitting, he patted his lap. "Rest your head and I'll give you one of my famous migraine-release massages."

She did as he'd suggested, and he began to tenderly rub her head.

"David," she said softly as the tips of his fingers gently eased her tension. "You're going to have to help me out with this kayak thing. I've never been in a kayak and I've no idea how they work."

"I'll be there, Laura. Every step of the way."

"David?"

He looked down.

"Do you think Gracie Schaffer is pretty?"

"Sure. What sighted man wouldn't?" He noticed the green-eyed monster beginning to emerge behind her wrinkled brows. "But inside, Laura, she's hiding some deep, ugly secret."

"What do you mean?"

"Something she told me about her father and how he was abusive to her mother. So much so that Patricia sent Gracie away to boarding school all her life."

Laura saw that look. The same look she saw on David's face when they first met and she'd told him about her stalker. "I'll have to learn to live with the fact that you'll always have a soft spot for women in distress." She sat up and kissed him. "But I draw the line at you pretending to be the fiancé of such a woman. Once was enough for that ploy, and it got you married to me."

"Let's go to bed, my beautiful damsel."

The next morning, bobbing gently at the water's edge, the kayak's opening hardly looked large enough to fit into. Laura gulped her trepidation and held the paddle behind her with both hands as per David's instructions.

Pink still brushed the sky. A lone walker ambled the shoreline. A little Yorkie tagged along, sniffing here and there, then scampering to catch up with its master. Most of the campground lay in an early-morning mist. It was the picture of sleepy pastoral serenity.

The water lapped cold against her feet. Goose bumps pebbled her arms and legs despite the windbreaker she wore over her black-and-red bathing suit. Her breath came in shallow spurts as she fought back the panic of her remembered near-drowning when she was thirteen. She wanted to be anywhere but here, right now.

"You sure you don't want to go for a run instead?" Was the opening getting smaller, the waves larger, or was her imagination playing tricks on her?

"Excitement. Adventure. Free-spirited. Remember?" David chuckled.

"Yeah, adventure, excitement. You're having fun with this,

aren't you?"

His laugh rumbled through her, setting off a chain reaction of desire and comfort.

"Kayaking is relaxing. It makes you start the day with a positive attitude."

"I don't think it's going to have that effect on me."

However, Laura could understand why David thought so. She used running on the beach for her positive-attitude fix. The communion with salt-sea air, tropical breezes, sandy earth, and the fire of the sun got her day off on the right foot while she was managing Big Pine Key Resort—even when it rained. There was something about letting the mind wander where it wanted in the openness of nature that did the body good. Maybe she and David could go for a run later—if she survived this ordeal by kayak.

"Can you promise me I won't get wet?" Laura asked, doubt pooling acid in the pit of her stomach.

David tried not to smile, but wasn't very successful at it. "Chances are you won't."

"That's real helpful."

He tweaked her nose playfully. "Don't think I'll let you try an Eskimo roll your first time out, though."

"How comforting! What next?"

"Squat down facing the bow."

Holding the boat steady, he waited for her to comply. "Reach across the cockpit and hook the thumb of your left hand—no, keep gripping the paddle shaft, too."

She felt awkward and clumsy with her maneuvering technique. "What do you think you married, an acrobat?"

She'd never been a great athlete, but neither had she been a total klutz. Now there seemed to be a short circuit somewhere between her mind and her muscles.

"You've got it. Hook your thumb under the coaming behind the seat."

"What's a coaming?"

"The lip around the cockpit. Keep your right paddle blade so it rests on the shore. Okay, now that you're balanced by the paddle, step sideways into the boat."

The boat bobbed harder under her inexpert movements and her brain fast-forwarded to an image of her splashing headfirst into the water, of the water rolling over her, swallowing her, dragging her down and down and down. She shuddered, dismissing the memory with a sharp shake of her head.

David steadied the kayak with one hand and her with the other. Her knees wobbled in response, setting the boat in motion again.

"You're doing fine. Lower yourself onto the seat. Extend your legs forward until your feet touch the foot braces. Feel them?"

She nodded, more aware of his hand on her lower back than the pegs beneath her rubber sports sandals. She was also aware that she had an audience. Some of the campers had gathered to watch the show—Laura Jennings, entertainment of the day.

David was aware she was distracted by the spectators. "Ignore them. Rest your knees against the knee braces. Swing your paddle around in front of you. There you go. You're all set."

"It's moving."

"It's supposed to."

She gripped the paddle with all her might, not budging a muscle, praying with fervency that the kayak wouldn't overturn. "Oh, God, David! I'm going to fall in."

"No, you're not. It's a very stable boat. I'm right here."

He waded into the water to his knees and stood next to her. He looked like a renaissance sculpture in his gray neoprene shortie—chiseled straight out of granite and not leaving much to the imagination. A suit like that on a body like his ought to

64

be outlawed.

Rubbing the back of her neck, he bent down as if to whisper a secret. A playful glint flickered in his eyes. A sexy smile and a wink followed the whisper that tickled her ear, "I love you, Mrs. Jennings."

She smiled. "Even now? Knowing I'm such a coward?"

"Always. Kayaking's not that hard. You'll get the hang of it in no time. The first of many fun adventures."

"Fun? Oh, yeah. I'm having the time of my life."

David got into his own boat with swift ease. His movements were graceful and effortless as he paddled next to her. The muscles in his arms gleamed in the soft morning light. She was struck once more with the lean efficiency of his body.

"Hold your paddle like so. Now all you have to do is make a cycling movement of your arms and shoulders so you alternate dipping your paddle in and bringing it forward."

"Easy for you to say. And just where did you learn to be such a kayak genius? Any other talents you're hiding from me?"

David gave her one of his infectious laughs. "Oh, honey, I have some talents for you I'm saving for the right time. My kayaking expertise came from a summer Boy Scout camp. Eddie and I learned together. We either learned or we knew we'd have to continue drooling over the Girl Scout camp across the Miami river."

He oared away and Laura almost reached out for the side of his kayak to keep it locked to hers.

"You're pathetic, David Jennings."

"Lean forward a bit," he called softly. His gaze narrowed past her and skimmed the campground's horizon. Did he see anything or anyone out of place? "That's good. Don't slouch. Keep your head up."

"What do you see?"

"Nothing. Don't look at the paddles, look ahead."

That was a mistake. Looking forward made it seem as if the horizon jounced, giving her a slight case of motion sickness.

Don't look at the shore, look at the water. That didn't help, either.

The water was wet, dark, slippery. The shallow, undulating waves appeared to form a sleek, pewter creature that slithered as it surrounded her, waiting to devour her should she make a mistake and roll this rickety craft over. The ripples from her paddle played on her imagination and gave the watery monster life.

Enough! Almost drowning, slippery stalkers, its all behind you now. You're with David. Your husband. He'd never let any harm come to you.. Make him proud. Give it your best effort.

Laura ignored her body's tension, the sweat slicking her palms, the dryness in her throat that needed constant lubrication, and concentrated on smiling and stroking the water with the paddle. The shaking in her arm made the right dip more difficult and sent the kayak in a less than perfect line.

"Don't stroke so hard with your left arm and it'll even out the path."

Right! Nothing was going to even out the rolling in her stomach. This was not fun. But she would do it. David's expectations of her were high. She wouldn't let him down. Make him regret he married her. He promised to be her protector till death did them part. She just hoped the death part wasn't going to be today.

David showed her various maneuvers—how to turn, how to slow down, how to reverse. Before she knew it, the shore was no longer within wading distance. Her movements grew easier. Part of her relaxed, giving in to the steady rhythm of the paddling, the slurp of water around the oar, the sibilant slip of fiberglass through water. Even the shore didn't seem to bounce as much.

"I can almost see why you enjoy this," Laura said, resting her paddle on the boat's bow.

"Kind of grows on you, doesn't it?" David took a break, too.

The current bobbed them slowly backward. The sun had burned away most of the morning mist and the resort was coming to life. "Terrie mentioned that a lot of the campers have paddled into the Atlantic."

"The Atlantic Ocean has a whole lot of dangerous currents." He pointed up ahead with his paddle. "I don't think you're quite ready for that."

He sounded distracted. His gaze remained on the boat ramp where the campground fish-cleaning area emptied into Salt Run. A truck and a sport utility van were parked in the lot. Two teenagers were unloading kayaks from the truck.

"What's wrong?" Laura asked, observing the scene, but seeing nothing out of place.

"That's Cory Marsh's SUV. Saw him get out of it yesterday."

The bright red paint gleamed in the sunlight. "Fancy."

"Got to impress the customers."

"Is it unusual for him to be here?"

"This early, yes, I think it's unusual."

"Want to check it out?"

"Might as well. We have to start somewhere and with someone about that curse verse."

They paddled closer to the shore. Cory sat on a boulder, dipping a fishing line into the water. As he spotted them, he waved a greeting.

"Up early?" David said as they neared. His demeanor ' friendly, but his gaze was all suspicion.

"Got to get some relaxation in before heading to th' How's the water?"

"Great!" Laura said, surprised that she meant the fish biting?"

"They're avoiding me." Cory laughed and shrugged. "Where are you two honeymooners off to?"

"Salt Run. Around the beach." Laura studied Cory's face, noted the slight rise of eyebrow.

Cory shaded his eyes against the sun with a hand, hiding his expression. "Revisiting the scene of the crime?"

Scene of the crime? An unfortunate turn of phrase or an unintended admission of deeper knowledge? Everyone had been told that Patricia's death was from natural causes. Laura shrugged as if Cory's statement went right over her head. "If romance is a crime, then yes, David and I are going to re-spark a memory."

"Sounds enticing." Cory waggled his brows at David, bobbed his line up and down in the water.

David's kayak bumped against hers. "Only problem is, at her rate of kayak speed, we may be old and wheelchair bound by the time we get there. She actually wanted to explore the Atlantic by kayak."

"That's not such a good idea," Cory said. "Some pretty dangerous currents out there—not to mention sharks."

"That's what I told her."

"He thinks I'm too fragile." Laura scrunched her nose in mock disgust.

"Fragile has nothing to do with danger," Cory said. He glanced at his watch. "Guess I better get going if I want to get a shower in before the happy campers end up at my office door."

"The office was short-handed yesterday," David said, still ~~dying~~ Cory's face. "If you need any help, give us a yell."

~~s~~, Terrie told me you jumped in and saved her sanity, ~~hanks.~~" He shouldered his fishing pole and waved. "See

~~ddled~~ away, Laura asked, "What do you think?"
~~?~~"

"Cory. Was he nervous and suspicious, or was he really fishing?"

"Hard to say."

"Then I say we need to find out more about him."

EIGHT

"The bone fragments are too charred and damaged to be identified as belonging to any particular person, but, no bones about it, human bone fragments they are indeed." Jeremy had the contents from David and Laura's beached bottle sprinkled on top of the kitchen table in his camper. "Where did you say you guys found this bottle?"

"On the beach," Laura said. "Our first day here."

"Feels kind of creepy knowing we've been carrying someone around," David added.

"And letting that someone sleep under our bed," Laura said.

Jeremy was only half listening as he moved the particles around with the tip of his tweezers. He still found it amazing how much bones could tell us, from how old the person was, where he or she came from in the world, and even what sort of job the human belonging to the bones may have had. "Uh-hum," was Jeremy's only response.

"Save your breath," Katie said. "He doesn't hear a word you're saying."

"I'd like if you'd show me exactly where on the beach the bottle came to shore," Jeremy said. "See, Katie? I was listening."

"Well," Katie replied, "ya'll can go bone beachcombing. I'm going for a swim. Care to join me, Laura?"

"I think I'll pass and stick with the boneheads."

Katie laughed. "Good one, Laura." She shared a high-five with Laura and left to change into her bathing suit.

David just grinned and shook his head. "You're becoming quite the investigator, aren't you, dear?"

Jeremy swept the dust and fragments from the table back into the bottle with a latex-gloved hand. "Ready when you are," he said.

"Should we just leave the bottle here?" David looked over his shoulder, concerned now that he knew for sure what was in the bottle.

Laura pulled him by the hand. "It'll be safe here. C'mon, I need to get some fresh, salt-sea air."

The beach area was somewhat rocky and a short distance from the campground. No cars were allowed here. Jeremy, David, and Laura worked their way over the rocks and down the wide, gently sloping beach that bordered the Atlantic Ocean. The March winds had stirred the waves as they rolled forward, smashing against the massive black rocks.

"Right over there," Laura pointed to the north end of the beach. "Just over the dunes past the roped-off area." This area of the beach was designated for beachgoers only. Again, no cars were allowed through. It was also the most secluded part of the beach.

David had his arm wrapped around Laura's waist. "She's right, Jeremy. I remember we had just passed over the ropes and headed to the shoreline when Laura spotted the bottle."

Jeremy had stopped to inspect the surrounding area. "Hey, come here, David!" The pure white sand he was sifting through glistened in the afternoon sun.

In moments, David and Laura were standing beside Jeremy. He wiped a small particle of whatever he'd found on the side of his shorts and held his find out to David. "A forensic anthropologist's gem," he said with a wide grin.

Laura peered closely at the foreign object now between David's fingers. "What the heck is it?" she asked.

"Same thing you probably have in your mouth," Jeremy replied.

"Pardon?"

David was rolling it lightly between his index finger and thumb. "Feels like epoxy or some sort of resin," he surmised.

"Resin," Jeremy patted David on the shoulder. "As in fillings found in teeth."

"Oh, you have got to be kidding me, Jeremy," Laura said. "How in the world can you determine that teeny thing to be a tooth filling?"

"Same way forensic specialists were able to identify victims of nine-eleven four years after the tragedy when some construction workers were sifting through gravel on top of the former Deutsche Bank that was being torn down."

David blew out a whistle. "Amazing stuff."

"What's amazing," Jeremy continued, "is that New York City has recovered nineteen thousand, nine-hundred and sixty-four pieces of human remains from the attack, and they were able to identify ninety-one hundred of them. Of the twenty-seven hundred forty-nine people who died at the trade center, there's still eleven hundred fifty-two victims who have no identifiable remains."

"Horrible," Laura said, wiping a tear away. "Listening to you, Jeremy, talking about bone fragments and identifying human beings with a piece of filling—it just brought me back to the awful reality of what really happened that day."

David wanted to try to move Laura out of whatever dark place her mind had her caught up in.

From behind her, he held her close, both arms wrapped around her midsection. He nuzzled her neck and whispered, "I love you."

She replied with a tug of his arms in her hands.

"If you're saying there were bone fragments in our bottle, are you saying this might be a filling from that same person?" David was becoming more and more engrossed.

Jeremy was brushing sand from his knees with one hand and reaching for his filling fragment with the other. "My guess right about now would be that the fragments in the bottle and this little find belong to the same woman."

"Woman?" Laura said, shocked.

"Excuse me?" Jeremy asked.

"Woman," David said. "You said you believed the bone fragments and that piece of filling belonged to the same woman. I thought you said the fragments were too charred to be determined as a human's."

"David, my man, I said the fragments were too charred to be determined as any *particular* human's."

"So what makes you think all this is the remains of a woman?" Laura inquired again.

"Examination of the bone fragments in the bottle determined that they belonged to an adult human female."

"An adult human female, as in Patricia Marsh?" David asked, more to himself than to Jeremy.

"Bingo!" Jeremy said.

"How could it be Patricia Marsh?" Laura asked. "There was an autopsy, wasn't there? How does one go about dissecting ashes?"

"There was," Jeremy said. "But keep in mind that the pile of ashes from a human also consists of bone fragments. Forensic examiners x-ray whatever fragments or body parts remain to get a closer look. X-rays, for instance, would determine if the individual died before the body was set on fire. If there were skeletal remains of the chest and the X-ray showed no soot, we'd know the person died before being set ablaze. Medical examiners scrutinize charred debris piece by piece."

"Are you saying that someone could have dragged Patricia

out here, set her on fire, dead or alive, all without being noticed by anyone?" Laura wasn't buying Jeremy's assumptions. "Not to mention the absurdity of someone shoving charred remains into a bottle."

"That's the intriguing clue for me," Jeremy said. "Think about it. Have you heard of very many men tossing romantic messages out to sea? *Nada.* That's something a woman would do. Whether it is a romantic gesture or, as in this case, a gesture of revenge, in my book it's a female gesture. If I were Detective Miles, I'd be paying close attention to daughter dearest."

As they headed back to the main part of the campground, David turned toward Jeremy and forced him to come to a halt when he took hold of his arm. "Wait a minute. You're not saying you believe Gracie murdered her mother, are you?"

Jeremy shrugged.

"But she doesn't fit the profile," David insisted. "Not even close."

"My belief is anyone is capable of murder," Laura said.

"She's right, David. The first thing you learn in homicide investigation one-oh-one is this—never make assumptions. Everyone is capable of committing a crime, given the right motivation."

David shook his head as they continued to walk toward their campsites. "I'm not sure I buy that. I've studied profiling, and—"

"Everyone," Jeremy continued. "You can trust your mother, David. But check her out first."

David nodded. Jeremy was as cynical as they came. Maybe that's why he was considered the best back in New York.

Still, David couldn't help remembering the way Gracie's lower lip had quivered when she was telling him about her mother's years of abuse.

NINE

At six A.M. on the dot Gracie awakened—again. She glared at the clock. At three in the morning she'd snapped wide awake in a cold sweat. It had finally hit her. Her mother was dead— murdered. Shaking with chills despite the flannel pajamas she wore to bed, she'd spent the rest of the night hugging a pillow and listening as flames crackled in her mind. A beastly roar of flames. She finally drifted back to sleep, but habit had awakened her. No amount of exhaustion would allow her to go back to sleep now.

Groggy and still irritable from her father's unexpected and unpleasant visit the day before, she tiptoed around in the dark so as not to disturb Cory. He'd been sleeping on the couch since the funeral service, and she wasn't quite sure how she felt about that. She wanted to go and comfort him, but she also wanted to be comforted. Cory always had a hard time talking about his emotions, and she didn't want to push him. By feel she selected shorts and a t-shirt and carried them to the bathroom. She glumly studied her face in the mirror. Her eyes were puffy, with dark half-moons under them. Her skin was blotchy and broken out from the stress of her tormented nightmares. "Not the gorgeous princess now," she muttered.

After she showered, dried her hair, and dressed, she opened the door a crack and peered out. She couldn't see Cory in the darkness. She wanted to let him sleep, but she had a camp-ground to manage.

The doorbell sounded. "Damn!" She looked at the clock. Who in the world would come to their house at seven in the morning?

"What is it?" Cory mumbled.

"Shhhh, nothing. I'll take care of it. Go back to sleep."

She swiped a brush through her hair a couple of times and snatched a black scrunchie off the top of the bathroom counter as she left the room. Twisting it around her hair at the base of her neck, she peeked through the peephole in the front door. The telescopic image of two men stared back at her. One was Detective Bradley Miles.

The police? Gracie's pulse picked up tempo. A visit from the police before eight o'clock in the morning couldn't be good news. "Cory, get up. It's Detective Miles."

Cory sat up and ran his hands through his tousled hair. Sleepy-eyed and dazed, he turned around to look at Gracie. "Well, don't just stand there, let them in. My mouth feels as dry as the Sahara Desert." He stood and stretched, then grabbed the bedding from the sofa and balled it up, tossing it into Gracie's opened bedroom. "Make some coffee, sweetie. I'll be out in a minute."

She unlocked the deadbolt and opened the door. Her eyes were drawn to the uniformed officer. He stood slightly behind Detective Miles, his young face freshly shaved beneath short-cropped hair. Strong, well-muscled shoulders filled out his shirt.

In front of Mr. Good-Looking Cop, Detective Miles held up his black wallet and shiny badge. He, too, was clean shaven except for a short mustache. In his late forties or early fifties, he wore a neat gray suit, white shirt, and the ugliest tie Gracie had ever seen.

The detective spoke. "Ms. Schaffer, I believe we've met. This is Officer Harrison with the Saint Augustine Police Department." The handsome officer nodded a silent greeting.

The detective went on. "We're here to ask you some questions. And Mr. Marsh, too." Detective Miles's head went from left to right as his eyes searched the perimeter of the room. "Is he in?"

The sound of the toilet flushing gave the detective the answer he wanted.

"He'll be out in a minute." Gracie didn't like the smugness Detective Miles exhibited. She wished he'd just sent the good-looking cop. She knew how to deal with his kind. *Probably a rookie in training,* she thought. "Please," Gracie said with as good a smile as she could muster. "Come into the kitchen. I'll put a pot of coffee on."

Gracie's tension lessened as Detective Miles actually managed to flash an easy smile. She stepped back and closed the door behind them as they walked through the cedar cottage and made their way toward the kitchen.

"Please sit down. Uh . . ." A pile of folders sat on the chair the detective was heading toward. She pointed to the breakfast bar that had three white wicker stools in front of it. "Maybe there?"

Detective Miles smiled. "That will be fine." He no more got himself seated beside Officer Harrison when Cory walked into view.

He still looked sleepy-eyed but had shaved, combed his hair, and slipped into jeans. "Good morning, all," he said, pulling a t-shirt over his head.

Gracie was pouring the officers coffee. She looked up and smiled, relieved that he had finally joined them. "Good morning, Cory," she said. "Detective Miles wants to talk with us." She put the coffeepot down in the center of the table, sat, and folded her hands in front of her like an attentive schoolgirl.

"This shouldn't take too long. I'd like to ask you both some questions."

Cory sat across the table from Detective Miles, aware of the officer who sat on his left and extracted a notebook and pen from his top pocket. "Sure, no problem, but I thought we covered everything. Is it really necessary to keep rehashing this over and over?"

"This is a complicated and unusual case, Mr. Marsh. Your wife was ill, refused to go to the hospital, and then her charred body ends up on the beach?" He mentally noted the way Cory's jaw tightened. "Forensics and the medical examiner didn't have much to work with. What we do know is that your wife . . ." He turned to look at Gracie, sitting slouched over the table. "Your mother, Ms. Schaffer, did not die from any illness, nor did she die from being set on fire at the beach. The cause of death was poisoning, which was discovered in the remains of her digestive tract."

The veins in Cory's temples pulsed. He bent to look Detective Miles in the eye. "Get on with this, Detective. Find out what the hell happened to my wife. And I think you should be having this conversation with Ken Schaffer."

"I assure you, Mr. Marsh, we will be talking more with Mr. Schaffer. Right now we're trying to validate his claim that he was nowhere around here on March fifth, but in West Palm Beach at some Club Med. I would appreciate it if both you and Ms. Schaffer here could go over that day again with me. Where were you? What were your activities? Who discovered the remains on the beach?" The detective watched the body language of both Cory and Gracie. Studying the way Cory was sitting back in his chair, arms folded across his chest, teeth clenched, head nodding up and down incessantly. Gracie remained quiet and sullen with eyes focused on the kitchen window . . . looking at nothing in particular. She just had a faraway stare on her face.

He refrained from giving either of them all the findings of the investigation. Like the grisly discovery of Patricia's liver, which was found fused into a lump of vertebrae, and her skull, shrunk down to the size of a baseball from the intense heat—heat that had to be well over twenty-five hundred degrees. Nor did he divulge the discovery of Patricia's left arm. Positively identified through DNA testing to indeed be hers. Charred, but intact. Except for the fourth finger on the left hand, which was missing.

"Ms. Schaffer—Gracie, we can start with you," Detective Miles said. "Could you go over the day's events from March fifth for me? What you did, where you went, and so on?"

At the sound of the detective's voice, Gracie turned her head away from the window. She swallowed hard against a dry throat. "I was here, Detective."

Officer Harrison flipped his notebook open; with pen in hand, he was ready for action.

"I know that, Ms. Schaffer. Could you please be more specific? What time did you get up? Where was your mother? Give me a rundown of your day from the time you awoke to the time you learned of your mother's demise."

"Her mother was with me," Cory chimed in. "In bed. She was pretty sick, and I was trying my damnedest to get her to go to the hospital."

"You'll have your turn, Mr. Marsh. Please, you were about to say, Ms. Schaffer?"

Gracie's eyes met Cory's. He was understandably becoming agitated. Had Cory been her father, he'd have already been arrested for brutality on the police. She gave him a wan smile, assured he'd return it. She would have liked to cry. Get it out once and for all. But her eyes remained dry. Perhaps her well of tears had become depleted through the years. Memories flooded her mind like a movie on fast forward. Memories banished from her consciousness for years. Or so she thought. When Cory's

It was her favorite.

"I went back to the kitchen, made her tea and also thought some saltine crackers would help. I brought a tray of tea and the crackers to her, set them down on the nightstand to prop up her pillows and help her sit up. I held the tea to her lips, and she sipped it down. She didn't want the crackers. After a few sips of tea she said she wanted to lie back down. I helped her get comfortable and brought the tray back out to the kitchen.

"I was planning to just sit beside her until Cory came home for lunch. Which I did. As soon as I heard Cory, I tiptoed out of the room and told him she was sleeping. He said he wanted to look in on her, which he did."

"When I did," Cory explained, "she looked rested and much better than she had in days. I went back out to the kitchen and made myself a sandwich. I asked Gracie if she could come back to the office with me just long enough to pay a few vendors."

"Did you, Ms. Schaffer?"

"Yes. I figured it wouldn't take more than a half hour or so."

"Why didn't tell us this before?"

"Tell you what?" Cory asked. He didn't like the way the detective seemed to be pointing the finger of accusation at him or Gracie.

"That you both had left Patricia alone."

"It was only thirty minutes," Gracie said. "When I got back, my mom was gone. I was panicked. I went through every room in this cottage looking for her. Then to her art studio out back. She was nowhere. I went outside and got on my golf cart to see if she was in the campground. Maybe taking a walk. She'd been laid up for weeks not feeling good. I thought she'd been all right. That whatever it was had run its course. That all the vomiting and diarrhea from the night before got it all out of her system.

"When I couldn't find her anywhere on the grounds, I went to the beach. I knew how much she loved the water. That's

Ten

"Look what I got." Standing in the living room of their motor home, Laura reached into her purse and extracted a silver box the size of her palm. She held it out for David's inspection.

"What is it?"

"It's a digital voice recorder. I bought it at the office supply store Katie and I went to. Look how small it is. It'll fit into my purse, or your pocket, and no one will even know it's there."

David chuckled. "My, my, you're turning into a regular Jessica Fletcher. What's your plan, baby?" David lifted a pencil from the coffee table and waggled it between his fingers in front of his mouth.

"We're going to the beach bash potluck, aren't we?"

He took Laura's hand and guided her to the sofa. "We cannot go around bugging people. Besides, I think it's illegal."

"It is not. They do it all the time on TV. And we'll be discreet."

Heaving a resigned sigh, David flopped down beside her. "Let me see that thing."

Laura passed the mini device to David. "I got this one because it has an external microphone. The recorder can be hidden, but the mic clips onto the strap. You got it!"

David had already figured the device out. He plugged a thin cord into the recorder and demonstrated. The microphone at the end was practically unnoticeable, as long as no one looked too closely. "I don't know," he said. "Maybe we should run this by Jeremy. He's the expert. Besides, I'm still not sure it's legal, and I'd hate for us to have to call your dad and tell him we were the main attraction at the Saint Augustine Old Jail."

"Gimme that!" Laura snatched the recorder from David and tossed it on the coffee table. "I hardly think we'd end up in jail, David. And I think Jeremy would find it a brilliant idea. I think you're just jealous that you didn't think of it."

"I haven't seen Jeremy today," David said.

"Pleading no comment on the microphone idea, huh?" Laura raised her feet from the floor and stretched out with them resting on David's lap. "Katie said he'd been on the phone all morning with some of his old colleagues. Probably conferring over that filling he found."

David massaged her feet, letting his hands roam a little farther up her leg. "Mmm, you feel nice and warm and soft."

"The feet."

"The heat."

They both laughed.

"Are they going to the barbeque?" David asked.

"Katie is. I don't know about Jeremy." She looked at her watch and dropped her feet back to the floor. "We better get going. It starts in twenty minutes."

"And will go on all day. What's your hurry, my pretty?"

"I swear, David, don't you ever get enough?"

"Of you? No."

At the beach, white-sneakered campers were already gathered in groups along the palm-lined waterfront. Laura spotted Stanley, the Cookie Lady, and Stella, who was tapping everyone she passed on the shoulder with her cane.

"Why do you suppose she even has that thing?" David asked. "She doesn't need it for walking."

Laura laughed. "No, she needs it for self-defense when someone eventually whacks her on the side of her head."

David looked around, trying to spot Jeremy. "I don't see Jeremy and Katie, do you?"

Laura scanned the beach. There was a group of children building sand castles. One particular little boy caught her attention. He was struggling with one arm that appeared to be weak as he lifted a handful of sand to the top of his castle. He looked proud of his architectural sand structure. "Lookie! Look, Mommy!" he was shouting. He reminded her of Eddie and Karen's little boy, Timmy.

"I don't see them," Laura said. "But isn't that Gracie?" She pointed straight ahead. Gracie and someone appeared to be in deep conversation as they strolled along the coastline.

"Looks like it," David said.

"I wonder who that is with her. Doesn't look like Cory."

David held his hands up to shield his face from the sun. The face of the man with Gracie was familiar. "I think it's her dad."

Laura gasped. "Her dad? What's he doing here?"

"How would I know? Why don't you take that little microphone of yours and see if you can get close enough to find out."

"How did you know I brought it?"

"I didn't. But I do know you, my love."

"Laura! Yoo-hoo, over here."

Laura turned and saw Terrie waving and carrying on as she struggled to make her way across the beach and down to the picnic area. She was toting a basket with one hand and waving to Laura with the other.

Laura waved back. "It's Terrie from the office," she told David. She motioned for the girl to join them.

When Terrie had finally made her way to where David and Laura stood, she was panting and sweating. "Whew! I forgot how hard it is to walk through this sand, much less try to run in it."

"The heat doesn't help. Here, sit down." David took the

basket from Terrie, and she collapsed onto the chaise lounge next to Laura. "Mmm, smells like fried chicken in here to me."

"It is. Help yourself," Terrie said.

"Don't tell him that," Laura said. "He'll leave nothing but bones."

David chomped his teeth into a drumstick and wiped his mouth with the back of his hand. "Speaking of bones, isn't that Gracie over there?"

"Where?" Terrie was craning her neck every which way. "Oh, I see her. Yep, that's her and her dad. He's really a creepy and scary guy."

"Why do you say that?" Laura asked. She fiddled with the recorder beside her and managed to turn on her little device without anyone noticing.

"He just is," Terrie said. "Norma, the other girl who works in the office, she told me she saw him slap Patricia—Gracie's mother." Terrie stopped and made the sign of the cross then continued. "This happened not long before Patricia got so sick."

"Did Ms. Queen Busybody tell you why he slapped her? And where was Cory when this happened?" David wiped his hands on a napkin and pulled his chair in closer. "More importantly, where is Cory now?"

Laura was in awe at how fast David had made Terrie come out of that little clamshell she lived in. He really had a way with women. Especially women he felt were being mistreated in any way or disrespected. It was one of his many traits that made her fall so deeply in love with him.

"David, please," Laura said. "You sound like an interrogator."

"Sorry, Terrie. I just . . ."

"Oh, it's okay, David. I like you and Laura. I did from the first time I met you guys. It's such a breath of fresh air to have you here."

David gave Terrie his best smile. "We like you, too. So, what else did Norma tell you?"

Laura heaved an exasperated sigh, then found herself hoping it didn't get caught on her recorder.

Terrie took a swig of the 7Up David offered her and continued. "Norma talks to Gracie a lot. I think they're kind of friends. Anyway, Norma told me . . . and please, don't tell anyone I told you. I'd hate to be thought of as a gossip."

"We won't," David promised, making an X across his chest with his right index finger.

Terrie turned and smiled at Laura. "He's so cute, Laura."

Laura returned the smile. "Yes, he is. Just a regular little Pooh bear, my David is."

Settled back into her chaise, Terrie told David and Laura what she'd heard from Norma and what she'd seen with her own eyes. "Patricia was afraid for Gracie. Afraid because her husband, Ken, was so abusive. She didn't want Gracie to be subjected to such violence so she sent her to a Catholic boarding school in Miami. At the time Gracie was only four. But Patricia would never allow her to visit at home because of Ken. She'd drive up to Miami to see her. Anyway, this went on for years. Finally, she got wise and left Ken. After twenty-five years of living with emotional and physical abuse."

"Hmmm, I wonder why she waited so long," David said. "I mean Gracie was already out of the house, so to speak."

"She met Cory." Terrie took another big sip of her drink. "They—Patricia and Ken—were living somewhere in Georgia at the time. Cory met Patricia just a few years ago and I guess he just befriended her. Felt sorry for her. He helped her battered and bruised soul to heal—I think that's how Norma put it. One thing led to another and their friendship soon turned into love. Patricia finally got up the courage to tell Ken she wanted a divorce. That's when, according to how Norma tells it, all hell broke loose."

David had seen it before. Women who felt trapped, frightened . . . and the men who thrived on such authority and dominance over these women. David's fists clenched. "Ken didn't want to lose his power and control over Patricia. That's what he was upset over," he surmised.

"Ken didn't want to lose the money," Terrie corrected. "That's what he became so violent about. Even went after Cory with a gun."

"Money?" Laura asked. "Did Patricia have money in her family?"

"No, Patricia had all the money from her paintings. She was an artist. Even had several of her paintings displayed in an Atlanta art gallery. She did beautiful work. For years. Then I guess she stopped painting altogether when the violence she lived with became stronger than her soul's inspiration. Cory is the one who got her painting again. He knew how much she loved the sea, and he talked her into buying this resort. He wanted her to always live with inspiration and beauty surrounding her. She did all the murals and art you see here.

"For years after their divorce Ken stalked them both—Patricia and Cory. Made their lives a living hell. Patricia kept getting restraining orders on Ken, but that never seemed to stop him. Once she and Cory moved here and married, things seemed to quiet down. That's when Patricia had Gracie come live with them. And that's when poor Patricia started to have more problems. With her own daughter. I guess Gracie got pretty mad with her mom over having to be in boarding school all her life. I saw her on several occasions get in Patricia's face and scream all kinds of accusations. Cory's too. She'd accuse him of just going after her mother for her money and all sorts of nonsense like that."

"Doesn't sound like Gracie," David said. "She seems kind of

quiet and reserved. And seems to get along fine with Cory."

"Oh she does . . . now. I guess she went through a period of adjustment. Had to get all that out of her with her mother. I know she loved her mother a lot. She was the one who cared for her when she got so sick. And I saw how devastated she was that day she came into the office, after being the one who discovered her mother's charred remains." Terrie made the sign of the cross again.

"I don't know," Laura said. "It just seems kind of strange now that Cory and Gracie appear so happy and are living under the same roof."

Terrie's eyes widened and she looked at Laura. "You think something's going on between them, too?"

"Too?" David asked. "Who else thinks that?"

"Well, everyone," Terrie said. "Gracie used to flirt with Cory all the time and he with her. When Patricia was still very much alive. No one knows for sure if anything was really going on, but I never saw anyone do a one-eighty like Gracie did about her feelings toward Cory."

David had evidently heard enough. "Terrie, you'll have to excuse us. We promised some other folks that we'd join them. I didn't realize it was getting so late."

An excuse if Laura ever heard one. But the look on David's face kept her from asking Terrie more questions. "Yes, we really should be trying to find where Jeremy and Katie are."

"I know them," Terrie said. "They're such a cool couple." Terrie sat back against the chaise and closed her eyes. "I'm going to catch some rays. They call me the Sun Goddess around here. You two go on."

They left Terrie sitting comfortably in her chair. Being on the same wavelength, they both headed in the direction of where Gracie sat under a wooden gazebo, with her father.

Click!

"What was that?" Laura asked.

"What was what?"

"That click."

"I think your recorder shut off, darling."

Laura pulled the device from the pocket of her beach robe and held it in front of her. "I forgot all about this."

David came to a halt. "Over here," he told Laura. "If we plop ourselves behind this banyan tree, we can hear what's going on."

"David Jennings. You are turning us into one of them."

"One of what?" he whispered.

"One of those gossipmongers we both despise."

"It's not gossiping, it's investigating. Big difference."

"Oh, okay, if you say so."

They sat about twenty feet from the picnic table occupied by Gracie and Ken. They didn't have to strain much to hear what was going on. The high-pitched tones coming from Ken and Gracie's obvious verbal sparring match were loud and clear.

"I don't want you talking to that detective again! You hear me? Not unless you have a lawyer present. Just keep your mouth shut for a change."

"Let go of me! You got some nerve . . . coming around here."

David craned his head from behind the tree to see if Ken was hurting Gracie.

Laura picked up on his concern. "She sounds like someone who can take good care of herself, David."

It was the way she said "David" that made him turn back around and face his wife. "Who? I was looking for Jeremy."

"Shush, this is getting good."

"Hey you two, what's up?"

Laura jumped and looked up to see Jeremy and Katie. She placed her hand over her chest. "God, you almost gave me a heart attack, sneaking up like that."

Jeremy looked over at Gracie and Ken. "Who's sneaking up on whom?"

"What is going on over there?" Katie asked. "All that yelling."

"Sounds like a little father and daughter bonding," Jeremy said.

"Well, as manager, I think Gracie needs to get over here and be a hostess to her campers."

"David," Jeremy said, "looks like you've got something on your mind. How 'bout we all go over to the Pirate's Cove and you can tell us what we missed."

Katie was quiet for a long time as she sat and listened to the three others. Finally she sighed. "You guys are all making way too much out of all this. Bottles washed ashore, poisoning, abuse, murder. My God. Can we not have fun and enjoy retirement? Leave the interrogations and suppositions and crime-scene investigations to the police." There. She'd said it.

Normally, Jeremy would have flared with indignation at Katie's outburst. But he didn't. He knew she was just feeling left out. Alone. Not interested in what he or his newfound partners in crime found exhilarating.

So he simply said, "Katie, I'm sorry. You're right. I was just getting ready to ask you for your female intuition, which is always so sharp. But you're right . . ."

"My female intuition about what?"

Jeremy wrapped his arm around her shoulder. "Nothing, dear."

David tried hard to hold in his laugh, but let it slip out.

"And what is so funny?" Jeremy asked.

"Nothing, man."

Jeremy looked into Katie's eyes. "Your intuition about Gracie Schaffer. What does your gut instinct tell you about her?"

Katie looked at David and Laura then to Jeremy. "Really? You guys really want my opinion?"

"Of course we do," Laura said.

"I think she's a very troubled young woman who has no business managing a campground filled with retirees. I also think she *is* trouble. Or looking for it."

"Meaning?" Jeremy prodded.

"Meaning I saw her this morning wrapped in Cory's arms."

David choked as he gulped down the frozen Tropical Breeze drink he had just started to swallow. "You saw what?" He was still choking as he spoke.

Laura patted his back. "She saw Gracie and Cory in an embrace."

"There's nothing wrong with that," Jeremy said. "They both lost someone very special to them. In a horrendous manner, no less. Consolation is hardly anything to be ashamed about."

"Jeremy's right," David said.

"I don't know about that," Laura said. "After what Terrie just told us."

"What did Terrie tell you?" Jeremy asked, dropping his arm from around Katie's shoulder.

"I got it all here," Laura said, pulling her recorder from her pocket.

"That's illegal," Jeremy said.

"Told you," David said.

"It is?" Laura proceeded to take the little device apart. "Then I'll just have to toss this battery with my recording away." As she pitched it toward a nearby trash can, Jeremy jumped and caught it in midair.

"I won't say anything if you don't."

David shook his head. "Our place or yours?"

"Mine," Jeremy said. "It's show-and-tell time. I have a few unearthed goodies myself."

"About what's in the bottle?" Laura asked.

"Yes ma'am!"

Eleven

The nightmare was coming back. The dark images crept into his sleep until he saw himself balanced on the edge of a black precipice. The rock beneath his bare feet cut into his flesh. He tried to pull himself out of the fog, to turn and claw for the rope that connected to him and safety, but it dissolved between his fingers and he teetered helplessly with nowhere to go but down into whirling, uncontrolled chaos.

Hanging on by sheer will, he watched as the flames engulfed them. First his mother, then Patricia. He couldn't reach them. Couldn't save them. He gripped tighter, holding onto the rock with the smallest of finger- and toeholds as the winds from the Atlantic beat savagely against him.

A large crack reverberated through the rock. He looked up. A figure, dark in silhouette, stood at the top of the Adirondacks, dangling a rope just out of reach. Laughter, cold and heinous, whipped at him along with the wind, loosening his hold.

Then it started all over again as the silhouette pushed the people he loved into the raging inferno of flames. *No! Stop!*

He reached out, trying to grab a hand, a sleeve—anything— that would stop the madness of this senseless dying. Something caught, jerked at his arm and pulled. He was falling. Down into the blazing inferno.

Cory awoke with a start to the sound of retreating thunder. Rain splattered through the screen of his open window onto the foot of the bed. A quick glance at the clock radio showed that it was barely eleven—not even an hour since he'd gone to bed. He got up to close the window. A blast of the March air pebbled his bare skin. In the next flash of lightning, he caught a reflection of his face on the glass.

Crazed.

Haunted.

Every time he failed to save them.

They'd both counted on him. He'd let both of them down.

And now there was Gracie.

She was the next victim, and his nightmare was warning him of a dire outcome.

He scraped a hand over his face, trying to erase the images. But they would always be there until he got answers to his lingering questions, until he was sure of Gracie's safety.

Needing a change of scenery, he pulled on a pair of jeans and headed to the living room to check the windows.

A teakettle purred in the kitchen, black against the red-hot burner. Dressed in one of her mother's oversized t-shirts and a white fleece cardigan, Gracie stood in the kitchen. Between the stove's light and the open refrigerator, radiance surrounded her like a halo, making her glow.

She was an angel. Offering hope.

He shook his head and dismissed the notion. She'd given him nothing but trouble since her arrival.

A bolt of lightning flashed blue through the cabin. Thunder cracked right on top of it. Gracie jumped, gasped. The light in the fridge surged, then died.

"Hang on. I'll find you a flashlight." He knew she didn't like the dark.

"Cory?"

"Were you expecting someone else?" He probed for the drawer, bumped his hand against her hip, felt a surge of heat—then guilt flooded through him.

"I thought you were asleep." A little tremor rippled through her voice, making him want to gather her in his arms.

"The thunder took care of that." He wouldn't sleep again tonight, not with the nightmare so raw and fresh on his mind. Lifting the flashlight out of the drawer, he flicked on the switch, then set it on the counter.

"Why are you up?" he asked.

There was a nervousness to her movement as she snagged a loose strand of hair behind her ear. "I was cold and decided to make myself a cup of tea to warm up." She whirled to the pantry and rummaged for the tea. She hadn't been thrilled about having to make a special trip to the store to replenish what the good detective had confiscated. "Did someone forget to tell Florida that it was March?"

He answered her smile with one of his own.

She breezed by him and it took all he had to keep from snagging her mid-flight and pressing her body to his. Chemistry, that was all. Emotions, feelings could be controlled with logic.

She plucked two mugs from the cupboard. "Join me?"

"Sure. Let me crank up the heat and see if we can chase the chill away."

Her smile faded and a flash of something warm and needy lit her eyes. Carefully she turned away. Her busy fingers ripped cellophane wrapping from the box of tea, turning the easy task into a marathon affair.

Walking away was difficult, but he did it. Giving in to lustful impulses would do neither of them any good. He went to the thermostat on the living room wall and turned it up a few degrees. "What are you making?"

"Making?" Her voice sounded a bit rusty.

"You were standing with the fridge open before the lights went out."

"Oh, yes. Well, there isn't much left. Orange juice. Lettuce.

Half a cucumber. A small chunk of cheese." She chuckled. "And some dark chocolate from Mom's secret stash."

"Secret stash?" Trying to ignore the sensations of his body at the sound of Gracie's voice, he went around and checked the windows again.

"In a coffee can behind the flour."

He smiled. That was typical Patricia. "Any crackers to go with that cheese?"

"I think we have some. I'll look." She was sounding more relaxed now.

The sounds of Gracie bustling around in the kitchen chased away part of the remnants of his dream and replaced them with frustration. Want. It was there, powerful and restless, stalking inside him like a starving beast. God, he missed Patricia. He wished he'd never allowed his testosterone to cloud his good judgment. He couldn't make the same mistake twice, even if he was now a free man. Free? Was he? Would he ever be free from the guilt? From being so taken by with Gracie's seductiveness that he caved in to his need and had an affair with his wife's daughter? Regret assaulted him.

Gracie took a quilt from the sofa and spread it out on the floor. She laid out a plate of cheese and crackers, and added some squares of chocolate. She went back to the kitchen, returned with two mugs of what smelled like peppermint tea, and handed one of them to him. The domestic tranquility should have lulled him into relaxation, but it didn't.

"You look like you're deep in thought," Gracie said.

He scrubbed a hand through his hair. "Look, Gracie," he said. "I know you went through a lot of trouble with this, but I think I'm going to pass on the food and call it a night."

Gracie reached for his hand that was gripping the back of the sofa. His gaze connected with hers. He silently spoke volumes with those compelling, magnetic eyes. But it was in a foreign tongue, not as easily decipherable as the secret, sensuous language they'd once shared. She wasn't sure what she was reading, or why she suddenly wanted to cry. *I understand,* she wanted to say, but the words got stuck in her throat. Instead she gave his fingers a squeeze.

"It wasn't any trouble," Gracie said. "You wanted something to snack on, I fixed it, and now I'll sit here and eat by myself. Not a problem."

He said nothing. She let her fingers slide back to her side. What had she expected? Appreciation? Understanding? Comfort?

"Good night," was all he said when he finally spoke. Then he headed toward his bedroom.

Trying to shove his rejection in the closet of painful things deep inside her, Gracie popped a slice of cheese into her mouth. "To hell with him," she mumbled aloud.

TWELVE

"Sure you don't want to go with me to Jeremy's?" David asked Laura. His hands were on Laura's shoulders as he looked over them. "What are you so busy with on that computer?"

"It's my travel journal." Laura tipped her head backward and smiled. "Full of adventure and excitement."

"What about sex?"

"What about it?"

"Did you put any of our *real* adventures and excitement in there?"

She clicked the file in Word, hit "save," and shut the computer down. "I put a few of those highlights in. Like how we discovered what those rest stops on the turnpike are *really* good for."

He swung her around in the swivel seat and stroked the soft skin of her cheek with his thumb.

"My visit with Jeremy can wait. How's about some afternoon delight?" He waggled his brows.

Laura rubbed the side of her head against his hand. "I'd love to, but I promised Terrie I'd help out in the office today. The Good Sam Sunshine group is arriving. Terrie said more than twenty-five rigs would be rolling in."

"The Good Sam what?" His invitation being turned down, he tucked his shirt back into his jeans.

"It's a caravan group of Good Sammers. The RV club?" Laura thought David had the cutest little-boy stare as he pretended to know exactly what she was talking about.

"Oh, yeah. Them. Well, have fun, with the Good Slammers and playing Sherlock."

"Sammers." Laura laughed. "I wonder what else Jeremy could have uncovered with the bottle. Maybe you can call me on my cell and let me know."

"Sure." His lips touched the back of her neck as he whispered, "I love vibrating you."

"Go on! Get out," Laura said.

As he headed out the door, he almost took a tumble, missing the first step of the motor home. "I keep forgetting my house is a vehicle with moving steps."

"Are you okay?" Laura asked. She couldn't help but let a laugh escape.

"I'm fine. You're loving this, aren't you? My husband—RVer in training."

"I love you," she said. "Catch you later, honey."

Honey, that's exactly what was going from her mouth to his ears. He shot her a wink and blew her a kiss and headed off around Stella's trailer and over to Jeremy's.

"What took you so long?" Jeremy asked. He was sitting at the picnic table outside his fifth wheel, fiddling with a digital camera. "How'd you like that rain last night?"

David sat sidesaddle across from Jeremy. "I loved it. There's nothing like the sound of rain humming against the roof of a motor home. Just kind of lulls you to sleep."

Jeremy looked over the rim of his glasses at David. "You're a newlywed, kid. There should be more than rain that lulls you to sleep."

David laughed. "Oh, there is, believe me."

"Come on," Jeremy said. "I'm tired of fooling with this camera. Let's go inside so I can show you something interesting in your bottle."

David carefully followed Jeremy inside, stepping into the fifth wheel carefully. He didn't trust these trailer steps much anymore. "So, what is all this?" David slid into the seat of the breakfast nook, studying the contents of the bottle that Jeremy had once again spread out. This time, however, he had separated the ashes and fragments into two piles, one larger than the other.

Jeremy handed David a pair of latex gloves. He took his tweezers and carefully lifted a charred piece of debris. "See this?" he said. "Metal."

"Resin? From the filling?" David moved his head closer to the object Jeremy was holding in front of him.

"Nope. This little gem is a piece of precious metal."

"Isn't that what's used to make jewelry?" David took the tweezers from Jeremy and tilted his head from left to right as he studied it. "This looks like it's still pretty strong," he said as he took his gloved hand and slightly wiggled the object between his thumb and forefinger. "I'd have thought precious metal was just that—precious and weak." He handed the tweezers back to Jeremy.

Jeremy set the charred piece of metal, the size of the tip of a matchstick, by itself and scooped the rest of the ash and fragments back into the bottle. " 'Precious metal' covers an array of metals," he explained. "This baby here proved to be the toughest. Platinum."

"I'm not even going to ask how you determined that," David said. "I see how trashed your trailer looks from all your little forensic goodies. But I'd love to know, if platinum is so strong, why just a teeny piece of it? Why wouldn't the entire piece, whatever kind of jewelry it was, be intact?"

"I'm going to turn you into a forensic genius yet, my boy." Jeremy loved David's curiosity, sharp wit, and above all, the way his acute, analytical mind always did just that—analyzed intelligently, before spouting off with something stupid. "First, platinum is alloyed with other precious metals to get its added strength and durability. Yesterday, when I decided to take another look at your find, I spotted it. Don't know how I missed it the first time. Anyway, I got my trusty little electron microscope out and it confirmed what I'd suspected it to be."

"That explains why you and Katie were late getting to the beach barbeque," David said, amazed at his new RV buddy.

"Yeah, well, back to why this could really be pertinent. You're right. There wouldn't be just a little piece recovered from such a strong metal unless there was some sort of brute force used to get the jewelry before it did go up in flames. This was probably some small decorative piece from the jewelry design that came lose or broke away easily from the twenty-five-hundred-degree intense heat." Jeremy pounded his stomach. "My gut, David. I always trust it because it's never let me down. And my gut instinct tells me that we need to get this information, the bottle, and us down to see Detective Miles as soon as possible. I think he needs to look into our new illustrious owner of Harbor Lights RV Resort, Patricia Marsh's husband, as well as old Kenny boy."

David sat in silent thought for a moment. He knew Jeremy was right about going to Detective Miles. He felt it should have been done the moment of the resin-filling discovery. "You're thinking this is murder committed by a male, because of the brute force used to get the jewelry, right?"

"Right. Just which male in Patricia's life . . . well, that's the detective's puzzle to figure out."

"But why the bottle, Jeremy? You said you thought it was a woman because of the symbolism of the bottle being tossed out to sea. Why would Cory or Ken or any other guy feel compelled to put a piece of jewelry into the bottle along with Patricia's remains?"

"Some of her remains," Jeremy said. "And that's for the criminal profilers to unravel." He smiled and sat back. "Maybe we should first call in Laura. That gal loves her profiling, doesn't she? That, plus her deductions and woman's intuition . . . hell, we might just be able to go to Miles with the case solved." Jeremy concentrated a moment on what he'd just said. "Hey, where is Laura? I'd have thought she'd want to be here on this."

"She's at the office. Something about some kind of Good Something Club coming in. They were a little short-handed and Laura volunteered to help during the rush. What about Katie?"

"Shopping. Souvenirs. I told her if she didn't cool it, our trailer was going to become a remake of that old Lucille Ball movie, *The Long, Long Trailer.*"

"Don't think I ever saw it," David said.

"Before your time. Rent it. You'll love the scene with Lucy's rock collection."

"I will," David said.

Jeremy stood and stretched. "So, what do you say? Up to taking a drive to the Saint Augustine Police Department?"

Feeling good about the possibility of finally getting to the bottom of what really happened to Patricia Marsh, David lifted an eyebrow, then pulled his cell phone from his pocket. "You bet. Let me just give Laura call. I promised her I'd let her know what was going on."

"Ha!" Jeremy said, as he slapped David on the back. "I knew she'd be here one way or another. Go on, call her. I'll wait outside."

Gracie was going over office procedures with Laura. She introduced her to Norma, her assistant manager; Terrie, whom she already knew; Linda, the activities director; and Virginia, the bookkeeper.

Norma was a chunky, tall woman who loved to wear Mickey

Mouse t-shirts and spandex shorts. When Laura helped out in the office the last time, Terrie had told her about Norma, how tight she was with Gracie, and that Norma did not consider herself to be overweight at all. Terrie explained to Laura that Norma defined herself as having been cursed as a big-boned woman.

"Thank you for helping out," Gracie said. "I have some things I need to do, and the club should begin arriving in the next hour or two."

"Then it'll be nonstop with them for the next three or four hours," Norma added.

"Well, I'm happy to help out," Laura said.

Terrie rolled her eyes at Laura as Gracie pulled Norma to the side. Within minutes, both women were huddled by the brochure rack. Forced to move from side to side to avoid getting in the way of the tourists interested in the brochures, the two headed outside onto the porch.

Laura craned her neck to see them. They were sitting on a bench. Gracie looked agitated . . . upset? It was hard to tell. "I wonder what's up with Gracie."

"She's been in one of her moods all day," Terrie said. "Best we can hope for is that she goes home and stays there."

Laura looked around. The activities director had left and the bookkeeper was balancing spreadsheets. Laura was envious. She'd been nicknamed the "Excel Super Gal" at Big Pine Key Resort, and loved it. "I don't see Cory. Is he here?"

"I heard my name," Cory said. He emerged from the back office carrying a handful of resort site maps. He plopped the maps down on the registration counter. "Here, Terrie," he said, "all the sites are marked for the club. Make sure they understand where their designated group will be." He then turned to face Laura. "Laura, right? Don't tell me Gracie recruited you to work in here. You're supposed to be on your honeymoon."

Laura smiled. "Not a problem." She glanced over at the site maps. "Good job you did on those."

"Thanks. Sounds like you're well experienced with this sort of thing."

"My dad has a camping resort in Big Pine Key. He enlisted me as manager. I empathize with you and Gracie."

"I appreciate the help, Laura."

Just then Laura's cell began to vibrate from the pocket of her jeans. Smiling, she retrieved the phone. "Will you excuse me for a moment? Phone call."

"You can use my office," Cory said. "Right there," he said, pointing to a room behind the counter. "I have to make sure everything's a go for the potluck dinner tonight."

"Thanks," Laura said.

She looked at the number on her caller ID and flipped open her phone. Sitting down in the black leather chair in Cory's office she said, "I thought you'd never call. What's going on?" Laura looked around to assure herself that she was alone in the room. Then she flipped through some papers in a folder marked URGENT as she listened to David's voice. She wasn't really snooping, just fiddling while she talked.

"Jeremy uncovered something, so to speak, in the ashes from our bottle. We agreed that we need to take what we've found to Detective Miles. Let's just hope the detective doesn't toss us in the slammer for obstruction of justice or something." David chuckled, but the possibility had clearly occurred to him. "We're getting ready to head to the police department now. You okay? Or, would you like to accompany your partner in crime?"

"You don't think that could really happen, do you?"

"That what could happen?"

"That you could be arrested for obstruction of justice."

"No. I think after what Miles hears from Jeremy, he'll just be happy to finally have a solid lead."

Laura breathed a sigh of relief into the phone. "Solid lead? Does that mean you guys found out more than you're letting on?"

"It just means that Jeremy has kind of narrowed the list of suspects. We can eliminate the female ones."

"David—"

"What are you doing in here, Laura?" Gracie entered Cory's office in a huff, making sure the door slammed behind her.

"Honey, I have to go right now. Please, don't forget to pick up the buns for the burgers. I love you. Bye." Laura snapped the cell closed.

"Well? I'm waiting." Gracie stood with her arms folded across her chest. "What are you doing at Cory's desk? In his office?"

"I had a call. Cory said I could take it in here. I apologize if sitting at his desk while I talked presents a problem." Laura couldn't help but wonder if Gracie had caught her fumbling through the folders on top of Cory's desk.

"It appears your conversation has ended. If you have to go, that's okay. We can manage with the club," Gracie said.

Laura stood. "Oh, no. I don't have to go. David was just calling to let me know he was going to the Publix supermarket and wanted to know if I needed anything." She headed for the door. "Excuse me," she said, as she flashed Gracie a smile in passing. "I'll get out there right away. I'm happy to help out."

As she closed the door to Cory's office behind her, Laura felt Gracie's unseen gaze go through her. The scent of suspicion was getting stronger.

THIRTEEN

"What do you mean? You got a lead on the charred remains on the beach?"

"Not a lead, Detective. Information." Jeremy squared his shoulders. "I don't know if you've met David Jennings."

David extended his hand. "Detective. My wife and I are honeymooning in your fine city . . . at Harbor Lights Resort." He firmly took hold of the detective's hand.

Detective Miles shook David's hand. "I think I've seen you around." He let go of David's hand and pushed two chairs from against the wall closer to the men. "Please, sit down."

David and Jeremy sat as Detective Miles walked around his desk and sat. He looked first to Jeremy, then to David. "I can assure you both, the Saint Augustine Police Department is trained in investigations of this kind, and we don't need help from civilians."

"We understand, Detective," Jeremy said. "Before we go any further, let me assure you that David and I are also trained in such investigations. I'm a retired forensic anthropologist from New York, and David is a private investigator who specializes in stalkers." He reached beside him and took hold of the bottle that rested on the chair. Lifting it, he continued, "David and his lovely wife had this wash up on the beach, at their feet, the day they arrived—"

David broke in. "At first we just assumed some kid had been playing with it, shoved some sand into the bottle, tossed it out to sea, and it ended up at our feet. After examining it more carefully, and meeting up with Jeremy, we discovered it wasn't filled with sand at all."

"What it is, Detective, are charred remains. Lab reports have proved they are the remains of a female human."

The detective held up a hand, and Jeremy and David fell silent. He reached across his desk and took the bottle from Jeremy. He studied the contents momentarily before putting it down in front of him. He then glanced up. "So, let me get this straight." He looked at Jeremy with both brows arched. "You come here from New York, a forensic specialist, and just think it's okay for you to begin an investigation of your own. Make conclusions and determinations. Then prance in here to tell me all about it."

His glance switched to where David sat. "And you. You're some PI who thinks he knows more than the local law enforcement. Instead of turning your finding here in to us . . ." He took hold of the bottle and, for emphasis, tapped it up and down on his desk a few times. ". . . you decide to go to have a pow-wow with your camping neighbor."

"Detective?"

Detective Miles cut him off. "I'm not finished. What I should do is throw you both in jail for tampering with possible evidence." The detective's face became red and blotchy from his anger.

"Detective Miles," Jeremy said. "We didn't tamper with anything more than a bottle that was washed ashore. Now, would it really have gotten your attention if we'd come to you a few days ago with nothing more than a bottle and suppositions? I doubt it. If you'd listen to what we have to say, you might realize we're here for one reason only. To find a murderer. We don't know his or her mental state, and this situation could be dangerous. We're here to help. Trained, as you and your department are." Jeremy sat back, crossing his left leg over his right, and resting his hands on the arm of his chair.

The detective was silent. Sitting back in his chair, he studied Jeremy and David, and then the bottle, which was still centered in the middle of his desk. He cleared his throat, looked at Jeremy, and said, "Start at the beginning. And don't leave anything out."

For the next two and a half hours Detective Miles was given a full account of the bottle's contents, the piece of resin filling discovered on the beach, and the charred particle of platinum that was identified earlier that day. He listened, sometimes tapping his pencil on his desk from sheer frustration and annoyance that David and Jeremy had not come in before now. At the same time, he was also elated they had.

"Let me ask you, Mr. Myers," the detective said to Jeremy, holding the bottle up. "Do you think the remains in this bottle are those of Patricia Marsh? Or is your conclusion that we may have two female unsolved murders on our hands?"

"For what it's worth," Jeremy replied, "my gut tells me you're holding the victim, Patricia Marsh, Detective."

Detective Miles stood. "Since the two of you are already into this case with interest apparently equal to my own, I'd like to ask if you could continue to see what you can dig up from the campers. What they may or may not have seen that day. I'm particularly interested in Cory Marsh and Ken Schaffer, Mrs. Marsh's ex. In the past two days I've patrolled the campground a number of times in an unmarked car, but always seem to be noticed by some old biddy."

David laughed. "Good old Stella Greenburg. Jeremy and I can get past her, Detective."

"Don't get too far past her," the detective said. "Someone like that might prove to be an unaware informant."

Jeremy stood. "We'll keep in touch, Detective. And you do the same."

"My wife, Laura, has been volunteering in the office and has already stumbled upon one interesting item that may or may not be connected." David pulled the folded piece of paper with the poem composed in the "Chiller" font from his shirt pocket and handed it to Detective Miles. "A little poem that fell from some shelves in a storage closet when my wife was looking for registration forms."

Jeremy looked at David. "Poem? You didn't mention anything to me about a poem."

"Sorry, Jeremy," David said. "I'd forgotten all about it. When you mentioned about coming here, I thought it might have some significance to the rest of the mysteries. I grabbed it when I went to call Laura to tell her what was up, and just now remembered it again."

"I'd like to keep this," the detective said. "Bag it as evidence with what you brought today."

"Mind if I take a look first?" Jeremy asked. Reading, he blew out a whistle. "I'd say it's a definite piece of the puzzle."

Discovering Laura wasn't at their motor home, David headed straight to the office.

"Laura, you were a lifesaver," Terrie said. "Again!"

Laura smiled when she saw David walk in. It had been a creepy afternoon with Gracie giving her evil looks, Cory and Gracie whispering in the back, and Norma and Gracie back and forth between the office and the outside porch. She just wanted to get out of there.

"Ready, my dear?" David asked.

"All done here." Laura waved to Terrie as she took David's hand and headed out the door.

David noticed a crack in the stair railing, but it was too late.

He grabbed for Laura. He caught the waistband of her shorts, felt gravity pull both bodies down. Holding onto her waistband, he sought to grip a stronger hold, snagged a fistful of t-shirt.

She clutched at his arms. The look on her face was the mirror image of the one she'd had when she first saw her father hanging from the stage of the clubhouse with Slippery behind him, armed to the teeth with her father's military weapons. Horror and fear pummeled David. He couldn't let her fall.

Laura's t-shirt ripped in his fist. He swore. She slid toward the thorny bougainvilleas below. He shifted his stance, braced his legs and slid one arm beneath her shoulders. Her fingers dug into his collarbone. Carefully he climbed over the splintered wood and stepped down on the slanted ground. Balancing her weight in his arms, he put himself between her and the ground beneath his feet.

"I've got you, sweetie."

She nodded, the soft blue of her eyes still wild with apprehension. "I'm okay."

If she'd fallen, the bougainvilleas wouldn't have saved her. They would have shredded her skin, then plunged her down against the embankment of concrete. No two ways around it, she'd have been hurt.

He'd vowed to love and protect her.

He'd promised her.

David glanced at the piece of wood railing staring up at him. Nothing out of the ordinary. Just the splinters of neglect.

Accident or planned incident? Not enough of an accident to kill her, but enough to terrorize her all over again.

Everything and everyone was suspicious to him now—even something as innocent as wood rot.

David's touch was immensely tender as he sought to disengage Laura from the thorns holding her prisoner. Laura hung on to his shoulders while he disentangled the branches clinging to the back of her ripped t-shirt.

"Are you sure you're okay?" he said once she was free again, concern evident in the wrinkling around his eyes.

The fall hadn't caused any real damage. A few cuts stung the backs of Laura's legs, but otherwise she'd escaped her misadventure unharmed.

"I'm fine. No damage done. Really."

Before letting her go, he held her deeper in the cradle of his arms. She brushed away imaginary thorns from her legs, taming the shivers still racking her body.

David examined the broken step of the office porch, filtering the decaying splinters of wood between his fingers. "Where's Cory? Or Gracie? Are they inside?"

Gracie, she thought, then quickly dismissed the notion. She was just about to say Cory was still there, when he emerged.

"My God! What in the hell happened?" Cory rushed to Laura's side, making sure she was all right.

"Rotten wood," David said, his voice rising a decibel or two. "Or a rotten something."

"I asked Sam, who takes care of maintenance, to replace this step days ago. I'm really sorry."

"Sorry doesn't cut it," David said. "Your responsibility is to your guests. Don't think that some lame statement 'not responsible for loss of property or personal injury' diminishes your accountability."

Cory raked his hand through his hair as he inspected the splintered, rotted wood. "You're right, David, I should have inspected this before an accident occurred. Laura, if there's—"

Terrie opened the door, and stood there with her mouth wide open. "Laura! Oh, my God. Are you hurt?"

"I'm okay."

"Get that damned thing fixed!" David said.

He wrapped his arm around Laura's waist and ushered her

back toward their motor home.

"You're sure you feel like going to the potluck tonight?" David wasn't sure Laura should go anywhere within this resort after what had happened. Earlier the thought of a potluck supper like the ones back at Big Pine Key had made his stomach growl in anticipation of the array and creativity of the campers' home-cooked dishes. Now all he thought about was Patricia Marsh, and the fact that she'd been poisoned.

As if reading his thoughts again, Laura said, "Yes, I'm sure I want to go. What's the matter? You think I'm afraid of being poisoned or something?"

A nervous chuckle escaped his lips. "Of course not. You're right, it might do us good to get our minds off your tumble with some good home cooking."

Laura laughed. "I thought so. I've never known your bottomless pit to pass up food for anything." She sat on the edge of their bed, dabbing peroxide on her cuts with a cotton ball.

"You're not going to wear this, are you?" David tugged at her ripped t-shirt.

"I thought I might. It'll make for interesting conversation."

He was happy to see her more relaxed, smiling. He helped her out of the t-shirt, gently rubbing his fingers over the scratches on her back. "Here," he said. "Give me the peroxide, and let me get the ones back here."

She handed him a dampened cotton ball as she strained her head over her left shoulder. "How bad are they?"

"Hmm, let Dr. David have a look." He ran kisses up and down her spine, groaning silently at his body's instantaneous response to her bare back. Every atom of his body responded to her softness with deepening hunger.

"That tickles," she said. Turning, she faced him, drew him closer, and kissed him repeatedly. She knew he'd feel responsible for the mishap with the office steps. "I'm all right," she whispered. Her hands traveled under his shirt, the tips of her fingers running up and down his back. "As long as you hold me, I'm all right."

He buried his face in her hair and held her tight as they toppled across the bed. "I love you, Laura."

Over the sounds of their ragged breaths came a knock on the door.

"Someone's at the door," Laura said.

David let out an exasperated breath as he sat up. "We definitely need to get us one of those signs for our front door."

"Signs?"

"Yeah. The one that reads, 'If the trailer's rocking, don't bother knocking.' "

She laughed as David walked down the narrow entryway running from the bedroom, through the kitchen, and to the front door.

A few minutes later he returned to the bedroom to find Laura changed into a clean red blouse and pair of black Docker shorts. "Who was it?"

"Some kid looking for his grandpa."

Laura burst into a loud laugh and tousled David's hair as he stood beside her in front of the dresser mirror. "We'll eat fast," she joked. "Then leave the rec hall and pick up where we left off."

That put a smile on his face fast.

David and Laura headed toward the recreation hall, Laura carrying a bowl of potato salad, David toting a pecan pie. Looking down at the pie, David was reminded of Laura's play with words when he'd called her earlier that day. "What was all that jabber about picking up buns when I called you today?"

"I was in Cory's office talking to you and Gracie popped in.

She looked a little annoyed, like she thought I was snooping around for something."

"Were you?"

"A little. What about you? You never said how it went at the police department."

"It went better than I'd expected. I don't think the detective was too thrilled about us sticking our noses into a murder investigation. Jeremy smoothed his ruffled feathers, and eventually Detective Miles saw that we could actually be a help and not a hindrance to him. He kept our bottle and that verse you found as evidence." David scooted around a group of campers. "I'll tell you all about it later. Looks like a big turnout here."

"These things always are. One thing I've noticed about campers. No matter what the activity might be, if it's free, there will be a turnout."

Sniffing appreciatively, David put the pecan pie on the long table then took Laura's dish from her and placed it beside the pie.

"The desserts stay separate," Stella Greenburg said. She picked up her walking stick and pointed it at the end of the table. "Over there."

David shook his head. "Yes, ma'am." He looked around the hall for a place to sit. "There's Jeremy and Katie. Let's go." He took Laura's hand and walked to the table in the back, close to the door.

Jeremy stood and pulled a chair out for Laura. "Where have you two been? We were beginning to think you were going to make it."

"Laura!" Katie said. "What in the world happened to your face and arms?"

"A little accident. Nothing serious."

David harrumphed. "Cory better get those front steps of the office fixed before someone sues him."

"Did I hear Cory's name mentioned?"

David turned to see Gracie standing behind him.

"Yeah," David said. "You did. Look what his carelessness in not getting your front office steps fixed did to Laura."

Gracie looked Laura up and down. "Cory told me she had a little spill. It doesn't look too bad. Let's not make a mountain out a little molehill." She smiled at David. "Enjoy your supper. I have to go find Cory."

David popped up from his seat as if ejected. His eyes glazed. His teeth clenched. *A little spill? Doesn't look too bad?* The more David thought about Gracie's comments, the tighter the anger coiled inside his gut.

Laura touched David's hand. "David, let it go."

He sat down. "Goldilocks and Papa Bear over there won't be smiling for long if they don't get that step fixed."

"Any time you want, you can tell us what all this about a broken step and Laura looking like she's wrestled with a tiger is all about," Jeremy said."

"Later," Katie said. "If we don't get in that line now, there won't be anything left."

"She's right," Laura said.

David and Jeremy followed Katie and Laura toward the table of food.

"Katie?" Laura asked. "I thought you didn't care for potluck dinners."

"I don't. But Jeremy has our trailer crammed so full with microscopes, skeletal structures, tubes, and skulls, I was afraid to eat anything in our refrigerator for fear it might be evidence of some sort."

They all broke out in a loud laugh. So loud, they suddenly realized all eyes were upon them.

The evening was strained at first. Conversation started slowly, and it seemed as if everyone was trying hard to avoid the obvious subject of what had happened to Laura, and why David appeared to be preoccupied with Cory and Gracie's table.

"Rude, that's what he was." An elderly lady gave a vicious nod that shook her tightly curled gray hair as she spoke. She was seated at the table right beside David and Laura's table.

Laura speared a twisty piece of pasta and a shrimp on a plastic fork. She stole a glance at the table with the yakkety older women. She kicked David's leg under the table, hoping he'd stop his attack on the fried chicken, potato salad, and green beans long enough to listen in. He didn't. He kept chomping away.

The elderly women continued. "I tell you, Lily, he ain't been right since Patricia died." She made a circular motion around her head with her index finger. "Don't even say hello when spoken to. Rude, that's what he is."

The one named Lily stiffened and drew out an outraged breath. "That Gracie is the one that's rude. Harbor Lights will never be the same without Patricia. Such a lovely woman she was."

Laura saw David hide a grin behind a chicken leg.

Stella Greenburg also sat with the elderly ladies. Her lips pursed as her chin shot upward. "It's scandalous, I tell you. Look at them. Sitting there all cute and cozy. They ought to be ashamed of themselves. This generation of young people certainly doesn't know the meaning of respect."

Katie tried not to laugh at the expression on Stella's face. The woman looked especially nice today in white capri pants and a pink blouse.

Stella's eyes focused on something over Laura's head. She shoved her chair back to get a clearer view, bumping Laura's chair in the process. "No respect for the Ten Commandments, either! It's a crime, that's what it is, a crime."

Laura turned her head, wondering what had caused such

venom in the old lady's voice. Behind her, people ate and chatted amicably. Several had returned for second helpings and hovered around the food, David and Jeremy among them. Some short, round guy stood talking to Cory at his table, while Gracie dabbed at her chin with a napkin. Laura's eyes then went briefly back to Stella, who was now whispering intently in Lily's ear. Laura rolled her eyes at Katie, aware she was taking in the whole thing as well.

"It's the world we live in," Lily was saying to Stella. "Cory and Gracie are struggling right now to deal with Patricia's death."

"Struggling is one thing," Stella snapped. "Wallowing in sin is another. And call it what it was. Murder. Patricia was murdered!"

David and Jeremy returned with their plates full of pecan pie and whipped cream. Both men came to a standstill at their table, having heard Stella's loud statement about Patricia having been murdered.

"Enjoying the potluck, Stella?" David asked with his best smile.

"Humph!" She pointed directly at Cory, who was now standing near the buffet table. Gracie was alongside him with her arm wrapped around his waist. "Just what do you think they're up to now, hotshots?"

In the split second that Stella had turned away from Cory and Gracie to address David and Jeremy, a ruckus broke out.

"First my wife, now you want my daughter!" Ken Schaffer hollered just before his fist met with Cory's face.

FOURTEEN

"Daddy, please! Stop!"

Ken Schaffer ignored his daughter's pleas, but David didn't.

David yanked the back of Ken's arm, halting the blows to Cory's face. "This isn't the place, Mr. Schaffer."

Campers scurried away in all directions, some out the two doors on the sides, others out the front, and a few ran out the back door. They only ran as far as the outside windows. There they pushed and shoved to get a bird's-eye view of what was going on inside.

Anyone who'd known Ken Schaffer could hear the time bomb ticking, ready to explode, as it just had on Cory. Wild with rage, Ken broke loose from David's grasp and smashed his fist once more into Cory's jaw, feeling the bones give.

"*No!*" Gracie screamed as she scrambled toward Cory.

Jeremy pulled Gracie away. "Get her out of here, Laura," he said.

Laura and Katie pulled Gracie away from the scene and headed out of the clubhouse.

David leaped, right foot extended, and gave Ken a snap-kick to his groin.

Ken went down. The pain in his testicles streaked up to his stomach. His lips twisted in a snarl. "Damn you," he moaned. "This is none of your business!"

"I don't give a damn if the two of you want to go outside and kick each other's guts out, but it damned sure is my business

121

when you start that crap in a room filled with women and innocent campers." David grabbed a fistful of Ken's shirt and yanked him upright before slamming him down in a chair.

Jeremy was tending to a dazed Cory, who was bent over on his knees. A pool of blood, not yet congealed, bloomed from his forehead in a small puddle. He pushed Jeremy's hand away. "I'm fine, man."

"Yeah, I can see you are," Jeremy said. He pulled Cory up into a standing position and dragged him across the floor toward the bathrooms and out of Ken's sight.

Gracie charged into the clubhouse, knocking over a few chairs that happened to be in her path. "Cory!" she cried.

"We couldn't contain her any longer," Laura said.

David was standing guard in front of where Ken sat. "Cory will be just fine. Jeremy is cleaning him up."

It seemed the worst was over. Ken was still trembling with rage but appeared to have control of himself. Gracie went to him, bent down, and held her breath in anticipation of his reaction.

His gaze, cold with disinterest, cranked back to the floor. She reached forward, tried to wrap her arms around his neck, to draw him into a hug, to inhale his powerfully masculine scent. "Daddy?"

But he shrugged away her hold.

Gracie fell back, holding empty space. Her insides squeezed, convulsed. She tried to hold back tears, and the bitter, familiar taste of abandonment.

"What . . . time . . . is it?" Ken asked, his words coming out slurred and painful.

Trying to shove his rejection into the closet of painful things deep inside her, Gracie glanced at her watch. "A-almost eight."

Did he not care for Gracie? Did he not love his daughter?

Don't think. Don't ask. Shut it off. Close it out. It's better that way. Who needs him? You've got Cory. Cory loves you.

Ken turned his flat blue gaze to her. "You're a . . . whore. Just like . . . your mother."

Katie gasped.

Ken shoved David's hold away, got up, and walked toward a window.

Campers scattered away like a mountain of ants that had just been intruded upon.

"It's been a long day," David spoke up. The controlled emotion ringing in his voice seemed to catch everyone off guard. "I'd say you got your verbal abuse fix as well as your assault high for one day. Let it rest."

Ken turned from the window and speared David with a withering look. "What?"

"You heard me. Get out of here. Or do you prefer a jail cell?"

Ken punched an ineffective fist on one of the tables. His reddened cheeks quivered with his anger. "This is family business. Not yours."

Laura reached for David. Why was he coming on so strong? "David—"

"No, Laura. Jerks like him have to understand they can't go around strong-arming anyone."

Laura knew David didn't mean *anyone;* he meant Patricia Marsh and the physical and emotional abuse she'd taken from this man for twenty-five years.

Jeremy emerged from the bathroom, Cory behind him.

"Are you okay?" Gracie asked, taking Cory's hand.

"There's your jerk." The veins in Ken's forehead protruded. "Trash. All of you." His eyes, blazing with fury, locked with Gracie's. "Say hello to your mother when you get to hell . . . because that's where you'll both rot." He turned and headed toward the door.

David was losing his patience with Ken. "If anyone's going to

123

rot in hell, Ken, it's surely you. It's high time someone woke you up, gave you a taste of your own brutality. Problem is, you can't seem to raise those fists too high when you're up against a man."

"What in the hell is going on out here?" Jeremy whispered to Laura.

Laura shrugged.

Gracie knew what was going on. A shift of power was taking place. Two men were drawing a line in the sand. But her father seemed to be no match for David Jennings. Ken seemed to know it, too, and he left the building.

Cory took Gracie's hand. "Come on."

Tightening her grip on Cory's hand, Gracie glanced over her shoulder. "Thank you," she said to David.

David nodded, and then turned to the others. "Let's get out of here. I've had about all the fun activities I can handle for one day."

Laura slid her arm around his waist. "I agree, let's go home."

As Cory led Gracie back to the cabin, he let her hand go. Stripped of purpose, his fist clamored for something to do. He stuffed it in his pocket, the feeling of the key chain Patricia had given him a comfort.

He looked at Gracie, her face down as she walked. She shouldn't have had to endure the abuse of her father, verbal or otherwise, as Patricia had. He shouldn't have had to endure the violent physical and verbal attack from Ken. It had been Gracie's choice, not his, to remain at the resort after Patricia's death. But ever since Patricia died, having Gracie in their house unnerved him and made him ill at ease. She was a constant reminder of the dull throb of grief and guilt in his mind.

Gracie's released hand fluttered like a leaf for a moment, then she shoved it into her shorts pocket, an unconscious imitation of his own stance. "You sure you're all right?"

"Yeah. Let's drop it, okay?"

As they climbed the cabin steps, Cory was reminded about another incident earlier in the evening. "Do you have any idea what happened to that office step today?"

Gracie pulled a key from her pocket and shoved it into the doorknob with angry force. "Is that a question, Cory? Or an accusation?" Inside, she tossed the key on a table and dropped onto the sofa.

He closed the front door with more force than he'd intended. When he'd settled himself beside her, he said, "It was just an inquiry. Nothing to get defensive about." He dropped his head on the back of the sofa.

"Then, no. I have no idea what loosened that railing and made sweet little Laura fall down." The sarcasm in her voice was evident. "I'm tired. I'm going to bed."

"Who said anything about loosening the railing?"

"You! You asked if I knew who loosened or tampered with the step at the office."

"I asked if you knew what happened. I never used the words 'loosened' or 'tampered.' " He sat forward and grabbed hold of her arm before she could get away and lock herself inside her bedroom. "If you know something I don't, you better tell me." Cory's voice rang with authority.

There was nowhere for her to go, so she straightened defiantly. "Or what? You'll interrogate me until I talk? Hmm, that might be fun." She ran her index finger up and down his arm.

He jerked his arm free. "Gracie," he said. His mouth opened as if he wanted to say something else more, but no words came out.

"Good night, Cory." Gracie sang the words as she went into her bedroom and slammed the door.

Cory got up and went into the bathroom. He flicked on the light and looked into the mirror. The bumps, bruises, and cuts reflected and wavered before him like a carnival illusion.

"Who the hell are you?" he asked the face in the mirror and was taken aback by the haunted sound of his own voice. He tossed cold water on his face, grabbed a towel, and dabbed it dry. Taking one more quick glance in the mirror, he just shook his head, then he turned the light off and headed to bed . . . his bed . . . their bed . . . where he last saw Patricia alive.

Fifteen

Yawning, David opened his eyes and found Laura looking at him.

"Good morning," he whispered. His hand glided over her thigh, up her hip, down to her waist, and up to her rib cage. He loved the feel of her skin, the scent of summer-heated flowers; he loved the way she responded to him. His hand paused on the flatness of her stomach, feeling the shiver of delight that rippled through her.

She licked her lips. "Ohh," she moaned. "It certainly is a good morning. I love you," she said against his body.

I love you. Her passion-filled voice echoed in his mind, seemed to reach deep inside him. He was alive, thoroughly, utterly alive. Every cell, every atom sang with the sensation. In his arms, he held the lost half of himself he hadn't even realized was missing until she came into his life. He was never going to let her go.

"I love you," he said, hugging her closer. "Now and forever."

In the afterglow of their passion, Laura sat at the foot of the bed tugging her t-shirt down to her knees. She was watching David bustle around the kitchen wearing nothing but an apron.

Turning, catching her staring, David shot her a wink. "Hungry?"

She smiled. "You're crazy, you know that?"

"Crazy in love with you, my dear. Come, breakfast awaits. We worked up an appetite."

She looked at the bowl in front of her. "What? Just oatmeal? No eggs? No pancakes?"

"I was busy this morning."

"Ah, so you were. And since when is making love with me work?"

His heart flip-flopped. He reached far across the table and placed his hand over hers. "It's not work, my sweet."

She tossed a napkin at him. "So, what's on the agenda for today?"

He looked at the seashell clock hanging above the refrigerator. "If you're still hungry, we still have time to catch the pancake breakfast at the clubhouse."

"Pardon?"

He was staring at the delightful play of light dancing on her cheeks when she looked up from her bowl of oatmeal. "You gotta admit the potluck was entertaining."

Laura was silent for a moment. Her mind traveling back to the scene at the potluck. All of it had happened so fast. No one saw it coming, especially Cory. "About last night—"

"Isn't there a movie titled *About Last Night?*"

She sat up straight and looked at him with her no-nonsense-I'm-serious look. "Seriously, David. What do you make of Cory and Gracie? Do you think all the gossip is true? That something's going on between them?"

David stood, taking their empty bowls to the kitchen sink, giving himself a few minutes to think about Laura's questions. "I'd say there's a pretty good chance there is."

"So do I." She was silent again.

He turned and went back to the table, standing beside her. He took her arm and examined the scratches she'd gotten the day before. Then he put his lips on her wrist and proceeded to place a kiss on all of them, right past her elbow.

"You give me goose bumps when you do that."

"I give myself goose bumps when I do that," he said. He pulled her up. "Let's shower and get dressed. I want to go to the office. Make sure Cory's getting that step fixed."

"Together?"

"Huh?"

"Do you want to shower together?"

With a wide grin, he waggled his eyebrows. "But of course, my dear. We must do our part to conserve water."

An hour later they were at the front of the office. There were a dozen or so campers mingling around, some in groups whispering, others in groups staring at David and Laura.

"Good morning," a few of them mumbled.

David just shook his head. "Is this the norm for campgrounds? I mean, don't any of them have a life?"

Laura started to sing, "Welcome to my world . . ." in a low voice.

Before allowing Laura to go up the porch steps to the office, David got on each one and bounced up and down. "Looks like he had them fixed." He reached his hand out for Laura. "Come on."

Inside, Terrie stood at the counter looking like a little puppy that had just been scolded. Her hands were shaking and she was walking from one end of the counter to the other, shuffling papers and looking at David and Laura as though they were her guardian angels.

Laura could hear the voices coming from Cory's office. "What's going on?" Laura asked in a loud whisper.

"Cory . . . and Gracie," Terrie mouthed. "They've been at it all morning."

"About what?" David asked.

"Shhh." Terrie put a finger over her closed lips.

They listened as the echo of Gracie's shrill voice trailed out from the closed door. "What's the matter with you, Cory? I don't understand. And don't shush me, dammit!"

Laura looked at Terrie and made a gesture of throat slashing with her hand going across her neck.

"What is it? The sex isn't exciting anymore? Now that Mom's dead . . ."

David leaned into Laura and whispered, "Does that answer your earlier question?"

"I think they're coming!" Terrie said. She began shuffling some papers.

The door to Cory's office flew open and Gracie stomped out. Her eyes met Laura's. "What are you looking at?"

"Nothing," Laura said.

"Me neither," David said. "Just came in to make sure that step was being taken care of." He looked at Cory. "I see it has."

Cory looked like a raccoon with puffy black and purple circles around both eyes. His forehead looked worse. And he appeared to still be dazed from the previous evening's blows. Or was it Gracie's verbal blows that had him looking so bewildered? David wasn't sure. The only thing he was sure of was that Cory looked beat up.

"Yes," Cory said. "Took care of it at the crack of dawn."

"Anything else?" Gracie snapped.

"Nope." David waved his hand over Gracie's head to Terrie. "Have a nice day, Terrie."

Laura wondered if Terrie's head was nodding as a gesture of good-bye or shaking from an intense case of bad nerves. She smiled at the girl, turned, and followed David out of the office.

David and Laura paused outside in front of the shuffleboard courts where a group of campers were bickering over who was going to be on whose team. Laura recognized one of them from the potluck dinner, an annoying fellow who had a too-loud laugh and a penchant for telling Polack jokes.

"Let's go," Laura said. "I feel a headache coming on."

"Uh-huh," David said. His eyes were focused on the path leading away from the office.

Laura nudged David with her elbow. "You didn't even hear me, did you?"

He shook his head. "Sorry. I was looking at them." He pointed to two nuns heading toward them. "I didn't know nuns went camping."

"They don't. At least none of the ones I knew ever did."

David smiled as they approached nuns. "Are you lost, Sisters?" he asked.

"No, I don't think so," one of them said. She extended her hand. "I'm Sister Mary Elizabeth and this is Sister Mary Magdalene."

David took Sister Elizabeth's hand in his, bowed, and kissed her ring. "Pleased to meet you. I'm David Jennings." With the nun's hand still in his, he turned toward Laura. "And this is my wife, Laura."

The nuns started giggling, and Laura laughed out loud.

"W-what?" David said. "Did I miss something?" He let go of the nun's hand.

"Mr. Jennings, I'm not the pope. I'm just a nun. It isn't necessary to kiss my ring."

David felt his face flush. "Sorry," he said. He was thinking now would be a good time to challenge Laura to a race back to their motor home.

Picking up on his embarrassment, Sister Elizabeth said, "Oh, don't be sorry, Mr. Jennings. For a second there I felt rather special."

"Are you two vacationing here in Saint Augustine?" the other nun asked.

"Yes," Laura said. "For another few weeks. Then we're heading to Alabama."

David was feeling more at ease but still felt like a jerk with his ring-kissing gesture. Like Laura, he'd grown up Catholic but had eventually become a lost sheep. Sister Elizabeth was tall, thin, and had bushy eyebrows and rosy cheeks. She wasn't a knuckle-cracking nun like those David had known in the second grade. He winced at the memory.

"What about you, Sister?" David asked.

"We're here to see Patricia, the owner. Such a lovely woman. We promised her if we were ever in the area we'd stop in and meet her husband and take a tour of their beautiful resort." Sister Elizabeth spread her arms out wide. "It's so picturesque."

David and Laura looked at each other, then at the nuns, then back to one another.

"You two look like you have something you'd like to say," Sister Magdalene said. She was much shorter than Sister Elizabeth, but also had rosy cheeks.

"W-well," David said. "It's about Patricia."

Laura noticed more and more campers were out and about. A few had even stopped and gawked at her and David chatting with two nuns. She looked over David's shoulder to a picnic area that was out of the way and quieter looking. "Maybe we could sit over there. Under the oak. In the shade."

The nuns turned their heads to follow where Laura was pointing.

"Yes. Let's sit there," Sister Elizabeth said. She glanced at her watch, then at Sister Magdalene. "We have plenty of time before our meeting with Father Jose." Turning back to David and Laura, she said, "We were chosen to give a presentation to the seniors at Saint Agnes High School in Jacksonville."

"It's quite an honor," Sister Magdalene added. "Our topic will be on an individual's unlimited potential."

"Congratulations," David said.

"Did you know Patricia Marsh a long time?" Laura asked as

soon as they were all seated at a picnic table.

Sister Elizabeth pulled a handkerchief from her pocket and wiped the sweat from her forehead. "Oh, yes. We've known Patricia for years at Our Lady of Perpetual Help School for girls. She brought her daughter, Gracie, to us when she was just a wee little thing. Stayed until just a few years ago when Patricia moved here from Georgia with her new husband."

"Gracie Schaffer was at *your* boarding school?" David asked.

Sister Elizabeth cleared her throat. "Uh, yes. You know Gracie?"

"She manages this resort," Laura said.

The nuns looked confused.

"Gracie still lives here?" Sister Elizabeth asked.

"You sound surprised by that," David said. He stretched his legs out from the outside of the picnic table bench.

"Not surprised," Sister Elizabeth said. "It's just that Gracie always seemed at odds with her mother. Blaming her for everything. Throwing tantrums when Patricia would come to visit. But, it sounds like she matured as she got older. I'm happy for Patricia."

She's dead, David thought. *Murdered.* He contemplated whether he should mention anything about that. They'd find out soon enough. Why not brace them for the shock?

Sister Magdalene let out a little laugh and covered her mouth, as if laughing was shameful. "I'm sorry," she said. "I was just thinking about how hopeful Patricia always was that Gracie would want to stay on with us. Become a nun. And maybe find a calling and purpose with Our Lady of Perpetual Help."

David chuckled. "That *is* funny, Sister."

Laura gave him a kick under the table.

"I think Patricia was afraid Gracie was too much like her father. The first time I met him, I thought he was the devil himself." Sister Elizabeth looked at her watch again and stood.

"We really should get over to the office so we still have time to visit with Patricia. It was such a pleasure talking with the two of you"

"Wait, Sister," Laura said. "We think there's something you need to know first."

An uncomfortable silence descended upon the table as Sister Elizabeth sat back down. A few seconds later, David took the plunge and began to tell the sisters what had occurred at Harbor Lights RV Resort since their arrival.

For the next thirty minutes David and Laura took turns. They were careful not to make any comments about where the suspicion rested for Patricia's death, stating only that Detective Miles did indeed feel foul play was involved.

Sister Magdalene sat shaking her head. "Tsk, tsk," was all she'd been able to respond when David and Laura felt they'd said enough.

Sister Elizabeth had lost the smile that had been on her face only minutes earlier. Her brow twisted, and her expression was pained. "Patricia . . . dead. Murdered." She let out a heavy sigh, then turned away and covered her face with a hand.

Laura reached across the table and patted Sister Elizabeth's other hand. "Are you okay, Sister?" Then her eyes brimmed with tears. "I'm so sorry."

"Sisters," David said. "You probably know Gracie better than anyone else. She lived at your school for a very long time. It might be a good idea if you contacted Detective Miles. I'm sure he'd be interested in talking with you both."

Gracie. Sister Elizabeth deliberately let her mind go backwards. As if a curtain had been ripped aside, she recalled Gracie, the child. The disturbed child. The cruel child. And Gracie, the teenager. The fear expressed from the other girls. The name that the other students had dubbed Gracie: "Little Lizzie Borden."

"Yes," Sister Elizabeth said. "We will certainly talk with the detective." She stood and forced a smile on her lips. "Thank you, David and Laura. I know how difficult it had to be for you to tell us about Patricia. You didn't have to, but you did. May God bless and be with you both." She shook their hands.

"We're sorry to have had to be the ones to tell you," David said. "Last we looked, Cory and Gracie were at the office. Maybe you'd like to say hello. Let them know you came by. I'm sure Gracie would love to see you both again."

"Maybe another time," Sister Magdalene said. "We really should be on our way."

"It's been a pleasure, Sisters," Laura said. "We'll light a candle in Patricia's memory."

"God bless you," Sister Elizabeth said.

The two nuns headed back toward the parking lot with their hands folded in front of them. Two campers in separate golf carts almost collided head on when they turned their gaze off the gravel road and toward the nuns.

"We'll light a candle?" David asked.

"Yes," Laura said. "Nuns like candles."

Sixteen

"What are you two sticking your noses into now?"

David and Laura turned around. Gracie stood, hands on her hips, with an accusatory look on her face.

"I don't have a clue what you're talking about," David said. A shiver ran up his spine. Had she been lurking around the big oak tree? Hunkered down and taking everything in while he and Laura talked to the nuns?

"You know damn well what I'm talking about!" Anger tightened her forehead. "Your little pow-wow with those nuns from the prison school for girls."

A group of campers headed up the path toward the beach. David and Laura had been on the same path after the sisters had left and before being halted by Gracie. There were also quite a few bicyclists wearing alien head-helmets and fluorescent spandex. A couple of the million-dollar motor homes from the camping club were rolling out as other RVs were rolling in.

"Those nuns were on their way to see your mother, Gracie." David was getting irritated standing out here in the high-noon sun, brushing no-see-ums from his legs and arms while listening to and watching Gracie make a complete sideshow for passersby. "I'd have thought you would have notified them of your mother's death. It sounded to me like they were very fond of her."

"It's none of your business!" Gracie whipped past them. "I'm sick of the gossip in this damn place," she yelled back.

Katie was walking up toward the office to check her mail when she was almost pushed into a bed of roses by Gracie. She spotted David and Laura in front of her. "What was that all about?"

"Sexual tension." Laura wiggled her hands. "It makes the air shivery. Crazy vibes."

"Or guilt," David said. He craned his neck over Katie's shoulder. "Where's Jeremy?"

"Where do you think? Poking around the beach where those bones were found. I think he was supposed to meet that detective there around three."

David looked at his watch. "Man, it's almost two now. Time flies when you're having fun."

"I was just on my way to check the mail when Hurricane Gracie tore past me." Katie turned as if to expect the return of Gracie. "Then I'm going to lie out by the pool. Care to join me?"

"That sounds great," Laura said.

David wanted to get out of the heat and humidity, get a cold Coke, and see what Jeremy was poking around for. Sitting at the pool with a bunch of catty campers was not how he wanted to spend the rest of the afternoon. "Why don't you go," he told Laura. "I want to catch up with Jeremy."

"I'll go home and change and bring us something cold to drink," Laura told Katie. "I'll meet you at the pool in five."

"There should be plenty of lounge chairs. I saw the sightseeing bus take a load of people from here."

Heading to their motor home, Laura waved to Katie. "Good. See you shortly."

Katie downed one of the cold bottles of water Laura brought to the pool. "Ahhh, that's good." She put the chilled plastic bottle against her face. "Man, it has to be a hundred and ten degrees out here."

Laura laid a towel across her lounge chair, rubbed some SPF-15 all over her, and flopped back in the chair. "This does feel so relaxing." She shielded her eyes with her hand and looked over to Katie. "You okay today, Katie?"

"Sure, why do you ask?"

"You just seem quiet."

There was something strange about Jeremy and Katie that Laura just couldn't pinpoint. They were a nice enough couple, even if Jeremy all too often allowed the chauvinist side of him to emerge. Ever since they'd all met and Jeremy had referred to Katie as his "traveling companion," David and Laura had debated over just exactly what a "companion" in a live-in relationship would consist of. Laura finally told David to just think of Dewey, someone Laura saw long before David and shortly after her divorce from Mac, because Dewey was the "companion" type. Remembering how that had clarified things for her and David concerning the mystery of Jeremy and Katie, Laura smiled.

"You and Jeremy didn't have a lovers' spat, did you?" Laura said, now downing a bottle of water herself.

Resting on her elbows, Katie lifted her head and turned to Laura. "A lovers' spat?"

"Well, did you?"

"Laura, Jeremy and I are . . . well . . . we're traveling buddies."

"He's a man, you're a woman. Katie, there *has* to be something besides this buddy stuff." She didn't want to press the issue or embarrass Katie. But woman's intuition told her that something was on Katie's mind. "How did you say you two met?"

Katie stretched back out on her chair, thankful that her dark sunglasses would hide any tears that might escape. "Okay, Laura. We're friends, so here's the real lowdown on the lives of Katie Green and Jeremy Myers, better known as—the odd couple. And I don't think I ever did tell you how we met. I was his administrative assistant. He liked my bones. His weren't bad, either." She let out a heavy sigh. "Hmm, where to begin.

"When I was younger, like you, when my body was firm and unscarred, when I was in my sexual peak, even then I never felt the tug of love and lust. Kevin, my ex, was more of a business partner than a soul mate. Lovemaking was a way to relieve stress, not share intimacy. But all that love stuff . . . I just never had the time or the inclination for such frivolity.

"Here I am, beyond middle-age, battle-scarred, way past the age when men ogle me on the street or lust after me in their hearts. Then I meet Jeremy, a man who put a flutter in my heart and a thump in my belly. The very first time I looked into those smoky-blue eyes of his, caught a whiff of his vibrantly masculine scent and was captured by his smile, I knew he was *it*." Katie frowned, then brushed her thoughts away with a sweep of one hand. "Oh, well, enough of this old broad's true confessions. Let's change the subject."

"You're *not* an old broad," Laura said. She sat upright in the lounge chair and put her hand over Katie's. "Look at you, Katie. You're the epitome of what it means to grow old gracefully." She raised her right hand and counted off, using her fingers. "First, I hope I look like you when I'm in my sixties. Second, you have a beautiful figure, and you dress in fashionable styles that compliment that figure. Third, even now, basking in the heat, and sweating profusely, you radiate beauty—"

"Please, don't stop there," Katie said. "Go on, I'm listening."

The sound of voices from the other end of the pool startled Laura. She turned her attention from Katie to the group of four sunbathers on the opposite side of the pool deck. One of them, a bone-thin woman in her seventies or eighties, was stooped over, testing the water with her toes. Two others, who also appeared to be seventy-ish, were cautioning the frail-looking woman to be careful not to fall in, and the other person in the group looked madder than hell. This was the one Laura's eyes and attention were focused on. The woman looked to be about Laura's age, in her mid-thirties, and was obviously arguing with the two beside her and very annoyed that they weren't paying much attention.

"Negative energy."

"Huh?" The sound of Katie's voice snapped Laura's attention away from the group across the pool.

"Negative energy attracts negative energy," Katie said. "Whatever you put out, that's what comes back." Katie was sitting up with her knees pressed against her chest and her arms wrapped around them. She nodded her head. "That woman you've been looking at. I could feel the vibes with my eyes closed. Negative vibes. My positive energy from all those wonderful accolades you were pointing out about me was interrupted by a spark of negative energy flowing across the pool."

Laura laughed and put her hand on Katie's arm. "See, that's another beautiful trait you have—your optimistic and intuitive spirit."

Katie lowered her sunglasses onto the bridge of her nose and looked over them toward the woman. "Not a happy camper. What do you suppose her problem is? PMS-ing?"

"I don't know," Laura said. "She looks familiar. I think I remember her from the office. Checked in with the others yesterday." Laura shrugged her shoulders. "Sorry about the distraction. Now, back to you and Jeremy."

"Jeremy is afraid of getting close, period. He doesn't talk much about his feelings or his past, so it makes it hard for me to figure out where he's coming from sometimes." Katie drew

140

in a long breath and let it out slowly. "It's just hard for me to know what he wants. What he expects from me . . . if anything." Katie shoved her lotion into her tote bag and pulled out her beach robe.

Sensing that Katie would just as soon drop the subject, Laura said, "What do you say we head on down to the beach and see what our handsome sleuths are uncovering."

"Sounds like a plan to me."

They slipped into their sandals, gathered their lotions, towels, and water, and stuffed them into their beach totes, then exited the pool area, heading toward the path leading to the beach.

Laura and Katie found David and Jeremy hunkered in a crouch with Detective Miles. They decided not to disturb what looked like an important discussion and just stood and observed in silence.

The three men were poking around in the sand with sticks. Detective Miles pulled a handkerchief from his pocket and wiped his face. Kicking softly at some seaweed, the detective scanned the ground. Jeremy and David had worked their way several feet away from the detective. Something had apparently caught Detective Miles' eye.

"Jeremy. David," the detective called out.

David and Jeremy came up behind Detective Miles, bending to look over his shoulder. Something odd and clumped caught their eyes.

"What is that?" David asked.

"I don't know," Detective Miles said.

"Looks like a piece of jewelry," Jeremy said.

The detective picked up a stick and poked at the caked sand, trying to break it loose from the object. A hermit crab scurried in front of him. A glint of gold appeared and what looked like a tiny sliver of metal. Detective Miles pulled a latex glove from his shirt pocket, slipped it onto his right hand, and lifted it.

"Look familiar?" the detective asked.

"Sure does. Like the piece I extracted from the remains in the bottle," Jeremy said.

David blew out a whistle. "The plot thickens."

A roar of thunder clamored overhead, causing Laura to jump and let out a loud gasp.

The three men turned to see her and Katie standing on the sidelines.

"Sorry," Laura said. "We didn't want to disturb you."

"One thing about Florida," the detective said. "One never knows when the storms will roll in."

Jeremy looked up at the sky. "Some threatening-looking clouds up there. Maybe we should start to head back. Wouldn't want the girls to get wet."

"We won't melt, Jeremy." Katie wrapped her arm inside of his.

"Besides," Laura said, "we're dressed for it." She whipped open her beach throw. "See?"

David made a wolf whistle. "A beach goddess. *My* beach goddess."

Detective Miles just shook his head. He walked back to check the area where he'd confiscated the sliver of gold. "I think we're all done here for today," he said. He turned and walked back toward the others.

"You better get the ladies back to the resort before all hell breaks loose from the sky."

"He's right," Jeremy said. "Where there's thunder, lightning's not far behind." He laced his fingers inside of Katie's hand. "We'll get together tomorrow, Detective."

They waved their good-byes and headed back to their RVs. David had Laura pulled close to his side as they walked. It started to drizzle as they cuddled in tighter. From behind them, Jeremy observed the couple. His hand felt empty, where just moments ago he'd held Katie's. She had slid her hand out of his to wave her good-bye to the detective. Jeremy wondered why she didn't place it back with his. He rubbed his palm on the leg of his pants. Her hand fit so well, so naturally, in his that it had made him feel like it was a part of him.

Emotions were dangerous. Jeremy knew that. His parents' example had shown him that. Especially this kind of emotion. The kind he had with Katie. Emotions distracted. They left a person weak and vulnerable.

His father had exploited his mother's unfettered emotions and broken her heart and her spirit. Katie's father had suffered a similar fate when his wife left him.

He should be continuing to examine his suspects, searching for more telltale clues hidden God knows where instead of dwelling on the fire Katie stoked in his blood with just a touch.

"Coming, Jeremy?" Katie was ahead of him, almost jogging toward their fifth wheel.

"Right behind you, sweetie." He stepped up his pace and was soon at Katie's side.

They all made it back to their rigs just as the downpour came.

That big deluge just before they entered their fifth wheel had caused Katie to get drenched. Her lightweight beach shirt plastered against her chest. It was rude of him to stare, but Jeremy couldn't stop.

Katie shook the dripping water from her body as she shed the wet cover-up and bathing suit and grabbed a dry denim shirt from the coatrack inside the doorway. She raised her hand to her right breast. "I had a mastectomy."

He gave himself a shake. His ears and neck burned.

She slid her arms into the dry shirt. She was smiling. "Managed to keep it from you this long, huh? Always able to divert your attention to other body parts. I thought I was okay with losing a breast. That I accepted my body and how I look. But I've been self-conscious about showing you my scars. Shoot, downright scared." Her fingers trembled while she buttoned her shirt. "Are you totally grossed out?"

Now that she was covered up, it was easier to look at her. He didn't know what to say. What kind of person was he? Living with her for the past month, sleeping with her, making love to her, but never noticing. God she must think he's a jerk. "What . . . what happened?"

"Breast cancer. I was fortunate. A mammography caught it in the early stages, before it metastasized—spread through my system. Unfortunately, it was an aggressive form and my oncologist didn't believe a lumpectomy would be enough. So I had a radical mastectomy, then chemo and radiation treatment. It worked. I then got divorced, looked for a job, and the rest, as they say, is history. I've been cancer-free for over four years."

All he heard was cancer. The Big C, the destroyer, that stinking ugly monster that ripped through healthy flesh and killed beautiful women and ruined lives. His throat felt as if it were swelling shut. His heart pounded so erratically, painfully, he knew at that moment he was having a heart attack. He clutched his chest and stumbled back.

"Jeremy?"

He couldn't breathe. Gasping and choking, he made it around the coffee table. He slumped heavily on the sofa. He choked and rasped for breath. An elephant was sitting on his chest.

Katie grasped his chin. "Good lord, you're dead white. What's the matter?"

"Chest . . . hurts . . ."

She picked up his wrist and pressed her fingers against the pulse points. Hell, she had no idea what she was doing or looking for. Damn. She recalled a scene from *House* and encouraged him to breathe deeply, slowly. "I'm calling an ambulance."

"No!"

"You might be having a heart attack."

"Don't care . . . no . . . ambulance."

She ran to the bathroom and returned carrying a glass of water and aspirin. She ordered him to take the aspirin and drink all the water. She grabbed his phone off his belt and began punching in numbers.

He snatched the telephone out of her hands and threw it as far as he could toward their bedroom. She stared openmouthed at him, speechless for once.

"No!"

"You are such a stupid, *stupid* man!"

She grasped his arm and helped him to his feet. Leaning heavily on her, he clutched his chest. Sweat dripped off his face. He was dying.

SEVENTEEN

"Anxiety attack."

Jeremy stared at the doctor. Anxiety? The chest pains had stopped during the ride to the hospital. By the time he entered the emergency room, he felt perfectly fine. Embarrassed as all get out, but fine. Still, the doctor had insisted on running tests. Now he held a long ECG strip as if Jeremy could make sense of the jagged printout.

"You're in remarkable shape, Mr. Myers," the doctor continued. "The heart of a twenty-year-old. Do you lift weights? Run?"

"Yeah," Jeremy said, numb over the diagnosis.

"It shows. Just to be on the safe side, I'd like to schedule a stress test. You are nearing sixty-five."

Curtain rings rattled and Katie peered into the treatment room. She'd fussed and fumed at Jeremy all the way to the hospital. Her anger touched him as much as it irritated him.

The doctor lowered the ECG strip and peered at Katie. "May I help you?" the doctor asked.

"She's my wife," Jeremy said. "Honey, I'm okay. No heart attack. I can go home."

The doctor patted Jeremy's shoulder. "Schedule the stress test. If you have another attack, give me a call. There are drugs available to treat anxiety." He flashed a curious smile at Katie, then hurried away.

"I'm so relieved you're okay," Katie said. "But grabbing that phone out of my hands and tossing it like you did was the dumbest thing I've ever seen anyone do. And believe you me, buster, I've seen a lot of stupid things."

He buttoned his shirt and slid off the exam table. Taking hold of Katie's elbow, he walked out of the exam room.

They passed by the information desk. "You filled out billing information, right? You didn't have my insurance card."

"I used a credit card."

They walked out of the emergency room exit doors and out to the parking lot. Jeremy held out his hand. "Can I have the keys? I'll drive. I feel fine."

Katie sat in the passenger seat, arms wrapped around herself. "I'm really glad you're okay. You scared me."

"I don't want to talk about it." A stupid anxiety attack. He couldn't believe it. Back in New York, as a forensic anthropologist, he'd earned the reputation for having ice water in his veins. As part of the homicide investigator team, he'd never burned out the way so many others had. Mr. Cool. The man who never lost his head.

"You don't have to be embarrassed."

"I'm not embarrassed," he mumbled.

"Do you want to talk about what happened?"

"No."

"It'll help." She rubbed his shoulder. "It's the mastectomy, isn't it? I shocked you."

Her silence seemed a palpable thing, nudging him, worming its way beneath his reluctance. He'd driven nearly five miles before conceding that she wasn't going to fill the silence with chatter.

"Cancer," he said. The word was bitter. It choked him and made his heart rate rise.

Lights from the dash barely touched her face. Her eyes were dark, gleaming. "Mmm."

"I never had an anxiety attack before. I thought I was dying."

"They'll do that to you. What is it about cancer that makes you so anxious?"

He'd never talked about it. Not to his friends, his family, or a priest. No one. Guilt over his cowardice festered inside him like a boil, pulsing and painful. Katie would be disgusted to know his shame. Or worse, she'd pity him for his weakness.

There was a dirt road up ahead. He slowed, then turned onto it. He killed the motor and the lights. He listened to the engine's *tick tick tick*. Without the lights of civilization, the night sky was inky, the ocean in front of them overwhelming in its vastness.

"I didn't know you had cancer."

"I don't anymore. Is it ugly? Revolting?"

Something in her voice made him look at her. "You think you're ugly?"

Shifting on the seat to face him, she showed her palms in a *you-tell-me* gesture. "My ex-husband thought so. He insisted I have reconstructive surgery. That's what he did, erased flaws, repaired imperfections." She sighed and clicked her tongue against her teeth. "I'm not certain exactly why I refused. Partly I wanted the reminder, sort of a badge of honor for finding myself, for finding God. I was humbled by all I'd gained. But mostly, I suppose, he made me angry. He saw me as flawed, mutilated, an imperfect thing that must be repaired or I was unworthy."

"He must be a real jerk," Jeremy said.

"It's the way he views the world. The path he must explore. Anyway, other than medical professionals, no man has touched me since my divorce. No man has looked at me, made love to me." She placed a hand on his forearm, letting it rest without pressure. "I almost had myself convinced that I wasn't afraid of what others would think when they saw the scar. But then I met you . . . and fell in love. I was very afraid."

Now he was a double-dirty, low-down dog. "I don't think you're ugly. Not ugly at all."

"I gave you a panic attack."

"I'm—I'm—"

"Shhh," she whispered and pressed a finger against his lips. "Don't apologize. Never apologize for how you feel. In a way you did me a big favor. Revealing my true self was a big step, and I survived. I feel bad for shocking you, but I'm not hurt or depressed or angry. I can handle your opinion."

He rested his head against the steering wheel. "It's not you, Kats, I swear it isn't. It's me." He swallowed the lump in his throat. "My wife died of cancer."

It was the first she'd known he'd even been married. The first time she realized how little they really knew about one another. She pulled back, sitting taller. "I'm so sorry."

He stared out the window at the billions of stars and waxing moon. "I let her die alone."

"What happened?"

Her gentle question held neither condemnation or horror. He couldn't look at her. "Her name was Lori. She was only twenty-eight. God, but I loved her. The first time I saw her, she crawled into my head and set up housekeeping. She was a research librarian. Worked at the New York Public Library. I came up with some really screwy questions just so I had an excuse to talk to her." He tapped his head. "Smartest person I ever met. We were married for four years. We were saving money to buy a house. Then she started losing weight. Hurting. By the time they diagnosed ovarian cancer, it had metastasized into her liver, lungs, and bones."

"Oh, Jeremy . . ."

He knuckled his burning eyes. "The treatments were terrible. Left her puking. All her hair fell out, her face swelled up. Nothing they did touched the cancer. It just grew and grew, eating her up. I couldn't handle watching her die, seeing her all shriveled and yellow, always in pain. Even touching her hand made her scream. So I . . . worked. I pulled every minute of overtime I could get. I buried myself in cases. Even went through old files, dead cold cases, anything to keep from witnessing her agony."

His gut ached. His heart was racing again. He deserved a real heart attack.

"Her mother called me. 'It's time,' she said. I sat at my desk and typed up a report. Typed it real carefully, checking for mistakes. When I finally got home, it was all over."

She snuffled. He whipped his head about. Her face was shiny with tears.

"Don't cry for me, dammit! She loved me, needed me, and I let her die alone. I'm garbage."

She fumbled around the vehicle, then finally wiped her face with her shirt sleeve. "Once upon a time, I never cried. I was rather proud of myself. I considered it a sign of strength. Avoiding one's emotions isn't strong at all. It's fear, pure and simple. I'll weep for you if I must, and for Lori, and for myself."

He pushed open the door. In the dome light, he glimpsed her reddened eyes and tear-streaked cheeks. He jumped out and slammed the door. He shoved his hands in his pockets and stared out at the Atlantic. Deep breaths of fresh salt sea air cleared his head a little. He expected Katie to get out of the SUV, to pester him into talking, to lay on him a bunch of silly platitudes like Band-Aids on a broken bone. He stood in the coolness for a long time, until it became clear she wasn't going to do anything but wait.

Something inside him said she'd understand, that she didn't condemn him or consider him a horrible human being.

Shivering, he slid back behind the steering wheel. He started the engine. He shoved the transmission into reverse, and backed out onto A1A.

Driving past small gift and souvenir shops, he felt oddly lighter. Confession had relieved him, at least a little. He wondered if Katie would give him funny looks from now on. Wondered if she'd drop the kidding around about sexual tension. Wondered if she still found him desirable.

"Where have you been?" Laura demanded. "David and I have been here for over an hour. I couldn't reach you by phone. We've been worried sick!"

Katie hugged Laura. "I'm sorry. We had a little incident. What's up?"

"What kind of incident?" David asked.

Katie exchanged a look with Jeremy. "The less you know . . ." She let the comment dangle, allowing David and Laura to imagine what they pleased.

David shot a glare at Jeremy that said he figured that whatever it was, it was his fault. "You guys missed all the action," he said. He looked at his watch. "It's getting late. But to fill you in, Detective Miles came by and took Cory away." He stood with hands crossed against his chest. "Do you believe that?"

"No," Jeremy said. "I don't." He twisted his neck in an attempt to crack away the night's tension. "Maybe he got something back on that gold sliver he found. Interesting."

"That's not all," Laura added. "After they drove away, Gracie was standing in the road in hysterics, yelling that she wanted to go with them. She had supporters, too." She looked at Katie. "Remember that younger, not-so-happy camper we saw at the pool today?"

"She was with Gracie?" Katie asked.

"Sure was. And Norma."

Jeremy took a seat at the picnic table in front of his trailer. "We're still going to meet with Miles tomorrow, aren't we?"

"You bet," David said. "I'm sure we'll find out then what this is all about with Cory."

"Maybe it had something to do with the potluck punch-out," Katie said.

"I don't think so. Not the way Gracie was carrying on." Laura gave Katie another hug. "Get some rest. You guys look beat. We'll talk in the morning."

"I'll walk with you to your motor home." Katie turned to Jeremy. "I'll be right back."

He waved at them. Watching Katie talking in soft tones to Laura as she walked away, he couldn't help thinking that if Katie were anyone else, he'd suspect she was gossiping about his cowardly past. He knew, as sure as sunrise, she'd never bring the subject up again. A comforting thought.

Katie returned. "I'm starving. How about you?"

He followed her inside. The last time he'd been inside, he'd thought he was dying. That he'd never see their home on wheels again. The kitchen table was a mess. Hell, the entire trailer was a mess with all his forensic equipment. A sketchpad sat on the kitchen counter with all the evidence and facts collected to date on Patricia Marsh. He picked it up and jotted a brief notation on the new information about Detective Miles carrying Cory Marsh away and the scene with Gracie's outburst. He closed the book and placed it on the overhead shelf in the living room.

Katie rummaged through the kitchen cupboards.

He approached her from behind and settled his hands on her shoulders. She stilled. Her hair smelled of honey and shampoo.

"I'm embarrassed. I don't think you're ugly. Or revolting, or any of that."

"Thank you."

"I didn't freak out because of you. The way you look."

"I know."

"The cancer . . . I can't go through that again. What I did to Lori . . ."

Lori hadn't actually been alone. Her parents and brothers had been there, and so had a member of Jeremy's family. When he'd walked in, they'd all murmured their sympathies, wept with him, but he'd felt their contempt for his cowardice. No one ever mentioned his desertion, but it was always there. He saw it every time he encountered them. It followed him, ever present, a cloud of guilt and shame. He'd even felt it at work. Seen it in the eyes of other detectives; heard it in the voices of friends.

He'd taken the first opportunity to get out of New York, away from his family, away from Lori's death.

Katie waited a few beats. "What you did was pretty bad. But understandable."

He flinched. That was the last thing he'd expected her to say. "I don't understand it."

"It's hard to watch a loved one in pain. Especially pain that's so difficult to manage."

"I've seen people die. I'm no stranger to pain. What I did was pure cowardice. I let her down. I loved her, but I deserted her. Now I can't . . ."

"Forgive yourself?"

"Yeah."

"I know the feeling." She turned to face him. He let his hands dangle at his sides. "I still haven't forgiven myself over a lot of things. Forgiveness isn't as easy as some would have us think."

She'd surprised him again. He'd expected, oh, you didn't do anything wrong, your guilt is misplaced, Lori was so out of it because of the drugs that she didn't know you weren't there anyway, blah, blah, blah. "So, uh, how does a person go about forgiving himself?"

"It's a two-step process. First, you have to make amends."

"How do you make amends to somebody who's gone?"

"Sacrifice, good deeds, helping others. Living a godly life." She tilted her head, staring into his eyes. "You gave up everything, didn't you? Your home, family, friends, a job you loved. Even God."

He backed a step. "Don't go there. I don't want anything to do with a god that fills a woman with cancer. A woman who never did anything mean to anyone, never said a bad word. A genuinely good person. It got so bad, even a draft of air on her skin was agony. What kind of freaky god does that?"

"God doesn't do it. These frail, fragile animal bodies we inhabit are the price we pay for the experience of living." She tapped the center of her chest. "Our spirits are imbued with all of God's love, and generosity and power and wisdom. Free will is our birthright, to do with those godly gifts whatever we wish. God isn't Santa Claus or a zookeeper."

Shaking his head, he turned away. "You honestly believe that."

"I do. I also believe that everything is a gift. Every breath we take, every idea, every occurrence. Even those things we fear or consider a tragedy."

Incredulous, he rubbed his nape. "Are you saying cancer was God's gift to you?"

"Yes."

"You're nuts."

"It's a possibility."

"How can something that horrible be a gift?" He practically shouted. His ears burned. He'd never met anyone who so flustered, infuriated, and engaged him—except for Lori.

She resumed rummaging through the cupboards. Finally deciding on tuna fish sandwiches, she pulled a can of tuna down from the shelf. "I woke up from surgery. There was no one in the room. It hit me hard that there I was, a respected wife of a physician. I lived in a million-dollar condo furnished with expensive antiques, with a full-time housekeeper. Yet I woke up alone. My marriage was empty. I hated my life. I had no friends, no family. For years and years anger sustained me. That anger manifested itself into breast cancer. On that day, in that lonely room, for the first time in over twenty years, I wept."

Dumbfounded by her brutal revelation, he sank into a chair.

"I cried a lifetime of tears that day. I was empty. In that emptiness, I realized I wasn't alone. The knowledge was so clear, so profound, it was blinding. Right at that moment, for the very first time in my entire life, I knew what it felt like to be unafraid. *That* was my gift."

"Wow." He leaned forward, his elbows on his knees. His intellect said she was nuts, but his gut told him otherwise. "So you gave it all up? The husband, the money?"

"I gave up all that was meaningless." She smiled. "It's an abundant world. I'm not deprived."

"Huh. So, uh, you said forgiveness is a two-part process. What's the second part?"

"The assertion in total confidence that you will never commit that particular sin again."

He stared at his hands and loosed a rueful laugh. "Then it should be easy. Because I'm sure as hell never putting myself in the position ever to do that again."

Stealthy noises roused Jeremy. He'd been up and down throughout the night, investigating every creak and rustle. The fifth wheel had only one door—he slept in front of it on the sofa. For some reason his gut had told him Harbor Lights RV Resort wasn't such a safe place. Not as long as Detective Miles was coming in and hauling the owner into custody for murder.

Adding to his sleeplessness was knowing Katie was in the bed they'd shared for the past four and a half weeks. Alone.

A night-light in the kitchen emitted a soft glow. Thin morning light seeped through the windows. Katie came out of the bedroom. She had a blanket wrapped around her shoulders. She went into the kitchen and made some coffee.

Her legs were bare. They were beautiful, long and strong and shapely for a woman in her sixties. As sternly as he told himself to behave, his body had other ideas.

"Good morning," he said.

"Good morning. I didn't mean to wake you."

A tiptoeing mouse could have awakened him. "What time is it?" he asked.

She crouched beside him. Bundled in the blanket with her hair sticking out every which way, he wouldn't have been surprised if she broke into some kind of shamanistic chant.

Why she was so damned sexy, he couldn't imagine. His male parts were doing enough imagining for ten people.

"It's probably around six. I'm up for the day if you want to go take the bed for a while."

Bed. *Don't say bed,* he pleaded silently. He stretched and rolled his shoulders and neck. Goose bumps prickled his back. "I'll get up." Might as well. In this state, he'd never get back to sleep.

Katie got up and eased past him to open the blinds. She gathered his jeans. "Here," she said, tossing them at him.

He draped the jeans over a chair. "Thanks."

"Stay there. I'll bring you a cup of coffee."

Then she shrugged off the blanket. All she wore was one of his shirts, the tails hanging to mid-thigh. Lace teddies and garter belts couldn't beat the eroticism of a woman wearing a man's shirt and nothing else.

He went to the kitchen. Glared at her as she handed him the coffee cup. She wore a grin he knew too well. A look that said he was an idiot, but she thought he was cute anyway. He was suddenly burning up inside.

He held out a hand. "Put the coffee down."

Still smiling that infuriatingly sexy smile, she placed the coffee cups on the counter. "No more games, right? I want you. All of you. From what I can see, the feeling is mutual. Is it mutual? Do you want all of me?"

"Yeah," he muttered. "Damn it." He gathered her into his arms.

EIGHTEEN

Detective Miles made it to his office early, not because he had anything special to follow up on with the Patricia Marsh murder investigation, but because he was hoping some new information would come through from the lab on what he'd collected from the beach.

"Hey, Detective," he heard, and then looked up to see Jeremy Myers just inside his office door, David Jennings standing behind him.

"You got something!" Detective Miles pounced at once, knowing it from the all-too-familiar grin on Jeremy's face. "What is it, and how helpful is it on a scale from one to two?"

"It's a definite one and a half," Jeremy laughed, coming forward with a stack of papers.

"Or, more accurately, maybe we should say *they* are. As in more than one," David chimed in.

Detective Miles took the papers fast and started to go through them. There were two separate files, apparently, and each file had an introductory fax above the rest of the stack.

"Two more of the fragments were identified by my former partner," Jeremy said, obviously too excited to wait for Detective Miles to read the reports for himself. "Early this morning I got that toxicology report from the fragments determined to be cells from the stomach lining, and it confirmed the coroner's preliminary findings in Patricia Marsh. Poisoning. More specifically, glycoside toxins."

David couldn't keep still; he needed to toss his own findings at the detective. Only problem was he didn't have much *real* evidence. Except what was in the bottle washed ashore. All he really had was a lot of "he said, she said" stuff and one really good assumption to add to what Jeremy just reported. "As in oleander poisoning. That stuff is growing all over Harbor Lights."

"From what we know," Jeremy said, "Patricia Marsh had all the symptoms of oleander poisoning. The nausea, vomiting, gradually worsening instead of improving . . ."

Detective Miles continued to read through the reports, looking up every now and then to listen to Jeremy and David. "The strain of severe abdominal cramps, vomiting, and diarrhea proved too much for her," he said. "Just like a bad case of flu would have done."

"Which is what Cory and Gracie and everyone else around the campground said Patricia had. A bad case of flu."

They sat silent for a moment. David thinking how terrible the last day of Patricia Marsh's life must have been.

Jeremy sat back. "Your turn. What have you found out? I understand you took Cory into custody."

Detective Miles closed the file folders and sat back with his hands locked behind his head. "I've been questioning people in the campground for close to two weeks, and Cory Marsh's name kept coming up." He sat forward. "It was just routine. I wanted him on my turf this time. I let him go after a couple of hours." His shoulders lifted a fraction. "Right after I let him go I had an interesting phone call from some nun. A Sister Elizabeth."

"My wife and I spoke with her and a Sister Magdalene," David said. "I gave them your contact information. I thought you might like to talk to them."

"You thought right," the detective said. "I find it a bit strange that Gracie went to their school for what . . . thirteen years? And the girl doesn't even let them know her mother was murdered?" He shook his head.

"Strange indeed," Jeremy said. "Do you think she did it?"

"Do you?" the detective shot back.

"She's pretty hostile and defensive with everyone."

Detective Miles shrugged. "Wouldn't you be?"

Yeah, Jeremy thought, he probably would. This was the part of the job he always hated. Placing the element of suspicion on the victim's family first.

"Speaking of defensive and hostile," David said, "did Cory happen to mention his confrontation with Ken Schaffer?"

"I heard about it from Gracie when I went to pick Cory up. She was a bit hysterical." He pondered on his words for a moment. "Don't understand why—the hysterics, I mean. Anyway, she was telling me I needed to be taking her father into custody, not Cory. Kept telling me to look at what her father had done to Cory."

David positioned himself more comfortably, stretching in his seat, then leaning forward with his elbows resting on his knees. "What about that note? The one Laura, my wife, came across?"

"I think it's part of very complex puzzle," Detective Miles said.

"Is there any way to find out who wrote it?"

"I sent it to the state police lab in Tallahassee, but I can guarantee it won't be a priority, and chances are they won't be able to tell much from it. The paper is your average copy store stock. The ink, even with the bloodlike Halloween font, looks like a common color printer type. If this person has more than an ounce of brains, he'd know to wear gloves while handling the paper. And you can buy latex gloves at any grocery store."

"Gracie deals with computers all day," Jeremy said.

"So do Cory, the other girls in the office, and the campers.

Who doesn't use a computer nowadays?"

"Yeah," Detective Miles said. Not knowing who they were dealing with was getting to him, slowly eating at him. Those he suspected he couldn't really see as harboring such evil. Except maybe Ken Schaffer.

"Well, someone really wanted Patricia Marsh dead . . . and they wanted it pretty damn bad." Jeremy stood. "Anything else, Detective?"

"Yeah. This is Saint Augustine, Florida. People come here to have fun. Take the day off . . . enjoy yourselves." He laughed. "And while you're enjoying, keep your eyes and ears open."

"We will." Jeremy shook the detective's hand, then he and David exited the office.

Just as quickly as Cory had entered the resort office and closed the door, someone swung the door open and came barreling in.

"You the manager?" A huge, bald muscleman stood inside the doorway. He sported no shirt under his black leather vest, exposing a large tattoo of an eagle with spread wings on his chest. He wore chaps over his jeans, thick-soled biker boots with fringe, and an expression of acute irritation.

Cory barred the biker's entry with his body. "No, the manager isn't available right now. She'll be in later."

The biker took a handful of Cory's t-shirt. "I said I need to speak with the manager. *Now.*"

Grabbing the biker's wrist, Cory pressed until the man released his grip. "What do you need? I'll take care of it."

"Is there a problem?" Gracie said, entering the office.

"No, this gentleman was just about to tell me how I can help him."

"Someone broke into my trailer," the biker said.

"What's your site number, Mr. . . . ?" Cory asked, keeping his voice low and calm.

"Red Dog Jackson. Site twenty-four."

"Anything missing?"

Red-faced, the biker scowled. His movements were choppy. "Yeah, something's missing all right, and I swear if anything's happened to Smoochie, I'll sue the hell out of this resort."

"Calm down, Mr. Jackson."

"*Doctor* Jackson."

"You're in luck, Dr. Jackson," Gracie announced, placing a hand on Cory's shoulder. "This is Cory Marsh, Harbor Lights' expert customer service representative."

The biker ignored Gracie and kept his frozen expression on Cory. "My pet's cage was open. Deliberately. And I know I locked the trailer door. I can't find Smoochie anywhere."

"We'll help you look for her." Cory pegged the good doctor for a dog man—a boxer, maybe a pit bull.

A shriek came from the back office. A chair crashed against the tile. Then there was a mad scramble.

"God, oh God." Norma exploded out of the back office, shoved Cory and Dr. Jackson aside, and ran out the front door.

Cory swiveled to run to Gracie's aid.

"Dr. Jackson?" Gracie's voice floated from her back office.

"Yeah?"

"What kind of pet is your Smoochie?"

"She's a six-foot boa constrictor. Just a baby."

Before Cory could reach Gracie's office, Gracie rounded the corner of the registration desk. A brown snake with irregular dark blotches was draped around her shoulders.

"I think we've found her," Gracie said.

Yelping, Terrie hopped on top of the counter and used Cory as a shield.

The transformation in Dr. Jackson was as different as night and day. His whole demeanor softened, turning this angry biker into a molasses-eyed Saint Bernard. "Smoochie, my sweet.

162

Come to Daddy."

Gently, Dr. Jackson relieved Gracie of her scaly burden and wound Smoochie around his own shoulders, kissing the reptile's face. "How did she get in here?"

"I have no idea," Gracie said. "She was under the bathroom sink cabinet in my office."

Dr. Jackson left, cooing at Smoochie. As Cory closed the door, the snake's elliptical pupils stared coldly at him. The reptile's long, curved fangs and forked tongue added to the impression of something sinister.

"Another satisfied customer," Gracie said, smiling. "Where's Norma?"

Terrie hopped off the counter. "Probably halfway to Jacksonville by now."

Cory shook his head. "Never a dull moment at Harbor Lights RV Resort."

"I'll be back in a second," Gracie said. "I'm going to see if I can find Norma. Poor thing."

Cory hesitated. Then, walking past the registration desk, he headed to his office. Gracie's office was just before his and he noticed she'd left the door open when she exited with Smoochie. Reaching out, he grasped the handle and started to pull the door closed. The 3-D flying objects screen saver on Gracie's computer stopped him. He looked to his left . . . then right . . . then entered Gracie's office and quietly pulled the door closed.

Sitting in front of the computer, he moved the mouse around to stop the screen saver and clicked the START button to shut her computer down. Instead, he found himself double-clicking the Internet Explorer icon. He moved the mouse to the top of the screen and clicked the down arrow beside the GO button. The first thing he saw was a Web site search for undetectable poisons.

A knock on the door caused him to jump.

"Yes?" he called out, and he swung the chair around, hoping his body would block the fact that he was messing around with Gracie's computer. If it was Norma, he was dead. If it was Terrie, the girl wouldn't say a word. "Come in," he said.

He smiled and relaxed when Terrie entered.

"I'm sorry," Terrie said. "I didn't know you were in here. I checked your office first."

"I was looking for the profit-and-loss sheets for last month. What is it, Terrie?"

"Gracie just called from her cell and said to let you know she found Norma, and the two of them are heading across the street to the Donut King and will be back in fifteen or twenty minutes. She didn't want you to worry."

"Thanks, Terrie. Anything else?"

"Nope." Terrie scanned the office. "Please," she said, "if you find any more pythons in here, let me know before you bring them out."

Cory smiled. "I will. I promise."

As soon as Terrie shut the door, Cory turned the chair around to face the computer again.

The glow from the monitor reflected like a veil of gauze on his face, casting murky shadows that disguised his features. Yet even the shadows revealed a man deeply absorbed in his work. Hunched over the keyboard, right hand scooting and clicking the mouse, Cory patiently and meticulously called up the recently saved files and notes from Gracie's Internet searches.

It was totally quiet, except for the muted tap-tapping of the keyboard and the soft hum of the tower processing unit. A few more files, and he would be finished. One by one he began to send the files on Gracie's computer to his computer in the next office. It had always been a practice for them to do this—share all incoming and outgoing files and documents. That way, no one would be in the dark as to what was going on within the resort's financial as well as customer-related activities. It was becoming clear to Cory that Gracie had ceased sharing her files with him soon after Patricia's death. Why? What was she hiding? The questions and uncertainties rattled around in his mind as he quickly continued to copy and transfer the files.

He looked at his watch . . . he'd been at Gracie's computer for close to fifteen minutes. She'd be returning soon, and the last thing he wanted was a confrontation over what he was doing in her office, at her computer. *Undetectable poisons. The autopsy showed your wife died of poisoning.* Thoughts were racing through his mind, settling in the pit of his stomach with a burning sensation. He cleared all traces of his activity from the computer, then returned everything to the way he'd found it.

Exiting the office, he turned toward the computer and waited a few minutes until he saw the flying objects screen saver begin. He closed the door behind him and walked back to the main front office just as Gracie and Norma entered through the front door carrying a box of donuts.

Cory smiled. "I hope there's a chocolate glazed in there." He nodded at the box in Gracie's hands.

Gracie placed the box on the registration counter and flipped the lid open. "Here," she said, handing Cory a chocolate glazed donut. "Are you okay? You look worried."

"I'm fine," Cory said, chomping into his donut. "Lot to do today, and this will help jumpstart me." Picking up a napkin from the counter, he wiped his mouth. "If you ladies will excuse me, I'm going to see if the maintenance crew showed up."

Norma walked behind the counter and flipped the reservation book open. "We have quite a few arrivals today, Gracie. Do you think we should pull in some volunteers?"

Gracie peered across the counter, turning the reservation book so she could see it. "It doesn't look too bad. I think we can handle it."

Norma shrugged. "I suppose."

"If we run into a rush, Laura Jennings is always happy to help," Terrie said.

"We'll keep that in mind," Gracie said.

NINETEEN

Norma Rowland had always been a snoop. It's what she thrived on most as a camper and employee at Harbor Lights RV Resort. She also loved the fact that Gracie and she had become such good friends—"soul sistahs," is what she called it. Norma knew more secrets about what was going on in and out of the resort than that Detective Miles or anyone else. When other campers referred to Norma as "Queen of the Busybody Club," Norma took it as a flattering compliment. The one place Gracie didn't invite Norma too often was her office. But today her chance had come. The chance to feed that gnawing urge and need to snoop.

"It doesn't look like our reservations are going to arrive any time soon," Gracie said. "I think I'll go see if I can find Cory and talk him into lunch at the Pirate's Cove. Poor guy's been through a lot in the past few days."

"How sweet," Terrie said. "Go on. Norma and I can handle things."

"Thanks. If you do get rushed and need me, call." Gracie held her cell phone up. "I always have it with me."

Just as soon as Gracie exited the office Norma jumped right in as next in charge.

Terrie was busy checking the online reservations to make sure no one had canceled and to open the sites up if there were cancellations.

"While you're doing that," Norma said, "I think I'll see if I can find some papers Gracie wanted notarized."

Without looking up from the computer, Terrie nodded in agreement.

In Gracie's office, trying her best to forget about the big, ugly snake that Gracie had emerged from here with, Norma scanned the room.

How could Gracie work like this? There were piles everywhere—on the desk, on the chair, on the floor, on the file cabinet, under the desk, in the closet—and none of them seemed to be constructed from a sense of logic. Financial spreadsheets were mixed with activity schedules, receipts for purchases with order forms, books with random pieces of paper. Rummaging through things, Norma'd even found something that looked like a high school essay. Even Gracie's desk calendar was three months behind. How did she find anything?

Norma recalled the many hours Cory had spent with Gracie after Patricia had died, setting up color-coded files to ease her task as manager, rearranging her desk and supplies in bins and organizers for maximum efficiency. His effort seemed to have been for nothing, Norma thought, shaking her head.

Gracie had confided in Norma about all the friction between her and her mother and told her stories about how her mother would send mean letters to the boarding school. According to Gracie, Patricia even blamed Gracie for her marital problems and abuse from Ken. Norma lapped up the tales like a cat eating tuna. The last time Norma was in Gracie's office alone was when everyone else was at the funeral. Norma had given a sad-sack story about not being able to handle such things. Told them she'd stay at the office and deal with the check-ins. Instead, she'd searched through the file cabinets and desk drawers in hopes of finding some of those juicy letters from Patricia to her daughter Gracie. But she'd found nothing.

Norma kicked at something under the desk that had fallen out of a file box. Bending, she picked up a legal pad. After clearing a space on the desk, she flipped up the first sheet. A piece of paper was divided into two columns—suspects and motives. It was obvious to Norma that Gracie had been busy doing her own investigation into her mother's death.

Leaning back in the black swivel chair, Norma read on, curious to know who Gracie had suspected in her mother's "foul play" demise. Gracie's notes were as disorganized and senseless as her other work habits. "Cory" and "Dad" were listed under "Motives," and the list of suspects looked more like a shopping list to Norma—tea, plants . . . What was Gracie thinking? Had she seen something? Known something?

The sound of giggling came through the closed doors. Norma hurried and shoved the legal pad back into the file box under the desk. She rose and opened the door quietly, her ear cocked in the direction of the laughter. Norma let out a sigh of relief. It was only Laura Jennings and Terrie.

"What's so funny?" Norma asked.

Terrie drummed the eraser of her pencil against a pad of paper. "Nothing. Laura was just telling me something that happened at the resort her family owns."

"Oh." Norma shrugged her shoulders. "So, what are you doing here, Laura?"

Laura turned from Terrie and looked straight into Norma's smoky-gray, catlike eyes. "I'm talking with Terrie."

"She stopped by to see if we needed help," Terrie added. "Wasn't that sweet of her?"

A nervous flutter still prickled in Norma's chest. She glanced back over her shoulder, then back to Terrie. "Just ducky," she said, focusing back on Terrie's comment.

"There's a few rolling in now," Laura said, pointing to the three motor homes that had just parked outside the office.

Norma looked out. "I think we can handle a few motor homes, don't you, Terrie?"

"Well," Laura said, "I should be going anyway. David wanted to drive around and see what A1A has to offer. Have a good day." Laura turned and headed out the front door.

Outside, Laura couldn't get Norma's apparent agitation out of her mind. She'd looked like a cat in a room full of rockers when she'd exited the back office.

Laura smiled at the campers and headed back to *Passion's Palace*.

David and Laura cruised down A1A Beach Boulevard. They'd only been over this road on the way into St. Augustine and to get groceries. David had said one day they'd have to just go cruising and see what else this coastal highway might have besides grocery stores, souvenir shops, and campgrounds. The small parking lot behind the gift shop Laura had wanted to stop at was full. Vehicles, many with out-of-state plates, lined both sides of the street. Pedestrians strolled along on the sidewalks. It was easy to tell the tourists from the locals. The locals were in shorts or slacks. Tourists wore bathing suits and cameras.

"Here's one," David said. He found a parking place on a side street a few blocks from the gift shop. "It's not that far to walk."

Laura yawned. "Sounds good. Maybe a walk will help wake me up."

"You were flipping and flopping all night. Something bothering you?"

They walked past the arcade. It was packed with teenagers playing electronic games.

"No. Nothing's bothering me. Guess I was just hyped up from the day." Laura pointed toward the arcade. "Look at the kids in there. Doesn't anyone go to school anymore?"

David shrugged. "Maybe that's some sort of PE for the homeschooled kids."

Laura laughed and took David's hand in hers.

An RV as long as a Greyhound bus took up three parking places in front of the drugstore. David and Laura stepped off the sidewalk in front of the RV and waited for a break in traffic. A car passed, and they stepped into the street.

Brake lights flared on the car. Tires screeched. Laura tensed for a collision, which didn't come. Backup lights glowed, the engine roared. The driver must have spotted a parking place, David thought. He pulled Laura out of the way.

A dark sedan stopped in front of them. The passenger-side window lowered with a faint mechanical sound. Every hair on Laura's body lifted. Her scalp tightened. An inner voice said *Run!* Her legs refused to obey until a movement in the shadowy car interior reached her brain. She pivoted, David's hand still in hers, and the both of them slammed back against the flat grill of the RV.

"What the hell?" David said.

Crack!

Aftershock smacked Laura's eardrums. Her nostrils caught a whiff of gunpowder. *Crack!* The ping of a ricocheting bullet spurred David into action. He pulled Laura from her frozen position into the street, around the RV, out of line with the sedan's passenger window. *Crack!* People screamed. David and Laura ran like hell.

They raced around the back of the RV. David helped Laura to leap over the curb onto the sidewalk. They continued to run, dodging people, frantically looking for a place to hide. The car backed up recklessly; oncoming traffic honked, screeched, and veered out of the way.

David and Laura darted around a corner and into the shadows.

Metal crunched metal. Glass shattered. A man shouted, "Get

him!" Other voices rose in a furious cry to battle. A siren wailed.

Laura pressed herself against David. Her heart pounded. Her mouth was sour with adrenaline.

"I've got him, dammit!" a man roared. "Back off! Hey! Yeah, you! Get off him. He ain't going anywhere. I mean it. Put those rifles away! All of you, move!"

Red and blue emergency flashers bounced off the buildings. People milled about on a street corner, seeking a better view. Laura sagged and patted her and David's arms and legs and upper arms, assuring herself neither of them had been wounded. *If it's my time . . .* she couldn't finish the prayer.

"Hey, you guys okay?" Detective Miles stood in front of them.

"We're fine," David said. "What the hell was that all about?"

The three of them walked back toward Beach Boulevard. The sedan was crushed like a demolition derby loser between two pickup trucks. Shop owners strutted in the street like wolves circling a fresh kill. A few carried rifles. Tourists and locals lined the sidewalks.

"I saw everything," a woman cried. She pointed at David. "That's who he shot! That's him!"

David caught a few words from the murmuring crowd.

"Shooting up our town . . ."

"Showed him . . ."

"Stupid sumbitch . . ."

Detective Miles tightened his hold on Laura's shoulder. They walked over to where Officer Harrison had a man, with his hands locked behind him, sitting in the back seat of the cruiser. His head lolled. Even with his bloody nose, swollen jaw, and split lip, it was clear to David and Laura that the man in custody was Ken Schaffer. Either he'd hit the steering wheel when the trucks smashed his car, or the locals had gotten in some blows. Either scenario was all right with David.

"Little tip for you, Schaffer," Detective Miles said. "This is a real bad place to be taking potshots at tourists."

Ken moaned. "I need a doctor."

"You'll need a lot more than a doctor before we're through with you."

A shudder racked Laura's body. She'd seen crazy people before . . . at the Big Pine Key Resort, as well as growing up as an army brat. She'd been stalked, sent death threats, and watched the violence from Norman Bateman unfold as he'd held her father at gunpoint. No one had ever shot at her before. Aimed a gun so close to David, so close to both of them, given chase, tried to kill David.

"You all right?" Detective Miles asked David.

"What the hell does he want to kill me for?" David asked.

" 'Cause you can't keep your face out of other people's business, Mr. Bruce Lee asshole," Ken shouted from the cruiser.

"Get him out of here," Miles told Harrison.

David placed a hand on the small of his back and arched against the ache. He studied the surrounding hammocks. The sun had risen an hour ago, but still hadn't topped the trees. Harbor Lights RV Resort was quiet, peaceful. David scanned the area; from where he stood, there wasn't one sign of any campers. Unseen birds cawed, whistled, and screeched.

Logic told him he and Laura were perfectly safe and unharmed. Ken was locked up in a jail cell, though it was David's thought that the guy needed to be in another kind of cell— one with padding. He wasn't hurt, Laura wasn't, and no one else had been.

Still, he'd slept poorly. Wind had rocked the motor home throughout the night, making it groan, creak, and rattle. Laura had been restless, too. Every noise had jerked her to nervous wakefulness.

David went back into the motor home. Irritation still frayed his nerves. Laura was in the kitchen making coffee.

"Good morning," she said.

David walked over to her and wrapped his arms around her waist, kissing her neck. "I suppose it could be defined as a good morning. We're still alive."

Laura turned and lifted her head to meet David's eyes. "Yes, we are alive. And we're not going to let that psycho Ken keep us awake anymore." Her mouth met his in a long and breathless kiss.

"You're right," he said.

Laura stood still, closing off her thoughts. Not saying what was on her mind—which was to tell David he needed to control his urge to jump in and save damsels in distress as he'd done the night of the potluck dinner. Ken was Gracie's father, and whatever the feud was between them or Ken and Cory was their problem. Laura thought it had been wrong for David to make it his problem and ultimately put himself in danger. Forcing all those thoughts out of her mind, her nervousness eased.

Hoping a shower would wake him up, David took a sip of freshly brewed coffee, then placed it down. "I'm going to take a shower. Are you okay?"

She kissed him again, this time more as a peck on his lips. "I'm fine. Go on. A shower will make you feel better, and then we can go for a walk or something."

He ran the water until it was steaming and stepped inside the stall. It was still hard for him to get used to the tiny bathing area. Even in a motor home as big as theirs, it still wasn't like taking a shower in a house. He stood under the hot spray, letting it pound the tension from his bones. He soaped up, scrubbed, rinsed, and began to feel like himself again.

Getting dressed, he began noticing an aroma of peppers and onions and that buttery oil Laura used for cooking. He heard singing. It sounded like the soulful voice of Kelly Clarksen belting out "A Moment Like This."

He walked out to the kitchen. Laura stood before the stove, waving a spatula over a frying pan as if it were a conductor's baton. Swinging her hips, her long, golden hair swaying, she sang. Her sweet, sultry voice made his jaw drop.

He had learned more about Laura in the two weeks they'd been at St. Augustine than he'd learned in a year.

She noticed him and smiled. He regretted the loss of her singing.

"Sit down. I made biscuits and omelets."

"Whole wheat biscuits, right?" The first meal she'd cooked for him after they were married was chicken and dumplings made from whole wheat and oats. He'd never seen such a thing and had been reluctant to eat them. Dumplings were supposed to be pillowy and white. She firmly believed that white flour was dead food, robbed of nourishment. Once he got over the texture, the dumplings hadn't been too bad. He was used to her cooking now.

She set a big cup of coffee in front of him, along with a cloth-covered basket of biscuits, butter and honey.

"You keep treating me like this, I'm going to get spoiled."

She smiled. "Like you spoil me? I can't have you cooking me breakfast all the time. I just felt ambitious this morning." She lifted the pan off the stove and slid a fluffy omelet onto a plate.

"You don't hear me complaining."

She set the plate before him. His mouth watered at the sight. She used brown eggs, and the yolks were so rich they were practically orange. The omelet was filled with green peppers and onions, and the outside edge was crispy, just the way he liked it.

Just as David brought the first bite of his omelet to his mouth, there was a knock on the door. "Who would that be this early?"

Laura put her plate on the counter and headed for the front

door. "I don't know."

As soon as the door opened, she saw Gracie standing on the metal steps. She wore a dark blue tank top tucked into denim shorts.

"Good morning," Laura said. She turned her head to where David sat. "It's Gracie," she called out.

"I'm sorry to bother you guys so early," Gracie said. "But I got a call from that Detective Miles late last night. He told me what happened . . . with my dad, and, uh, I wanted to apologize and see if you're both okay."

David stood behind Laura, his hands on her shoulders. "We're fine. Would you like to come in?"

"No, I can't. I have to go down to the police station. The detective wants to talk to me."

"Do you need me to help out in the office while you're gone?" As soon as the words escaped her mouth, Laura regretted them. She'd just finished telling David they'd do something special today, and she wanted to do just that—something that would make them both feel like they were actually on their honeymoon.

"That's really sweet of you to offer, Laura, after everything that's gone on. If you're really sure, Terrie and Norma could use the extra hand. We have another club arriving today," Gracie said.

Laura turned toward David. "Do you mind?"

"Not at all. Go ahead."

"I shouldn't be too long," Gracie added.

"I'll get dressed and be there shortly," Laura said. She pulled the door closed.

Gracie called out her thanks as she walked away.

David went back to the table, hoping the omelet wasn't completely cold. He sat down and cut off a big chunk with his fork and shoved it into his mouth.

"If that's cold, I can nuke it," Laura said.

David nodded his head, declining. "It's fine," he muttered with a full mouth.

They finished breakfast and David washed the dishes while Laura got showered and dressed. She emerged in a sleeveless white cotton dress, her hair pulled back in a ponytail. David smiled, remembering how she'd looked when they first met. All prim and proper, every hair in place, dressed for success. He was happy to see her looking more relaxed, more like she was enjoying life.

"You look all comfy and summery, my dear."

"Thanks." She looked down. "I thought I'd wear this so we could go out and do something when I get back."

"Anything in particular?" he asked.

"Well, anything except strolling along Beach Boulevard. I think I had all that kind of fun I can handle."

David laughed. "Agreed. Your wish is my command."

Laura snatched a set of motor home keys from a hook by the door. "I'll take these just in case you're out when I get back."

"Good idea. I want to see what Jeremy's been up to. Clue him in on the latest excitement."

"You think he hasn't heard already?" Laura nodded toward Stella's trailer across the way. "She sees and hears everything."

"I stand corrected," David said.

TWENTY

In the office, Laura found Norma conversing with a woman in her mid-thirties who wore pale green capris with a short-sleeved white eyelet top, white sandals, and the face that Laura and Katie had seen at the pool. She was imperceptibly shaking as she clutched the counter. Terrie looked relieved to see Laura.

Norma turned her attention from the woman to Laura. "Good morning, Laura. This is Becky Nelson. Gracie's cousin."

A satchel from Norma's shoulder fell to the floor when she turned, and Laura bent over to pick it up. When she did, a book fell from the bag. "I'm Laura Jennings," Laura said, extending her free hand. "I'm sorry to meet you under such circumstances." She handed the book and satchel to Norma.

"Thank you," Becky said, removing her hands from the counter and sinking into a nearby chair. "Cory called a few days ago and told me what happened."

Norma shot an *I'm-handling-this* stare at Laura. "What's that?" she asked, glancing at the book.

Laura looked at the book quickly, saw the word *Reflections* written across the cover, put it under her arm, and said, "Sorry. Nothing . . . that's mine."

Norma snatched her satchel from Laura. "Terrie, why don't you see if we have some iced tea in the fridge for Becky," she said.

"Sure thing," Terrie said.

"I saw you at the pool a couple of days ago," Laura said.

"You were with two other women."

"Yes. My mom and grandmother. I drove up here from Miami and picked them up in Daytona." Becky shook her head in disbelief. "It was such horrible news."

Laura couldn't help but remember the women at the pool. To her, they looked as though they were having a good time, all except Becky. "Yes, it was horrible. More so because it doesn't seem to ever go away. The campers and employees . . . well, my husband and I have only been here a couple of weeks and it's all we hear about."

Terrie came back from the supply room with a glass of tea and handed it to Becky. "I put a slice of lemon in it."

"Thanks." Becky took a sip. "My mom never got along well with her sister. I think there was a lot of jealousy or something over Patricia's success as an artist. I don't want to air out all our family's dirty linen, and I'm sure you've all heard enough anyway. About Aunt Patricia's ex-husband Ken, and Gracie being stuck in that boarding school all her life." She looked up at Laura. "Aren't you and your husband the ones Ken shot at yesterday?"

"Yes, we are," Laura said.

Terrie gasped. "Laura! I didn't know anything about that? What happened?"

Norma let out a big sigh. "Not now, Terrie. I'm sure Becky is upset enough."

"I just don't understand," Becky said. "I mean, my aunt was the kindest person I knew. To me and my mother. She never acted like she was so successful, and I always felt sorry for her—being imprisoned and tortured by that jerk Ken. I just know he had something to do with Aunt Patricia's murder."

"Some around here are pointing the finger at Cory," Norma said. "Saying he did it for the insurance money."

"Yes," Becky agreed. "The other night, when that detective

hauled Cory away, Gracie said she'd even suspected he had something to do with it. I don't know Cory that well, so I can't make any judgments. But I do know Ken Schaffer, and I've seen him in action."

Terrie's head turned from one person to the next.

"Well, I don't buy it. Cory is the sweetest person I've ever known. He wouldn't hurt a fly." Norma looked at Terrie. "Isn't that right?"

Terrie shrugged. "I guess. You've known him and Gracie far longer than I have."

"Where is Cory?" Laura asked.

"He went to the police station with Gracie. That's what I mean," Norma said. "He wouldn't let her go alone."

The chimes above the door jangled, and they all became quiet when two elderly women walked in.

"Here you are, Becky," one of them said. "We're ready to roll when you are."

Becky got up from the chair and put her empty glass on the counter. Then she introduced her mother and grandmother to the others. "Ladies, this is my mother, Harriett, and my grandmother Esther."

"Pleased to meet you both," Laura said.

"We really have to get going," Becky said. "Mother needs to get back to help her woman's club put together some charity."

"Not *some* charity," Becky's mother said. "For neglected children. Like your cousin Gracie was."

Embarrassment flushed Becky's face and neck. "It was nice meeting all of you," she said. She turned to Norma. "Thank you for all you've done, and please thank Gracie and Cory again for us."

Norma gave Becky a hug. "I will. You drive safely. There's a bunch of crazy spring breakers out there still."

Norma waved as they drove away from in front of the office.

"Okay, girls, time to get to work," she said as she made her way up the steps and back inside.

Laura was already busy at the computer, checking the online reservations. Terrie was ringing in the cash drawer at the register. Laura looked at Terrie and just rolled her eyes as Norma stood behind them both like a drill sergeant.

Officer Harrison pulled his cruiser into the parking lot of police headquarters promptly at seven-forty-five. Yesterday, he'd arrived a few minutes past eight and received a lecture from Detective Miles on the necessity of developing good investigative habits. The detective considered punctuality right up there near the top of his list. "Being late implies laziness, and there's no room on the force for a lazy investigator."

Harrison endured the dressing-down silently, aware that a half-dozen pairs of eyes watched covertly from behind cluttered desks around the room. He had to remind himself he was lucky to be working with Miles, who reportedly changed partners more often than a teenage girl changed clothes. He was beginning to see why. Not many men would willingly perform all the grunt work and chases like yesterday's Schaffer idiot, while the arrogant detective refused to dirty his hands.

But Harrison would suffer that and worse to learn from the best investigator in the state. One day he hoped to lay claim to that title himself.

He picked up the folder containing the notes he'd printed off at home last night. For the most part, his work so far in this case had been great. He'd faithfully recorded notes of every conversation, every interrogation Miles conducted. Their case file was growing. True, they didn't have much to go on yet, but the detective's techniques were inspiring. Now, with the help of a qualified and interested big New York forensic anthropologist offering his retired know-how, they didn't have to concern themselves with budgets on lab tests that would otherwise be too low to help them.

Harrison made his way down the hallway toward the crowded room where Detective Miles's desk was located. The lab report they'd received yesterday had indicated no evidence of toxic oleander in any of the tea bags they had confiscated from Cory Marsh's and Gracie Schaffer's kitchen. Nor did it come up with anything conclusive on the lab reports from the fragments found in that bottle.

Miles was already at his desk, reading through a typed report. He looked up when Harrison approached, his eyes fixed on the folder. "Those yesterday's reports on Schaffer?"

"Yes, sir."

"Good. I needed them an hour ago."

He snatched the folder. Harrison bit back a sharp retort as Miles pulled out the neatly printed pages and scanned them. Yeah, he was learning a lot working with Miles. How to act like a good investigator. And how not to act like a total jerk.

Tomorrow he'd be here at seven.

He stood while Miles scanned the notes. The detective chewed on the corner of his lower lip while he read. When he finished the last page, he gave a nod. "Looks like it's all there."

That was as close to a compliment as Harrison was likely to get. "Thanks."

Detective Miles shuffled the papers and pulled a two-hole punch from his drawer. "I've got Gracie Schaffer coming here any minute."

"But we already—" Harrison cut off his argument mid-sentence at a glance from Miles.

"I want to talk to her again, especially since having had my chat with those nuns." The detective punched holes in Harrison's notes and slid them onto two metal prongs inside the folder he'd been reading when Harrison arrived. "Then I want to see if the commissioner has gotten me the court order yet to go through Ken Schaffer's house." Since Ken lived out of the jurisdiction, in Daytona Beach, they had to go the red-tape route, taking forever to get a search warrant.

Harrison's cell phone rang. With an apologetic grimace at Detective Miles, he unclipped it from his belt and glanced at the display. His parents' number. Before eight o'clock in the morning? Something must be wrong.

He flipped open the cover. "Hello?"

"Brian." Relief saturated his mother's voice. "I'm so glad I got you."

The speed of his pulse picked up a notch. "What's wrong, Mom? Is Dad okay?"

"Why wouldn't he be? He's out in the garage, as usual, tinkering with the lawn mower."

Officer Brian Harrison felt the weight of Detective Miles stare. He turned his back. "Mom, is this important? I'm working."

"Of course it's important. I wouldn't be calling otherwise. I need you to come to the house for dinner tonight."

"Dinner?" Officer Harrison lowered his voice and took a couple of steps away from the detective's desk. "Why is that important?"

"Because I've invited someone I want you to meet, and this is the only evening she can make it."

He closed his eyes. Lately his mother's efforts to see him married off to a nice girl had crossed the line of mere nagging and become downright frustrating. "Mother, I am not coming to dinner tonight to let you parade another girl in front of me."

An outraged puff sounded in his ear. "Are you taking a tone with me, young man?"

He took pains to reply calmly, "I'm in the middle of an important case. I don't have time for this right now."

"But will you come tonight? I promised Betty Lou you'd be here."

"Then you'll have to call her back and unpromise her."

"I can't do that!" A hint of desperation crept into his mother's voice. "The poor girl will be so disappointed. She's already made plans to be here."

"I hope you have a nice time with her," Officer Harrison said, leaving no room to continue the argument. "I'll be working late."

"Honestly, who would have thought that such a sweet, compliant little boy would become such an irritating man?" She humphed. "An irritating, *unmarried* man."

Officer Harrison raised his eyes to the ceiling. "Good-bye, Mom. Tell Dad I said hello."

He closed the cover and clipped the phone onto his belt. When he turned, he found Detective Miles watching him, arms folded across his chest.

"Whenever you're ready to get to work," the surly detective said, "we have something a little more important than your love life to attend to. Like a murder to solve?"

Gracie parked her car in front of the police station. She was beginning to feel like this particular parking spot had been reserved just for her. It was always open when she came here, and lately it seemed she'd been coming here to police headquarters a lot. She pushed her way through the front door, and a jangle of bells announced her presence.

A head appeared over the top of a cubicle, and a young woman peered at her from behind dark-rimmed glasses. "Can I help you?"

"Uh, yeah. I'm here to see Detective Miles. He's expecting me."

"I'll tell him you're here. And your name is?"

"Gracie Schaffer."

The woman pointed at a bench behind Gracie. "You can have a seat over there, Ms. Schaffer," she said. "Help yourself to some coffee."

Gracie shifted her weight to her other foot. "I'm fine. I'm also in a hurry. I'll wait right here."

Fifteen minutes later, Detective Miles and Officer Harrison emerged through a door on the other side of the cubicles separating the front office of the police station from the personnel offices.

Detective Miles unlocked a door and moved aside for Gracie to enter. "Thank you for coming, Ms. Schaffer." He motioned to a back office. "Come in, please."

Gracie took a seat next to Mr. Good Looking Cop. The officer flipped open his notebook, crossed his left leg over his right knee, and waited.

Detective Miles sat back in his swivel chair, hands locked behind his head. "We have some questions to ask you about an incident that happened yesterday. One in which your father was very much involved."

"I'm not my father's keeper," Gracie said, sitting up straight and folding her hands in her lap. "What does an incident with my father have to do with me, Detective?"

Miles unlocked his hands and sat forward. "The incident in question involved the attempted assault on two of your campers, David and Laura Jennings? Names sound familiar?"

Gracie cleared her throat. "Yes, the honeymooning couple. I still don't understand what all this has to do with me. I've had very little contact with my father in my life. I've probably seen him more since the murder of my mother than I have in years. If you expect me to have answers as to why he attempted to run over the Jenningses, I'm sorry, I don't."

Officer Harrison's eyes shot up from his notebook to Detective Miles. He knew exactly what was coming.

"Ms. Schaffer," the detective said, "I didn't mention anything about what kind of assault was attempted on Mr. and Mrs. Jennings's. You seem to already be aware of the fact that your father tried to run them over and shoot at them."

Gracie let out a deep intake of air. "Of course I know, Detective Miles. I live at a campground, remember? I'm the manager. My mother was the owner. She was murdered. It's no secret that my father has a violent temper and that he's been coming around stirring up trouble ever since Cory and my mother bought that resort. Harbor Lights is no different from any other campground . . . it's a breeding place for gossip and innuendoes."

The detective's eyes held Gracie's across the desk. "Ms. Schaffer, where were you yesterday?"

Gracie was becoming agitated. Why were they questioning her about something her father had done? She glanced at Officer Harrison, whose eyes remained on his notebook, his expression grim.

"I was at the campground," she answered. "All day and all night."

"Can anyone verify that?" Detective Miles asked.

Gracie cast an irritated glance his way. "Hmm, let's see," she said with sarcasm oozing from every syllable. "There's Cory, Norma Rowland, my assistant manager, Terrie Snyder, my office clerk, and probably a few dozen campers."

"You didn't leave the campground at all?" Detective Miles asked.

"No . . . well, yes, just for a few minutes. I went with Norma to get some doughnuts and coffee. What's this all about, Detective? You don't think I had anything to do with what my father did to the Jenningses, do you?"

"Do you own a gun?"

"No." Gracie turned her head to look at Officer Harrison. "What's this about?" she repeated.

"Ms. Schaffer." Detective Miles forced her to look back at him. "The Glock that your father used for target practice on the Jenningses is registered to you. That makes you an accessory."

Gracie reeled. "But . . . but . . . that's impossible!"

"You didn't answer my question, Ms. Schaffer. Do you own a Glock Safe Action pistol?"

"Uh, yes. But I've no idea how my father might have gotten it."

"Why did you get it?" Detective Miles asked.

"Why does anyone get a gun, Detective? For protection."

"Protection from whom? Or what, Ms. Schaffer? Seems to me a Glock pistol would be . . . excuse the expression . . . overkill, in terms of protection."

Gracie shifted her body in the chair and cast an agitated look at Officer Harrison before turning her attention back to the detective. "Detective, my mother was murdered. For all I know her murderer could still be lurking around the campground. I am not going to leave myself unprotected should some psycho decide to do me in like he did my mother. If the Saint Augustine Police Department would do their job rather than harass crime victims, I wouldn't need a gun. I'm sorry my father somehow got hold of my gun and used it for reasons of his own. If you're going to arrest me for my father's crime, go ahead. If not, I'm a busy woman with a campground to manage."

Detective Miles stood and walked around his desk to stand in front of her. "You are not being charged with a crime, Ms. Schaffer. I simply needed your statement, since the gun was registered in your name."

Fighting to breathe past a sudden lump in her throat, she asked. "Could I see my father while I'm here?"

The detective and Officer Harrison eye's met at Gracie's

request, then Harrison bent his head down and started jotting notes again in his little notebook.

"Of course," the detective said. "Come with me."

Gracie was escorted into a small waiting room equipped with only a card table, three folding chairs, and an American flag in the corner.

"Wait here," Detective Miles said. "I'll go get your father."

"Thank you," Gracie said.

She sat drumming her fingers on the small table as she scanned the diminutive room. This place gave her the creeps, and she wanted to get out of there as fast as she came in. But first she had to find out what in the world her father was up to and why he continued to implicate her in his wrongdoings.

Detective Miles opened the door with Ken Schaffer at his side. "You've got ten minutes," he said.

Ken sat in a chair across the table from Gracie, staring at her with a look of disdain. "What are you doing here? I know it ain't to bail me out. Not with half a million dollars as bail."

Gracie looked up at Detective Miles. "Do you mind if we have those ten minutes alone?" she asked.

"Not at all," he said, and closed the door . . . remaining on the other side.

"I was called down here because you used *my* gun to take potshots at two of my campers." Gracie spoke in a whisper. "I want to know how in the hell you got your hands on my gun."

Ken sat back, arms folded across his chest. "I must say, I love your daughterly concern."

"Damn it, Dad! I'm not kidding. I'm tired of always being smack in the middle of your crap. Now, how did you get my gun?"

"From the top drawer of your nightstand, sweetie," he said with an evil grin. "You really should lock your doors when you and your lover-boy stepfather are at the office."

Gracie looked away. What did she want from him? An apology? Some gesture of concern and fatherly adoration?

"Hey, don't look so worried, baby. No harm done. I just wanted to put a scare into that big shot David Jennings. The guy thinks he's some hero. He's nothing but a jerk. Bet he thinks twice before jumping in on someone else's fight next time." He leaned forward and whispered, "What did you tell that detective?"

"The truth," Gracie said. "That you're a bastard." She pushed her chair back and stood up, walking around the table and in front of her father.

A reflex reaction made Ken stand up as well, as if he expected to have some sort of boxing match with his daughter. He stared at her hard, with his hands on hips. "Is that it, little daughter?"

She pushed her right index finger into the center of his chest. "You're damn right this is it," she said. "As far as I'm concerned, you can rot in here." She backed away and headed toward the door. Before opening it, she turned to give Ken another once-over. "And stay out of my campground as well as my life. Got it?"

Ken gave her a military salute then called out, "We're done, Detective. You can open the door now."

The door opened, and Detective Miles escorted Ken back to his cell. When he returned, he told Gracie she was free to leave.

"We may need you to make another statement," the detective told her as she headed out the door. He handed her a business card. "Call if you have any sudden plans to leave town."

Gracie pushed the card back at the detective, "I have several of those you've given me. Good day, Detective."

Gracie heaved a sigh of relief when she walked out the doors of the police department and into the bright spring sunshine. The past two hours had been the most frustrating of her life. First they'd made her wait in some room more sterile than a hospital, and then left her sitting alone for thirty minutes. Detective Miles and his sidekick had treated her like a criminal, as if they considered her as having a part in the terrible act her father had committed. She boiled with anger and humiliation.

Twenty-One

Gracie arrived back at the campground office and found Terrie alone, juggling a number of tasks, frazzled and frenzied as she did so. Multitasking definitely wasn't one of Terrie's strongest work skills.

Gracie placed her purse on a shelf under the registration counter and proceeded to take the daily cash-balancing task from Terrie. "So, where's all the help I left you with?" she asked, licking her right thumb as she began counting the stack of currency in her hands.

Terrie grabbed a handful of mail piled inside the in-box crate and started to sort the campers' mail from the campground's. "The rush calmed down and Norma told Laura she could leave," Terrie explained. "And about fifteen minutes ago Norma said she was going to take your golf cart and do a check to make sure all the sites were free for the remainder of the RV club that hasn't arrived yet."

Gracie took a bank deposit slip and started to log the daily cash deposit. "What about Cory? Has he been in today?"

Terrie didn't look up from sorting the mail. "He was in earlier, right after you left. He didn't stay long or say much." Terrie put the handful of mail down and looked at Gracie, who was busy writing out the deposit. "Is he okay, Gracie?"

"Is who okay?"

"Cory. He didn't look okay."

"Meaning?"

"I just mean he looked . . . uh . . . well, kind of spaced out."

Gracie stopped what she was doing and looked at Terrie. "Spaced out? That doesn't sound like my Cory."

My Cory? Terrie found that a rather interesting comment.

"Like I said, he was only here for fifteen or twenty minutes. In his office. When he came out, he looked like he was in a trance or something. Said he was leaving, and he left."

Gracie shrugged. "Well, I'm sure Cory has a lot on his mind with all that's been going on. We all have—"

The conversation was interrupted when Norma came barreling through the door. "Man, you won't believe what's going on out there. Old Mrs. Conner is drunk as a skunk, and I had to pull her out of the bushes on site four-seventeen and then drag her onto the golf cart and dump her at her camper. Then I stopped by the clubhouse, and the craft ladies were having a gossip fest—without me." Norma stopped talking long enough to take in a deep breath. She looked at Terrie, and then turned to Gracie. "Did I interrupt something?"

They stood silent for a moment. Terrie's gaze was on Gracie, Gracie's was on Norma, and Norma's gaze kept zigzagging between Terrie and Gracie.

"Well," Norma said, "somebody say something."

"Terrie was just telling me why no one was here to help out." Gracie went back to her deposit, slipping a rubber band around the bills.

"I was here," Norma said. "I just stepped out to—"

"Gossip and see what kind of new dirt you could dig up," Gracie finished for her.

Norma put her clipboard down on the counter and grasped Gracie's arm, forcing her to stop what she was doing. "What's the matter with you? It wasn't like it was busy. And I certainly didn't go out in the campground to dig up dirt, as you so rudely put it."

Gracie pulled herself free from Norma's hold and shoved the deposit into a bank bag. "Look, it's been a long morning, okay? Just forget it." She shoved the bag toward Terrie and headed to the back toward her office.

Thirty minutes later the door to Gracie's office flew open. Startled, Gracie swung her chair around and turned, just as Cory entered.

"Where the hell have you been?" Gracie asked.

Cory slammed the door to her office. "At the cemetery. I thought I'd see you there, then I realized that was way too much to expect from you."

"Look," Gracie said, "if you want to run out to the cemetery every day and play the grieving widower, go right ahead. Don't expect me to play the same game." She swung her chair back to look at her computer.

Cory placed his hands on the back of the chair and turned her back to face him. He took hold of her arms and pulled her up. "Today is your mother's birthday, for God's sake. Did you even know that? Have you ever given a damn about your mother?"

Gracie looked shocked. *My God,* she thought, *what must he think of me? How could I forget your birthday, Mom?* "I'm sorry. Yes, I forgot, Cory. I was at the police station—being implicated as an accessory in my father's crime." She let out a long, deep sigh. "I gotta get out of here." She pushed past him and the door, almost knocking Norma over as she exited.

"Whoa," Norma said, bracing herself against the wall of the hallway. "Where's the fire?"

Gracie ignored her and sailed out of the office.

Sitting crossed-legged on the bed, Laura opened the journal and turned the pages, stopping every now and then to ponder the emotions felt by whoever the journalist was. The past and the present seemed to blend in a sweet-and-sour cocktail of pictures and emotions.

Would the answers everyone was seeking in connection to Patricia Marsh's murder be found inside these pages? What would Laura discover? Daily routines? Photographic details? Parts of the writer's soul?

"Laura?" David's unexpected voice should have made Laura jump, but it didn't. She looked up from the journal's cover and spotted his head poking over the kitchen counter toward the bedroom. "Hey, whatcha doing?"

"Investigating."

He climbed up the three steps to the bedroom. He was wearing nothing but cut-off shorts, showing his hard pecs and his washboard stomach. He sprawled beside her. "Okay, Detective, what do you have?" He scooted closer and craned his neck to look over at the journal.

Laura was pondering whether or not she should be prying into someone else's private musings.

She held the volume in her lap, her hand over the cover. "A journal."

David looked at her. "Oh? With all your secrets?"

"It's not my journal. And I don't have any secrets. To you, my life's an open book." She leaned over and kissed him.

"Okay, I give," he said. "Whose journal is it then? And how did you get it?"

"It fell out of Norma's bag, and when I picked it up and tried to hand it to her, she looked at me like I was nuts. Said it wasn't hers. So, I brought it here."

He bent his knees and scooted himself back against the headboard. "What have you found out so far?" he asked, pointing at the journal in her lap.

"Maybe answers. I don't know. I'd just started going through it when you came in." She pushed herself back, sitting beside him. Their shoulders were separated by no more than a thought.

"Can I see it?" David asked.

"Of course." She handed him the journal. "You're more experienced with these things than I am. Maybe you can figure out whose journal it is."

"The real expert on this kind of stuff would be someone like Jeremy." David opened the cover. Unlined pages stocked the inside. The journal was filled with words and drawings. Whomever it belonged to had started the book with a title page bearing the words "My Life: Reflections of Revenge" in deep red print. The second page held, along with sketches of trees, leaves, a beach, and flames, a word list consisting of "Meadowsweet," "Slippery Elm," "Nettle," "Clover Blossom," "Buchuu," "Comfrey," and "Chamomile." The last word told David it was a list of herbal teas.

Laura rested her head on David's shoulder. "What do you make of all this?"

David blew out a whistle as he twirled his right index finger around his temple. "The journalist's choice of titles alone is enough to tell me this person isn't someone I'd want to get on the wrong side of."

"My guess would be that this book belongs to Gracie. But the handwriting isn't at all like hers. So I don't know," Laura said.

Still thumbing through the book, David stopped at a page that had a verse written in red and pictures of what he supposed were intended to be blood splots dripping from the words. "Look at this," he said, pointing to the poem. "Isn't this the same verse that you found in the office?"

Laura glanced over the poem then shook herself, imitating a shiver. "Sure sounds like the same poem. Maybe we should hand this over to Detective Miles."

"First I'd like to show it to Jeremy." He closed the book and laid it beside him, then reached across the bed to the nightstand and snatched up a pen and a piece of scrap paper. "Number one, talk to Jeremy. Number two, swing by police station."

After watching him jot down the note, Laura smiled. He was meticulous when it came to his to-do lists. Picking up the journal, she returned her attention to the book. A loose page floated out. "Listen to this," Laura said. " 'I hate when people around here think I'm mean or cruel because I tell the truth. Tell it like it is. They call it gossip. Ha! As if they should talk.' Maybe it is Norma's. She is the resort's queen busybody."

David leaned closer to peer at the page. "Hmm, interesting. Norma strikes me as a chronic gabber, but a crazed lunatic like some of those other entries indicate . . . ? I don't think so. But then again, I could be wrong."

Laura read a few more entries, gaining insight to life at Harbor Lights RV Resort as well as the author's wry and angry view of life. "The entries stopped just about the same time as Patricia's death," she said, flipping to the journal's last page. "Coincidence?"

"Let me see that." He took the journal from her, and read the last entry, then frowned. "The last entry doesn't even sound like it was finished. Look, it stops in midsentence. 'Something about the way Cory . . .' "

He thumbed through the pages. Laura read along with him.

The author had documented a series of near-accidents, a feeling of being watched, and a growing paranoia. The writing stopped abruptly two days before Patricia Marsh was found by her daughter, charred to death on the beach.

"Look here," David said, pointing at the second-to-last entry. "They mention someone had erased files on their computer. This has to belong to someone in the office."

Laura took the scrap of paper and pen from David's lap and scribbled a note. "And we know the poem that fell out of the closet in the office was done on a computer. I think we're onto something."

"We know not just anyone has access to the office supply closet. And you said yourself that the office has at least three computers that you knew of."

Laura drew a box around the word "office," connecting it with a line to a box with Cory's name, then Gracie's. "The office is also the location of at least two of the detective's suspects."

"Cory and Gracie," David said. "Seems no matter what the situation, it always goes back to those two playing the starring roles."

Laura hopped off the bed. "Let's go show this to Jeremy. See what he thinks. Then we can all take a ride to the station."

She headed into the bathroom to brush her hair and freshen her makeup.

David watched her as he went to grab a t-shirt from the top drawer. He slipped the shirt over his head and pushed his arms through the sleeves, walking over to the bathroom.

Via the mirror, Laura watched him staring at her. Finally, she asked, "What?"

"Nothing."

"You're starring at me like you've never seen me put makeup on before."

"I never realized how sensuous an act it was, or . . . why you want to cover up perfection."

She smiled at him through the mirror and mouthed a kiss. "I'm not covering up anything. I'm accentuating what I have."

He wrapped his arms around her waist and began to sway her back and forth as he snuggled into her neck. "My love, you are a goddess . . . with or without the war paint."

Laura lifted her head and met his lips. "You're a goof, and that's why I love you so much. Come on, let's go."

★ ★ ★ ★ ★

Katie was sitting outside at the picnic table lingering over a cup of coffee when David and Laura arrived.

"Morning, Katie." David said. "Where's Jeremy?"

"Hey, guys," Katie said, patting the picnic table bench. "Come on and sit down. Jeremy's inside." She scooted over to make room for Laura. "Jeremy," Katie called out. "Bring a couple more cups out, please. And the coffee carafe."

Moments later Jeremy opened the door to their fifth wheel, doing a balancing act with the cups and carafe of coffee. He held packs of cream and sugar under his chin.

David laughed, grabbing the cups. "Let me help you."

"I'll never understand how waitresses carry all those items," Jeremy said as he sat the carafe and condiments on the table. "What are you two up to today? No more strolls along Beach Boulevard, I hope."

"Funny, Jeremy—" Laura said.

"We have something we want to show you. Something that fell at Laura's feet. In the office."

Jeremy looked down to where Laura was sitting, staring at her feet. "What is it with those feet, kiddo? First a bottle with charred remains, then gothic verses, and now . . . what?"

Laura smiled. "A journal."

Jeremy waggled his eyebrows up and down. "A juicy journal, I hope."

Katie poured David and Laura a cup of coffee and then warmed up her own. "That's all this guy ever thinks about," she said, nodding toward Jeremy.

David pushed the journal across the table toward Jeremy. "Take a look."

Jeremy picked up the journal and began to flip through the pages. It appeared that the more he read, the deeper his interest became. Ten minutes later, he closed the journal and set it down.

"What do you think?" David asked.

Jeremy raked his hands through his hair, then poured himself another cup of coffee. He took a sip, swallowed, and picked up the journal. "What I think," he said, "is that whoever this belongs to is one sick and dangerous puppy."

"We thought we should turn it over to Detective Miles," Laura said.

"Can I see?" Katie asked, reaching for the journal.

Jeremy passed the book to Katie.

"Ewww, creepy title," Katie said.

"Creepy prose and drawings, too," David added.

"I agree," Jeremy said. "We should pay Miles a visit with this."

Katie shook her head as she flipped through the pages. "I can't look at any more of this stuff." She handed the journal over to David. "I have an appointment in a half hour at the beauty parlor. Will you please excuse me?" She stood and wiped her hands on her peach-colored shorts, as if to wipe away the journal's contents.

"Go right ahead," Laura said.

"Y'all have fun, and puh-leese, stay out of harm's way." Katie bent over to kiss Jeremy on the cheek then headed inside to get ready for her appointment. She no sooner closed the door to the trailer than Cory drove up in his golf cart.

"Good morning," Cory called out.

Jeremy turned to face him. "Morning."

David took Laura's hand in his. "I hope you're not here to ask for Laura's help," he said. "We were just getting ready to head out for the day."

Laura folded her fingers around his and instinctively placed her free arm over the journal in a gesture meant to hide it from

Cory's view. She leaned her head on David's shoulder. "Good morning, Cory. Is everything okay?"

Witnessing their affection gave Cory a tight feeling in his chest. His marriage had lasted less than two years. He'd meant to stay married forever. He was facing all three of them from where he sat in the golf cart, but from the corner of his eye, he peeked at Laura. In a way he couldn't quite define, Laura reminded him of his wife. Not in appearance. Patricia had been brunette and tiny; Laura was blond and willowy. Perhaps it was the calm self-assurance, or the easy way she had around people.

Hope was sneaking around him, hiding in the shadows like a cat, ready to pounce and infiltrate when his back was turned. Hope that the grief and guilt would end. Hope that he wouldn't have to spend the rest of his life alone. He didn't deserve hope. Just as Patricia didn't deserve what had happened to her.

"Cory?" Laura asked, noting that Cory seemed to have something serious on his mind.

Cory shook his head, forcing himself back to the present. "I'm sorry," he said. "Got a lot on my mind today. I didn't come here to snatch your lovely wife from you again, David. Though she is an asset to the office. I was looking for Gracie. Have any of you seen her this morning?"

"I haven't seen her since early this morning," Laura said. "When she came by the motor home to ask if I could fill in at the office for a couple of hours."

"Is something wrong?" Jeremy asked. He was all too familiar with the roller-coaster emotional mood swings of Gracie; he'd just about convinced himself that the girl was definitely bipolar.

"No," Cory said. "Nothing wrong. She just left in a bit of a huff and I was concerned. I'm sure she's around here some-where. I apologize for the intrusion."

"No problem," David said.

Behind Laura, Katie gave a quick, "Hello, Cory," on her way

out of the trailer.

"Good morning," Cory said. He smiled and put the golf cart in reverse and headed back toward the office.

"Is he okay?" Katie asked.

"Yeah, he's fine. Just looking for his stepdaughter," Jeremy said. "You heading out now?"

Katie leaned over and kissed him on the cheek. "Yes. And stay out of trouble while I'm gone."

Jeremy gave her a pat on the butt. "Without trouble, life would be a bore."

It was just a few minutes past noon when they arrived at the St. Augustine police department.

"Tell me you got something," Detective Miles said when he came out to greet them. "Because all I have is one huge puzzle with a lot of missing pieces." He motioned for them to follow him back into his office.

David dropped the journal on the detective's desk. "Maybe this will help fill in one of the missing pieces," he said with a grin.

Detective Miles picked up the book and plopped down in his chair. "What's this?" he asked, quickly skimming the pages.

"It's a journal," Laura said. "It dropped out of a satchel carried by a woman named Norma Rowland. She works in the office. When I tried to give it back to her, she claimed it wasn't hers."

The detective looked at Laura over the rim of his glasses. "So you took it?"

"Yes, sir," Laura said.

"Anything yet on the lab reports out of New York?" Jeremy asked.

Detective Miles was apparently engrossed in something he'd stopped to read in the journal. "Uh-huh," he said, his eyes remaining inside the journal. "Came in overnight."

Noticing the detective's sudden interest in the journal's contents, David broke in, "If you look toward the back, you'll find the same verse that Laura found in the office. The one I gave you."

Detective Miles turned to the back of the book.

Jeremy leaned forward and flipped the pages to where the verse was. "What did you find out?" he asked.

After several minutes, Detective Miles closed the book and looked up. "I'd say you definitely brought me something useful." He turned his gaze to Laura. "How much do you know about this Norma person?"

"Other than the fact that she's dubbed the queen of gossip, not much. I know she's pretty tight with Gracie and Cory."

Miles leaned back in his chair and clasped his hands at the back of his head. "Hmm, interesting. I thought I had talked with everyone in the office weeks ago. With the initial investigation. Don't recall anyone named Norma."

"She should have been there," Jeremy said. "Or at least mentioned to you. She's the assistant office manager."

The detective sat forward and opened the top drawer of his desk. He pulled out a thick file folder. "Got all the interview transcriptions," he said, flipping the pages. "Yep, right here. No mention of Norma."

David looked at Laura and then back to the detective. "Damn, that is strange. Norma's always front and center with everything at the resort."

Detective Miles jotted down some notes on a piece of paper and slipped it into his pocket. "Are you still working in the office, Mrs. Jennings?"

"From time to time," she said.

"Well, keep up the great work when you are in there." The detective lifted the journal from the desk. "I'm going to keep this. Maybe I can get it dusted for prints."

"If you read through it," David said, "you'll also find some freaky drawings as well as a list of teas."

"Teas?" the detective said.

"Thought that would get your attention," Jeremy said. "After you got the lab tests on the oleander poisoning. And speaking of lab reports, you started to say something? The fax?"

"Sorry," Detective Miles said. "Yes. The reports on the metal discovered within the bone fragments. The DNA scrapings were a match to Patricia. The medical examiner also stated that no jewelry was found on Patricia. The killer obviously removed it, and we've determined from a small design still apparent on the piece of metal found when we were at the beach that it was some sort of ring."

Jeremy let out a whistle. "I see what you mean about the puzzle getting larger and the pieces all being scattered."

David stood. "We don't want to keep you, Detective." He reached across the desk and shook Miles's hand.

Detective Miles turned his gaze to Laura. "Keep up the good work. It's beginning to sound to me like that office is a breeding place for secrets."

Laura smiled. "And gossip."

"I know how rumors and stories have a tendency to spread in a place like a campground," Detective Miles said. "Hard to tell fact from fiction, especially when everyone is spooked. That's why I'm grateful to have the three of you as . . . uh . . . silent partners."

"Glad to help out," Jeremy said, extending his hand.

Detective Miles walked the three of them out to their car. He opened the back door to Jeremy's SUV for Laura. "Keep the eyes and ears open," he said, closing the door.

"Will do," David said. "And to think I thought the camping lifestyle would be boring."

Jeremy turned the key in the ignition. "Let me know if anything comes through on those reports," he said.

"You got it." The detective smacked the top of the SUV and waved them off.

Detective Miles considered investigative skills a gift, like being able to draw or turn your tongue upside down. The three who'd just driven away had the gift. They were brilliant investigators. As canny as he himself was.

TWENTY-TWO

"I'm older than dirt," Stanley Parsons told Laura, pounding his cane into the ground in front of his pop-up camper. "A person shouldn't let himself get so old and useless. It ain't right. What did you say you came here for? I know it wasn't just to hear me complain."

Laura smiled at him. She felt certain he didn't mean half of what he said. She'd seen him with Stella Greenburg. He was teasing her. He had that glint in the corner of his eye and a slight curve to his mouth. His white hair and mustache were too well-groomed for a man who had given up on life, and the perimeter around his camper blossomed with his well-kept garden.

"Terrie told me you've been coming to Harbor Lights for years. That you're perhaps the longest returning guest here." Laura tried to settle in the outdoor cushioned chair, but it threatened to swallow her whole. She pushed herself forward.

"That's right. Been coming here for thirty-two years. Ethel, God rest her soul, loved coming here. Called it her paradise."

"You've heard about Patricia Marsh's murder?"

"I said I was old, young lady, not deaf, dumb, and blind. Or dead. What kind of hole do you think I live in?" He adjusted the glasses that had slipped to the end of his nose and gave her a quick once-over. "I've got myself cable TV, and I can still see good enough to read the newspaper and hear well enough to know what's going on here."

205

Laura blushed, feeling thoroughly put in her place. "David and I got here just after the memorial service, and since then we've heard an array of stories about Patricia, Gracie, Cory, Gracie's father . . ."

"And you're trying to sift through all the yappity yap." He nodded his head and took up a corncob pipe that looked as old as he was, stuffing it with tobacco. Then he leaned forward and fussed through a stack of newspapers on the table next to him. "Where is that dang lighter?"

Laura retrieved it from under the edge of a *Trailer Life* magazine on the table beside her and handed it to him. He seemed a little too agitated. "I used to manage my family's campground in the Keys, and I know from experience that the ones to get something besides gossip from are the ones you don't see in every nook and cranny buzzing like bees."

He flicked on the lighter and sucked the fire down into the bowl of tobacco, watching her over the pipe, but he didn't say a word. He just let the smoke puff out of his mouth and around the stem.

"Norma told me you were always talking with Patricia. Real serious talking."

"That Norma talks more than she should."

"Maybe. But it made me wonder about Patricia. What she was *really* like."

"Some people, no matter how hard you try, can't be saved," he said more to himself than to her. "That's a life lesson, young 'un. You'd do well to learn it now."

"What did she need saving from?"

"People make choices, and gosh darn if they don't act all surprised by the consequences. Does that make sense to you?"

"What choice did Patricia make?"

"How much pit bull you got in your lineage? You're as directed as my old dog, Rocky. He'd tree a cat and sit there as long as it took to get him down."

"I'll take that as a compliment, if you'll let me."

He grinned. "I did love that old dog, but why're you diggin' around about what happened to Patricia? Leave that for them big-shot detectives. Can't do you or nobody else no good. Times change and the world moves on. God, but Cory did love that woman." His eyes filled with tears.

Obviously, Cory wasn't the only one who had loved Patricia.

"Shame's a powerful motivator," he went on. "We used to have too much of it. Now we don't have enough. You think there might have been some time in between when we got it just right?"

"I doubt it. What was Patricia ashamed about?"

"Did I say anything about Patricia being ashamed?" His eyes narrowed.

"No, but I thought you meant—"

"Sometimes people think too much. You one of those people?"

"Most definitely."

That made him laugh. A snicker turned into a belly laugh. "I think I like you. You and old Rocky would have made quite a pair. You say that you been working in the office?"

"Yes, I have. Just when they get short-handed or have a club arriving."

"Hmm, hmmm, hmmm. You don't have no better sense than to be in that breeding pit for doom and gloom?"

"The office? It's not that bad. Besides, you're in there a lot. Or you were, when Patricia was alive."

"But I didn't *work* there. Only the once."

"When?"

"Cory was going to close up the office the day after the murder. I volunteered. Maybe was just my way of being able to say good-bye to Patricia."

"In the office?"

"Tradition. How I was raised. Patricia had been there. I felt her presence. Her spirit."

"So you just stayed there? Alone?"

"Somebody has to sit with the spirits of the dead. Wouldn't be right to just leave them alone."

Little shivers prickled up Laura's arms, even in the heat of the afternoon sun.

"But everyone was at her memorial. No one was even around."

"Guess it wasn't really work I was doing, huh? Patricia and me were friends."

"Weren't you . . ." The words had escaped her mouth before she could stop them.

"Scared?" He chuckled at her. "Lots more than spirits to be scared of, child. Spirits, they come to you, chat a while, and move on. They don't mean no harm to the living. It's people you should be afraid of, if'n you have a mind to be afraid."

"It's just that I didn't think people still did that."

He puffed slowly on his pipe. "Most don't, but I ain't most people."

"And Gracie? Did you talk to her much? She had to be devastated. From what I've heard, she was caring for Patricia when she was sick."

"Humph! Some people have their own definition of caring. I don't know if Gracie, or even Cory, knew Patricia as well as I did. I lost a daughter, Shelly, when she was only ten. I saw a lot of my baby in Patricia. Don't know what she saw in me. But we was always real close."

"I'm sorry about your loss, Stanley."

He waved his hand in front of him, as if driving away a painful memory. "No need to be sorry. She's in a better place. Just like Patricia."

"She and Cory hadn't been married long. How was Cory

while Patricia was so ill and after . . . ?"

"I helped him."

"Pardon?"

"Cory took Patricia's death real hard. He did what had to be done, making the memorial arrangements, the reception at the clubhouse afterwards, but that night when no one much was around, I heard him sobbing. Ever hear a grown man sob from grief? He was just over there." He pointed toward the hammocks that led to the beach. "Sitting by himself. I went over to see if I could do anything. When I got closer, I could hear he was talking to Patricia. No need for him to be like that all night. If he'd had anything important to say, he should have said it while she was alive. You don't do that, Laura, do ya? You got somethin' to say, you tell it to a person while they're living. You can't be sure how much they hear after they're dead. No need making confessions and amends then. I helped him back to his cabin. Got him out of his trance."

"What kinds of confessions?"

"Now that would be between the three of them."

"Three?"

"Cory, Patricia, and God. Ain't none of my business."

"You knew Patricia so well. Tell me, who hated her enough to murder her?"

"Now you're asking me to see into the hearts of men. I don't rightly know who might have done somethin' to her. Didn't seem to me nobody was even aware of her one way or another when she was alive. Murdered, everyone was aware. Sort of what happens to some of us when we get older. No one much cares one way or another if we're dead or alive. You got to plant your good deeds early, so they have time to blossom in your old age."

The metal on the camper rattled with what Laura assumed was a knock.

"Back here," Stanley yelled.

Lively old Stella with her shriveled, dimpled face and a Styrofoam container appeared around the corner of the camper. Her face went slack when she saw Laura, but she recovered quickly. "Oh, I'm sorry, Stanley. I didn't know you had company," she said, handing him the container. It emitted an aroma of tomato sauce and peaches.

"What you got for me today, Stella?"

"Spaghetti and meatballs with salad and fresh cobbler."

"Gosh darn it! Didn't you tell them that I said spaghetti doesn't travel well?"

"The message was delivered. Aren't any of those cooks at the clubhouse professional chefs like you," Stella reminded him.

"They get a free site, don't they?"

"Yes, I suppose they do."

"Then they get paid, and that makes them professionals. They should know their business. Don't take a whole lot more to do a job well than to just do it."

"Do you want it now or should I put it in the fridge?"

"You can throw the danged thing in the ocean for all I care," Stanley fussed.

Stella winked at Laura. "That means put it in the fridge." She disappeared for a moment, then swished back outside, paused from the end corner of Stanley's camper, and waved. "See you tonight, Stanley. If we're still on for *Wheel of Fortune.*"

Stanley waved. "Yeah, yeah, we're still on."

Laura fought to prevent a laugh from escaping. She couldn't help but notice that Stella didn't have her cane. It seemed she periodically had moments of miraculous healing.

"She's a right nice lady," Stanley said, "even if she doesn't listen worth a hoot."

"I can tell," Laura agreed. "Norma seems like she has moments of being nice, too."

"She can be nice. When she keeps her mouth shut."

"The police have her down as one of the suspects in Patricia's murder."

He shrugged.

"Well, what do you think? Could she have done it?"

He chuckled at her. "Norma is a lady. No matter how much she plays that school-girl crush thing with Cory, she'd never want to see Patricia hurt. Even if Patricia despised her gossip and got on her all the time about it."

"What is it with Cory? The attraction, I mean? Doesn't Gracie also have a crush on him?"

"Don't know nothin' about that stuff. Sometimes you just suspect somethin' but you don't move quick like. Later you wished you'd trusted your instincts."

"What are you saying? Did you suspect something? Something you wished you'd told someone? Maybe Patricia?"

Stanley's face turned hard. "I'm not saying nothin'. Just an old man ramblin' on, is all." He placed his pipe in an ashtray and pulled himself up. "Got to go watch CNN," he said.

"It's been a pleasure talking with you. Stop by and visit David and me sometime."

He waved with one hand as he made his way up the steps.

David met Laura on the bike path. He squeezed the handle brakes and stopped. "Hey, good looking, where you been all my life?"

"Looking for you," she said.

He patted the handlebars. "Wanna ride?"

"Not on those things."

"Okay, I'll walk." He hopped off the bike. "Where were you? I was getting worried when I didn't find you at the office."

"I was visiting with Stanley. Nice old guy. What's going on at the office?"

"The mystery of the missing Gracie was solved. She was in there cracking the whip."

"I found out from Stanley that he had a very close friendship with Patricia. Eerily close. I think he believed she was his dead daughter reincarnated."

"Well, he's in the right town for all that spirit and ghost stuff."

"He knows something," Laura said.

"Like what?"

"I don't know. But he definitely knows something he's not telling."

"If he was so close to Patricia, maybe it's some sacred confidence she told him?"

Laura nodded. "I don't think so. It's almost as if he's afraid to say what he's thinking."

"Maybe it's in the journal somewhere."

"Maybe," Laura said.

David stopped in front of the clubhouse, where a long line of campers were standing patiently. "Hey, how about we go to the clubhouse. Spaghetti is the day's specialty."

"Don't you know spaghetti doesn't travel well?" Laura chuckled.

"Huh?"

She pulled him along with the bike in the direction of the aroma. "Come on, let's take the bike home and see if Jeremy and Katie are in the mood for another clubhouse dinner."

Thirty minutes later, Jeremy, Katie, Laura, and David joined in for the clubhouse spaghetti fest. Just inside the door, at a table where campers were to stop and pay the five-dollar dinner charge, Norma sat alone, a glass of what looked like iced tea beside her, looking dazed and confused.

"Are you all right, Norma?" David asked.

Norma looked up, then took the ten-dollar bill David was

holding out. "I'm fine," she said, putting the money in the cash box. She tore off two ticket stubs, stamped them paid, and handed them to David.

Laura placed a hand on Norma's shoulder. "You don't look fine. Are you sure you're okay?"

It wasn't Norma's nature to be sitting alone. She thrived on people, especially people who could feed her juicy gossip. For her to be sitting at a table, playing the part of cashier, away from the groups of gossipers, struck Laura as not only odd, but out of character for Norma.

Norma nodded. "I'm okay."

Gracie and Cory appeared behind Laura.

"Norma," Cory said, "this is a first. How did you get stuck with cashier duty?"

"She didn't get *stuck* with anything," Gracie said. "We needed a cashier, and I assigned the duty to her." She tapped Laura on the shoulder. "Are you in line?"

"We already paid," David said, taking Laura's hand.

They waited for Jeremy to get his two tickets, then they headed to the kitchen area where another line formed to get their dinners.

"Gracie seemed awfully snippy, didn't she?" Katie said.

"Bitchy is more like it," Jeremy said.

David was observing two campers squabbling over who had squatter's rights at a round table toward the back. "These functions give a whole new meaning to 'dinner theater.' You never know what kind of entertainment there will be."

Jeremy laughed. "You got that right. Never a dull moment."

They got their plates and headed to a table in the center of the hall.

"Well," Laura said, "there's definitely something going on between Gracie and Norma. Usually the two of them have their heads stuck together about one thing or another."

"Gracie seems to get flakier by the day," Katie said. She nodded toward the entrance of the clubhouse. "There she goes again, playing the disappearing act."

David turned to watch Gracie's exit. He shook his head and turned his gaze to Laura. "She and Norma were going at it earlier in the office when I went to see if you were there. Maybe it's the full-moon phase."

Jeremy watched Cory get two plates of spaghetti from the kitchen then walk out the side door.

"Looks like our host got his dinners as takeout," he said, shoving a forkful of twisted pasta into his mouth.

"Forget them," Laura said. "Let's enjoy our supper for once." She looked over at Katie. "What a cute haircut you got."

Katie combed her fingers through her hair. "Thank you. Low-maintenance style. That's what I asked the girl at the Mane Event to give me."

Laura still couldn't get her mind off Norma. The woman had not looked good earlier in the evening. "I'm going to run over and check on Norma," she told David. "You go on. I'll meet you at the motor home."

"I don't mind going with you," he said.

She waved him on. "I'll be fine. I won't be long."

Laura walked up the three metal steps to Norma's camper. She tapped lightly on the door but heard no sound. She opened the screen and knocked loudly this time.

She thought she heard a sound from inside, like a moan, or a soft cry. The hair at the base of her skull prickled. Should she go in? What if nothing was wrong and she barged into Norma's trailer uninvited? But what if something was wrong? With a glance around the empty yard, she twisted the doorknob. Unlocked. She pushed the door open a couple of inches and called through the crack.

"Norma, are you home?"

Again she heard a moan from somewhere within the trailer—this time she was positive. Norma was in pain. Setting her jaw, she opened wide the door.

"Norma, it's Laura," she said in a voice loud enough to carry through the trailer. "I came over to see if you're all right."

Silence.

"I'm coming in, Norma."

She stepped across the threshold and heard a crash. Anxious, she hurried through the small living room, following the sound.

The strong odor of vomit hit her like a physical slap when she stepped into the short hallway. She took a momentary step backward. Then, bracing herself and breathing through her mouth, she hurried toward the back of the trailer. The door to the small bathroom stood open, displaying evidence someone had been too violently ill to make it all the way to the toilet. She fought a gag reflex as the stench nearly overpowered her.

In the bedroom just beyond, she found Norma lying lengthwise across the bed, her nightgown saturated with vomit and sweat. An alarm clock lay shattered in pieces on the hardwood floor as though she had been trying to reach it. A telephone also lay on the floor, the receiver under the bed with the base upended. Norma looked at her with glazed eyes and moaned.

Laura rushed to the bed, swallowing hard. She ignored the soiled nightgown and took Norma's hand.

"It's okay, Norma. I'm here."

A vein in Norma's throat pulsed with a wild rhythm, and her hand felt clammy. Sweat dampened her forehead and neck, and her skin was chalky-white. Her mouth moved to speak, but Laura shushed her.

"Don't try to talk. I'm calling nine-one-one. You'll be all right as soon as the paramedics get here."

Laura grabbed the phone from the floor and held the button

in until she got a dial tone, then dialed 911. After giving the name of the resort and site number and a description of the emergency, she ran to the bathroom and snatched a washcloth off the towel rack. As cool water ran over the cloth, she thought, "*Oh, God. Tea. Like Patricia. Norma had a glass of iced tea in front of her at the clubhouse.*

Back in the bedroom, she sat on the mattress and wiped Norma's face, whispering soothing words to the barely conscious woman the way her mother used to do when young Laura was hurt or frightened.

"It's going to be okay. Don't worry now. You're going to be fine." She gently wiped at Norma's face then asked, "Norma, were you drinking that tea tonight that was in front of you?"

Norma nodded and moaned, "Just a little."

Minutes later, Laura heard the ambulance's siren screaming down the road. She ran out to meet it and then was politely but firmly pushed aside as the paramedics went to work. Campers were now scattered in front of Norma's trailer. Laura spotted David and waved him toward her.

"What in the hell's going on?" David asked, taking Laura in his arms.

She pushed herself free. "I'll tell you later. Wait out here."

Orders were shouted, a gurney retrieved, and Norma strapped onto it. As they whisked Norma away, one of the paramedics quickly told Laura what hospital they would be taking her, explaining that it was probably nothing more serious than a bad case of the flu that was going around. Then they were gone.

Hours later, with Cory locked away in his bedroom, Gracie sat on the sofa, TV remote in hand, channel surfing. She struggled to keep her eyes open as she searched for something on television to hold her interest. She finally stopped the remote at a channel showing a medical drama. She reached over to put the remote on the coffee table, her eyes catching a glimpse of Detective Miles's business card. She lifted the card and twirled it between her fingers a few times, then picked up the cordless phone resting beside her on the sofa. She glanced at the wall clock, which read eight-thirty-five P.M., hoping Miles was still at police headquarters.

She dialed the number on the card. "Detective Miles, please," Gracie said into the telephone.

Though the detective's home number lay scrawled across the back of the card he'd given her, the memory of the hint of suspicion in his gray eyes earlier that morning, which had left her feeling as though she was in the hot seat, made her angry all over again. She would not call him at home in the evening. Nor would she call Officer Harrison, especially when she remembered his smug manner as he took notes during her questioning. Instead, she'd dialed the number of Detective Miles's office.

Predictably, the man who answered the phone informed her, "He's not in. Can I help you with something?"

"Uh, no thanks. Does he have voice mail?"

"Sure does. Hang on, I'll put you through."

A moment later the detective's deep voice requested that Gracie leave a message, which he would return as soon as possible, or to call his home if it was of vital importance. *Beep.*

"Hello, Detective Miles, this is Gracie Schaffer. I thought of something I didn't mention earlier today. About my assistant manager, Norma Rowland. Actually, a couple of things came to mind. A journal of hers I saw in her purse a few days ago, and also the fact that I'd caught Cory on several occasions instant messaging with Norma from her home computer. Thought you might want to question her. Uh, that's all. Good-bye."

Her hand rested for a moment on the cradle of the receiver

after she placed the phone back into it. There. Her duty was done. Now she could forget about the day and try and get some sleep.

Rolling over in bed, Gracie peered through squinted eyes to read the red numbers on the digital clock on the nightstand. *Eleven-thirty-three? In the morning?* She thought, rubbing her eyes as she tried to come awake enough to get a sense of whether it was still night or late morning. The sun glaring through the cracks of the vertical blinds confirmed it was late morning. She tossed the covers back and slid out of bed and into the bathroom.

Twenty minutes later she was dressed and standing outside the office, coffee mug in hand, and still feeling dazed from oversleeping.

The office door was propped open to let in the clean, fresh, ocean-scented breeze. Gracie heard the sound of a woman's sobs and Terrie's soothing voice telling the person to calm down. She put her coffee mug down on the wooden banister and stood still. Obviously someone had come to the office quite upset over something. Should she go inside and see who was crying? Or should she leave them in privacy? Terrie was much better at this stuff than she was.

She sat down on a chair just outside the window, pretending, for all the passersby who stopped briefly to wave hello, to be taking in the gorgeous spring morning. She felt like an eavesdropper as she listened to every word from inside.

"What's happened, hon?" Terrie asked. "Did something happen to one of your parents?"

"N-no," sobbed the woman. "They're fine. It's . . ."

Gracie sat straight up. She knew the voice. It belonged to the newest suspect in the murder of her mother.

Norma Rowland's tearful hiccup trailed out of the office to

where Gracie sat. "It's nothing like that. I was in the emergency room half the night with some flu . . . then . . . the police were at my trailer this morning. Oh, Terrie, they said terrible things. They think I killed Patricia! That I'm having an affair with Cory!"

The pain in Norma's voice made Gracie cringe. She'd never heard Norma cry before. She was always such an upbeat person. Gracie knew how Norma felt. When the police had questioned her yesterday, she'd shed a few tears of her own. A mixture of guilt and compassion stirred inside her. She knew what it was like to be questioned by pit-bull Miles.

"That is ridiculous. I'm sure they don't think any such thing." Terrie's voice sounded louder, as though she had turned toward the office doorway. "Why don't you just sit down here and have some coffee while you tell me all about it before it gets too busy in here."

"O-okay."

Panic gripped Gracie's insides. Would Norma blame her? The police had never even heard of Norma Rowland until she impulsively told Detective Miles about the journal and the instant messaging between Norma and Cory.

She was not prepared to face Norma right now. She needed time to compose herself, to get her thoughts in order so she could ask the right questions and lead the conversation the way she wanted it to go. At that moment, Terrie stepped out onto the porch, her arm around the shoulder of sobbing Norma.

Norma took one look at Gracie and the tears evaporated. "You!"

Gracie's insides sank as Norma stared daggers in her direction. *Damn!* Gracie thought. Apparently, her name had come up during the questioning.

Norma took a step toward the wooden seat, and Gracie leaned as far back as the chair would allow. Norma looked angry enough to slap her. Terrie stood with her arms hanging at her sides, her attention ricocheting between the two of them.

Norma pointed a finger in Gracie's face. "You sent the police to my trailer. You told them terrible lies about me."

"I did not," Gracie shot back. "I only told them what I know."

Terrie took a step forward. "Gracie? What does she mean? What did you tell the police?"

Norma whirled. "She told them I was having an affair with Cory!"

Terrie gasped, her eyes going round as melons. "Gracie, you didn't!"

Feeling blood flood her face, Gracie drew herself up. "I did not say that. Not exactly."

"Not *exactly?*" Terrie repeated. "Then what *exactly* did you say?"

Gracie did not want this confrontation to be overheard by the passersby, so she walked inside the office. Terrie and Norma followed, with Norma slamming the door behind her.

Inside, Gracie found it difficult to look at the accusation in Norma's face, so she kept her gaze fixed on Terrie. "I told Detective Miles about catching Norma sending instant messages to Cory and how my mom even wondered what was going on." She cleared her throat. "And I might have mentioned that I saw your journal in your satchel and that he might find some answers in it."

Norma sobbed, and Terrie stepped forward to put an arm around her shoulders. She guided her to a chair and seated her, then glared at Gracie from above Norma's light brown hair.

"Well, it was the truth," Gracie said, allowing a touch of anger to creep into her voice.

"I'm sure there's an explanation." Terrie's hand rested protectively on Norma's shoulder.

After a few moments of quiet crying, Norma shook her head

and made a visible effort to choke back the tears. This didn't look like a murderess. The righteous anger, the devastated sobs, the dejected slope of Norma's shoulders all had the unmistakable feel of a woman unjustly accused. Gracie shifted her weight in her chair. What if this all backfired? Blew up in her face with all fingers pointing in her direction?

She pulled a tissue from the box on the desk in front of her and reached to offer it to her sobbing assistant manager and now, for sure, ex-friend. Norma stared at it a moment, as though afraid it might be poisoned, and then took it without looking up. She blew her nose and took a shuddering breath.

"I don't own a journal. Never have. I hate writing. That's why I talk so much. I told the detective that." She blew her nose again and dabbed at her eyes with the tissue, then gazed at Gracie. "You know that to be true, Gracie. I told Detective Miles if anyone had a journal with secrets spilled out on the pages, it was you."

Terrie squeezed her shoulder once, and then went to the counter to pour a mug of coffee. She set it down, and Norma took a grateful sip before continuing.

"As for Cory and sending the instant messaging, it was all innocent, and only done when your mother was so sick and Cory didn't come to the office. Nor did you. He'd be on his computer and if he saw me online, he would send a message on what had to be done at the office." She balled the tissue in one fist, the other hand clutching the handle of her mug. "If anyone was having an affair with Cory, it was you! And I told that to your detective, too!" The words came out like venom as she stared straight into Gracie's eyes, eyes that were as wide as a crackhead's.

"Well, obviously Detective Miles didn't believe you. If he had, I'm sure he'd have been at my door, too, this morning." Gracie tried to sound self-assured and convincing, but her resolve wavered. She had to think faster, even though she already felt as though her thoughts were on fast forward. Norma knew too much. The two of them had been close since Gracie had arrived at Harbor Lights. What was she thinking when she made that call to Detective Miles? *Be cool. Don't act paranoid,* she demanded of her thoughts.

"Maybe he did. Maybe Miles is at your place right now. Talking to Cory." Her face a mask of misery, Norma sniffled. "I thought we were friends. Sisters, you called us. How could you betray me like that, Gracie?" She looked up, first at Gracie and then at Terrie. "If Cory is being questioned again, he could fire me. Thinking I stirred this all up. He's always getting on me about gossiping and my overactive imagination." She sniffed. "I can't afford to get fired or thrown in prison. I'm barely making the bills now, and my parents need me."

Gracie wanted to crawl under the desk. What kind of worm would accuse her best friend of murder? The Mother Superior at Our Lady of Perpetual Help school for girls had been right about Gracie not thinking before she acted. Like now, the fault had always backed her into one corner or another.

With her heart in her shoes, a wave of compassion ran through her. Gracie reached across the counter and took Norma's hand. One way or another, she had to get Norma back in her corner. "I'm so sorry, Norma. I was way out of line. I don't know what came over me. I shouldn't have told Miles what I saw. Or planted the suspicion in his mind about you."

Norma's chin quivered. Her stare was so direct, Gracie felt as though she was being examined from the inside out. She kept her gaze steady, hoping Norma would believe in her sincerity.

Finally, Norma gave a hesitant nod. "I guess you only did what you thought was right. And maybe you were suspicious when Cory and I were sending instant messages."

Terrie, however, didn't seem ready to forgive. "What were

you doing anyway, creeping around in Norma's trailer? Peering over her shoulder while she was on her own computer?"

Gracie bit back a sharp retort. Instead, she bowed her head and said truthfully, "Snooping." She looked at Norma again. "Actually, that was the day I had so much on my mind. With my mom getting sicker and everything. I wanted to talk to you. But when I saw the computer communication going on between you and Cory . . . well, I thought you were holding back. Not being honest with me."

Norma nodded. "It was a bad time for everyone. A bad time turned gruesomely tragic. But why all the stuff about me and some journal?" Her lips twisted into a grimace.

"The journal you keep in there." Gracie pointed to the pink satchel bag resting at Norma's feet.

Norma picked up the bag and held it open. "What journal, Gracie?"

A chill shot down Gracie's spine. She grabbed the bag and started rummaging through it. "It was in here. I saw it a couple of days ago."

Terrie leaned forward and peered into the bag. "Your purse is worse than mine," she said.

"Wait a minute," Norma said. "I remember something. Some book. The day your aunt and cousin were leaving." She pulled her bag from Gracie's grip and turned her attention to Terrie.

"Remember the day Gracie's cousin Becky was in here? She was upset. Laura Jennings was in here, too."

Terrie put a hand over her mouth. "I remember. Your bag dropped from your shoulder and something fell out. A journal?"

"Yes, a journal," Norma said. "Laura picked it up and tried to give it back to me. I told her it wasn't mine."

Gracie was chewing on the skin beside the pinkie finger on her right hand. "So, what did she do with it?"

"Huh?" Norma said.

"The journal! Where did Laura put it?"

Norma shrugged. "I don't know. I was busy calming Becky down. I wasn't paying any attention."

Terrie got up and walked to the back of the office where a large cardboard box sat. It was marked in big black letters, LOST AND FOUND. "Maybe she tossed it in here."

Gracie jumped from her seat and sprinted toward the box. She started tossing things out and digging through it as if the box contained a buried treasure. "It's not here! What did she do with it?"

"What are you getting so riled up about?" Terrie asked. "Because it was yours, wasn't it Gracie?"

Terrie dropped down from her kneeling position by the box and stared at Gracie openmouthed. "You planted your journal in Norma's bag?"

"I didn't do any such thing. And it wasn't my journal!" Gracie stood and smoothed out the creases in her slacks. "I'll be right back. I want to see what's keeping Cory this morning." She was out the door and down the front porch steps in seconds.

"How much you want to bet she's not checking on Cory at all?" Terrie asked.

"I'd bet what little I have that she's on her way to the Jennings's motor home right now."

TWENTY-THREE

"Good morning. It's David and Laura, right?" Lorraine Reed, seated behind the library's front desk, looked over the top of a pair of half glasses. "Haven't seen you two in a while."

"We've been kind of busy the past week or so," David said with a smile of greeting.

"We got some new books in a few days ago, and there are a couple I think you'll like, Laura, on the New Arrivals shelf."

"Great, thank you," Laura said.

David and Laura went over to the new row of computers. He pulled a chair out for Laura, took one for himself, and then opened the online catalog. He rubbed his hands together, "Ready, Sherlock?"

Laura smiled. "Hurry," she whispered.

David typed the word "oleander" and clicked the search button. The computer returned a list of three titles. Two were fiction, but the last on the list looked like exactly what they needed. David read the title out loud. "*Poisonous and Deadly Plants of Florida.*"

"It says it's available," Laura said. A stack of scrap paper and a short pencil lay beside the computer, and Laura jotted down the call number.

They made their way through the 500 aisle, scanning the numbers until they came across the right place.

"It's not here," David said.

Laura made a quick search of the surrounding shelves. "Nothing," she said.

Laura's pulse picked up speed as her mind ticked through reasons the book might be missing.

"Maybe a library page or one of the other librarians shelved it in the wrong place," David said.

"Or maybe the computer was wrong, and someone had checked it out. But who?"

David stopped searching the shelves and turned to face Laura. "The murderer, that's who. More than likely he or she just waltzed in here and took it. A killer wouldn't want a record of research on file at a public library."

Their jog up to the front desk drew curious stares from a couple of patrons. David and Laura ignored them.

"Lorraine, can you check something for us?" David asked.

Lorraine looked up from her book. "Sure. What is it?"

"This." Laura slid the paper across the desk. "The computer says it's available but we can't find it."

"Well, let's see." Bright pink fingernails flew across the keyboard. Lorraine's brow puckered. "Poisonous plants, huh? The police called yesterday afternoon to ask about books on oleander. I checked the catalog then and told the officer this book was available. It should be here. Are you sure it isn't?"

"We're sure." David tried to sound casual. "Maybe someone has it. Can you see when the last time was that it was checked out?"

Lorraine's mouse clicked. "That book hasn't been checked out in over five years, nor have any other books about poisonous plants or oleander. Except for the fictional title, *White Oleander*. I told the police that, too." Her brow creased. "I don't understand. The book should be on the shelf."

"Has someone asked for it recently?" Laura asked. "Maybe they walked out with it by accident."

"No." Lorraine shook her head. "I don't remember anyone

asking about poisonous or deadly plants except that detective. It has to be there. I'm sure you just missed it."

She rose, and David and Laura followed her back to the 500 aisle where they conducted a thorough search.

The poisonous and deadly plants of Florida were nowhere to be found.

The moment David and Laura got back to the campground, David ran for the phone. He punched in Detective Miles's number. This information was too important to leave on the voice mail.

"Hello, Mr. Jennings. What can I do for you this afternoon?"

It still threw David when someone knew his name before he identified himself. He and Laura still didn't have caller ID, but everyone else in the world seemed to.

"You're not going to believe what Laura and I found out," he blurted.

He told the detective about their trip to the library.

"So a book's missing. So what? Unless someone saw who stole it, that doesn't do us any good."

Did he have to spell it out for him? "You could search people's trailers. Campers are avid library patrons. If you find the book, you'll have proof."

"And whose trailer would you suggest we search?"

"Norma Rowland's," David shot back. He told him about Laura's visit with old Stanley and about how quiet Norma was at the spaghetti dinner. Detective Miles did not seem impressed.

"That woman is not a killer any more than you and Laura are. I talked with her early this morning. The only thing she's guilty of is being a gossipmonger. Unfortunately, that's not a crime or something I can haul her in on."

David drummed his fingers on the kitchen table. "Hmm, then what about Cory?"

"Actually," the detective said, "I was just on my way over to see Mr. Marsh when you called."

"Did something come in? Anything on that journal? Or the fragments from the bottle?"

"Confidential, Mr. Jennings. I'm sure you know I can't discuss evidence."

Evidence, David thought. Then he *must* have gotten some information. "I understand, Detective. Sorry to have bothered you. I just felt this particular stolen library book might have been pertinent to the case."

"I appreciate you keeping me informed. And, yes . . . under the circumstances surrounding the murder of Patricia Marsh, a stolen library book titled *Poisonous and Deadly Plants of Florida* is very pertinent information."

David grinned. "Always glad to help. We'll be around today if you want to talk to us after your meeting with Cory." David was just about ready to say good-bye when he remembered something else. "One more thing, Detective," he said. "About Ken Schaffer. What's going on with him?"

"We don't have the room here," the detective said. "He'll most likely be transferred back to Daytona. I wish you and Laura would change your minds and press battery charges. Without something solid, he won't be incarcerated long."

"The guy's a total jerk," David said. "I can't see pressing charges and having him hold Laura and me up from our travels. Sooner or later he's going to mess with the wrong person. Then he'll get his just punishment."

"What goes around comes around. It's a universal law far greater than any law enforcement agency's. Anything else?"

"No, sir. Have a good day." David said good-bye and hung up the phone.

"Well?" Laura asked.

"I don't know," David said. "I think Detective Miles found

out something. He's just not saying what it is."

Detective Miles parked the cruiser in a visitor slot close to the campground office. He got out of the car, and Officer Harrison fell into step beside him as they walked up the sidewalk. The egotistical detective exuded confidence; Harrison had to give him that. He walked with a steady step, his head held high, eyes constantly sweeping his surroundings. Nothing got past the guy.

Officer Harrison followed Detective Miles into the office. Directly in front of them stood the registration counter piled with stacks of folders. Detective Miles saw Norma Rowland's face go snow-white when she saw them enter the office. He tried to reassure her with a smile, but she turned quickly away.

Without a moment's hesitation, the detective crossed the front office to the first desk opposite the registration counter. He smiled down at Terrie.

"We're here to see Cory Marsh."

Terrie's eyes slid to Officer Harrison and back to Detective Miles. "Is he expecting you?"

"No, he isn't. We took a chance that he would have some time to talk to us."

"Just a minute and I'll see if he's free."

She disappeared for a few minutes then returned, smiling at the detective. "Come this way, please."

She led them down the hallway behind the registration counter. The nameplate on the first office read CORY MARSH, PARK MANAGER.

Inside, Cory sat in a high-backed chair, his desk empty except for a neat stack of papers in one corner and a month-at-a-glance calendar in the center. A matching computer desk behind him held a computer and several pictures of Patricia Marsh. In front of his desk were two comfortable-looking visitor chairs.

Cory looked every bit the part of campground manager. A

white polo shirt bearing the name Harbor Lights RV Resort complimented his dark Florida tan. When he came around the desk to shake their hands, the tan, well-creased camp shorts spoke of a person who appreciated comfortable but neat-looking clothing. His physique revealed a man who obviously joined in on all the physical activities the resort had to offer.

"Good afternoon," Cory said. "Have a seat. Terrie, would you close the door, please?"

Detective Miles sat in one of the chairs facing the desk, and Officer Harrison took the other. He pulled a small notebook and pen from his pocket, ready to record any pertinent information the interview would reveal.

"Now, what can I do for you? I thought I told you everything I knew in the last three interviews."

Detective Miles sat with his elbows resting on the arms of the chair, his fingers steepled before him. "We're here because some new facts have come up that pertain to your wife's murder."

Cory shook his head, his lips drawn into a sad frown. "This has really rocked the resort, not to mention how it has rocked me. I still find it hard to hear the word 'murder' and my wife's name in the same sentence. I can't believe anyone would want to harm her."

The sympathetic smile—the one that said *I'm you're friend, you can tell me everything*—appeared on Detective Miles's face. "We actually received a tip this morning that we need to check out with you."

"Me?" Cory's eyebrows rose.

"Yes. You see, we've been made aware of a possible, shall we say, extramarital relationship that could have a bearing on this case."

Officer Harrison watched closely. The surprise that leaped into Cory's face could not be faked. Norma must have been right about the affair.

"You must be joking. Me? Having an affair?" He sat back in his chair and gave a low laugh. "That's ridiculous."

Detective Miles spread his hands. "Nonetheless, we do need to follow up on every lead. I'm sure you understand."

"Of course. But tell me, who am I supposed to be having an affair with?"

Miles's expression did not change, but Harrison felt his intensity increase as he focused on Cory's face. "Your stepdaughter. Gracie Schaffer."

Cory threw his head back against the high backrest and laughed out loud. "You've got to be kidding! Where in the world did you hear that? My God, the girl is twenty-five years younger than me. Do I look like a pedophile to you?"

Detective Miles' smile tightened. "From someone who saw you both in a rather compromising position."

At that, Cory sobered. He leaned forward and looked Detective Miles directly in the eye. Harrison watched for any sign of dishonesty, any guilt.

"Gracie is having trouble dealing with her mother's gruesome murder. She's had a very difficult life—an abusive father, being in a boarding school. Never having any semblance of a family except for nuns." He took a breath, and continued. "Compromising position? Yes, maybe I hug her more than I should. Maybe she responds to those hugs more intensely than *she* should. I have made it a point to let her know I am here for her whenever she needs or wants a friend. People here talk. More so now that Patricia is gone. They realize Gracie and I are now living by ourselves . . ." His lips twitched. "I'm aware of the gossip. The rumors that have spread throughout this resort like a cancer, eating away and destroying innocent people's reputations."

Cory swiveled in his chair and picked up a picture alongside his computer. "Do you see this woman? She was the sweetest, most loving and caring wife a man could ever have. I would never do anything to hurt her. Not while she was alive, and not now either."

Harrison shifted in the comfortable chair.

Miles's fingers tapped against one another. "Have you and Gracie been arguing a lot? Since Mrs. Marsh's death?"

"Arguing?" Cory shrugged and placed the picture of Patricia on the edge of his desk. "I wouldn't call it that. The girl has always been . . . um, difficult. She reminded me of a small, untamed, and wild animal. I tried to tame her as did her mother—with genuine affection and concern. But I never carried that affection into some illicit affair, if that's what you're thinking." He ran his hands through his hair and sat back. "Gracie might have misinterpreted that affection from me. And, to be honest, I found her passionate advances and flirting flattering. There were a few times I did allow my hormones to overrule my brains. I kissed her once. I shouldn't have, but I did. That was the extent of anything remotely close to an affair, Detective. I continue to discourage her advances and, yes, sometimes that may sound to others like we're arguing."

Officer Harrison detected nothing in Cory's manner to make him doubt the truth of the man's statement. Cory did not flinch, nor did he flush. He held his gaze steady, and that wasn't easy to do while being examined by the best detective in the state.

"Do you have a computer at home, Mr. Marsh?"

An abrupt switch to a new topic. Harrison recognized this tactic, used to throw the subject off balance. Cory's expression did not change.

"No, I don't." He nodded toward the one on his computer desk. "I use this one for business, and for the occasional personal e-mail. It's a notebook, so I can take it home if I need to."

"Would you mind if we took a look?"

Cory shook his head. "I'm sorry. I have access to confidential guest records and financial data. I can't let you use my computer without a search warrant."

"We'll get one if we need it. Of course that means we'll return with a sheriff to serve it." Detective Miles smiled. "Sheriffs' deputies aren't exactly quiet when it comes to delivering warrants, you know."

For the first time Cory's expression changed. An angry red flooded his cheeks. "What do you want to see on my computer?"

Detective Miles's shoulders twitched upward. "Just your Internet history."

"If you're looking for porn sites, I'm not into that. Anyway, we have a filter here that prevents us from accessing sites like that."

"Does it block you from Web sites on oleander and poisonous and deadly plants in Florida?"

His lips a tight line, Cory glared across his desk. "Fine. Check it right now. With me watching."

At Miles's nod, Officer Harrison set down his notebook and rounded the desk. Cory swiveled his chair around to watch as Harrison opened Internet Explorer and displayed the history list. The guy obviously didn't do a lot of surfing. The list only showed about two dozen sites, mostly on camping supplies Web sites and news sites, like *CNN* and *USA Today*. Nothing that looked like a site on poisonous plants. Harrison clicked over to the Options window, then turned to look at Detective Miles.

"It's set to keep history for seven days."

Detective Miles gave a humorless smile. "Inconclusive, then."

Cory's face remained impassive. Harrison closed the window and returned to his seat as Miles resumed his questioning.

"Do you mind telling me where you were from six A.M. on March third until ten-thirty A.M. the same day?"

If the detective hoped to rattle Cory's composure by bouncing from topic to topic, it didn't seem to be working. "As you well know, I answered that question the first time you interrogated me. I was up all night the night before because Patricia was very ill. The next morning, the morning in question, she was resting and I had to leave to get some things done at the office. Gracie said she'd be there and would look after her and call me if anything happened or if Patricia got worse. The next thing I knew, she was running over here in hysterics. That was about ten. Patricia had wandered off while Gracie was notarizing some papers that Norma brought over. When Gracie realized this, she went searching for her mother and found her, burned to death on the beach."

Detective Miles's eyebrows rose. "You just left her? Your wife, I mean. Not knowing how she'd be when she woke?"

"I have a resort to run," Cory reminded him. "I don't always have the privilege of being able to be where I want. I had checks that had to be signed for vendors and activities that needed my approval."

"Was anyone else here with you?"

Cory shook his head. "It was early. Six A.M. The office personnel don't arrive until seven-thirty or eight. If you need proof, I'm sure the office security cameras recorded my arrival. You can probably get the records from our security service and see when I turned the alarm off to get in the door."

Officer Harrison didn't need Detective Miles's glance to tell him to write down that piece of information in his notebook.

"Who is your security service, sir?" Harrison asked.

"Interceptor. I'll call and tell them to give you whatever you need." Cory looked at the detective again. "All I ask is that you be discreet as you verify my statement. As I've told you, a campground is breeding ground for gossip. As the owner and operator of this resort, I don't need a scandal racing through the grapevine or to have something picked up by the media."

"Of course," Detective Miles assured him, and then he rose.

Officer Harrison got to his feet as well, pocketing his notebook and pen.

Cory stood, but remained behind his desk. "I have an early meeting with the Florida Association of RV Parks and Campgrounds tomorrow in Tallahassee, and I planned to drive up this evening to spend the night. Leaving town is acceptable, I assume?"

Tight lines around the edges of his lips were the only signs of the man's anger at having to ask permission to leave town.

Detective Miles shrugged and then gave a single nod. "We'll be in touch," he said as he opened the door.

Even to officer Harrison, it sounded like a threat.

Twenty-Four

David and Laura had had their fill of clubhouse potlucks. They had spent the afternoon with Jeremy and Katie barbecuing hot dogs and hamburgers, laughing and joking, and finally relaxing, putting murder on the back burner for the day. When they arrived back at their motor home David hit the play button of their recorder.

"Hello, David and Laura? This is Lorraine Reed at the Saint John's County Library. Remember that book we looked for yesterday? I found it. It was mis-shelved. Someone put it under fiction, in the Cs. I can't imagine how that happened, because the author's name starts with an F, not a C, and obviously an encyclopedia on poisonous plants isn't fiction. Anyway, I've put it on hold for you guys, if you want to come by and pick it up. Thanks. Bye."

"Wow!" David said. "This is big, really big."

"Here we go again," Laura said.

"No matter what Lorraine thought, no library worker would make such a mistake."

Laura plopped down on the sofa. "Maybe some lazy patron dropped the book on the wrong shelf."

"I don't think so."

"The gut-instinct thing again?" Laura asked.

"Yeah."

Laura smiled as she watched David pick up the phone and dial what she presumed was the detective's number.

"Meet us at the library, Detective," David said into the mouthpiece of the phone.

Laura stood up and grabbed her purse off the dinette table. "To the library, I gather?"

"Come on," David said.

Twenty minutes later David and Laura catapulted through the library door at something just short of a run to find Officer Harrison waiting for them. He stood leaning against Lorraine's desk, dressed in jeans and a blue t-shirt.

"Odd place for a meeting," he said with a grin.

David stopped in the middle of the floor. He'd hoped to find Detective Miles, not his sidekick, waiting for them.

Lorraine rose from her chair. "Hi guys, I see you got my message. I put your book over here on the hold shelf."

"Don't touch it!" David said, a little louder than he'd intended.

The librarian turned a surprised expression David's way, her hand hovering above the book. "Why not?"

"Yes, Mr. Jennings," said a familiar voice from behind. "Why don't you tell us all?"

David whirled to see Detective Miles striding through the door, his ever-present smile plastered to his face.

At least the detective could make things happen. David took two steps toward the man and grabbed his arm.

"Detective, we found the book Patricia's killer used to identify the poisonous oleander."

Detective Miles's attention turned from David to Laura, and then to Officer Harrison, before settling back to David. "Since the book turned up here and not in the killer's possession, how can that help us find the killer?"

Laura jumped in to reply before David could open his mouth. "This book is a plant encyclopedia with pictures. The killer came here to find pictures of deadly plants that grow in Florida. Like oleander. Oleanders are all over the resort. They got the book, found the pictures, drew them into the journal I found, then hid the plant book in the fiction section before anyone saw him or her reading it."

Detective Miles nodded slowly. "That is a plausible explanation, but how does that apprehend the murderer?"

"Don't you see?" Laura stomped her foot. "Fingerprints! Dust the book for fingerprints. That's what *CSI* would do."

David smiled. He loved it when Laura got passionate about something. There was no stopping her.

"*CSI* has Grissom, Mrs. Jennings. We do not."

"Are you saying you can't dust for fingerprints?" David asked.

"Of course we can dust for fingerprints. And we collected a good set of prints from the cover and pages of the journal as well. But AFIS didn't have a match."

Officer Harrison explained, "In order to identify an individual using fingerprints, they must be on file with the criminal justice system database that stores the prints of—"

Laura cut him off. "I know what AFIS is."

"Ah, yes." Detective Miles awarded her a long-suffering smile. "*CSI* again."

Laura wanted to scream. Was it because she was a woman that they wouldn't listen?

"At least you could try," David said. "If nothing else, you might be able to match some prints on the book with the ones you got from the journal."

The detective gave a tiny nod. "All right. Anything that can help us piece together the killer's steps leading up to the crime will help." He looked up. "Harrison, bag the book."

Laura let out a whoosh of breath. Thank goodness.

Officer Harrison retrieved the evidence kit from his police car and placed the book in a big zipper bag. David saw that it was an oversize paperback with, thankfully, a coated cover that would with luck yield a good set of prints.

"Hey," said Lorraine as they turned to leave. "You can't take that book without checking it out. Library policy."

They all froze. Harrison and Miles exchanged glances, momentarily stumped.

"I guess we could call the judge at home and get a warrant," Officer Harrison suggested.

Honestly, men could be so simpleminded at times. Shaking her head in their direction, Laura reached into her purse for her library card. "Here you go, Lorraine. I'll be responsible for the book."

"That's my girl," David said.

At twelve-thirty the following day, Laura parked her car a block from Pizanno's Italian restaurant. The resort took a vote as to where this month's ladies luncheon would be held, and Pizanno's won hands down. As she locked her car and headed down the street, she remembered how upset everyone was that she was going to the luncheon.

David, Jeremy, and Katie had tried to talk Laura out of it, David reminding her of her promise to man the office. "Cory's there," she'd argued. "Besides, the office won't be busy midweek."

She had not been happy when David reached into the purse draped over her shoulder and pulled out her digital recorder.

"Well, you're not taking this with you," he'd said. "Illegal recording devices. You're getting carried away with this case."

She tried to get it back from him, but to no avail. "Keep it," she'd told him. "I won't need it anyway."

She hurried down the street toward the restaurant. She was ten minutes early, and hopefully Katie would be here soon. Or Terrie, or Norma, or somebody. Laura's stomach twisted tighter than a noose at the thought of facing Gracie alone. The girl had been acting squirrelly for the past several days. Laura had even caught her snooping around their motor home the day before. When Laura questioned her about it, Gracie gave some lame excuse about looking for a ring she'd lost in the flowerbed around their site.

"Psst. Mrs. Jennings."

Laura's step slowed as she approached the corner of the red brick building that housed the restaurant. She surveyed the small parking lot, but she didn't see anyone.

"Over here."

From inside a dark blue sedan, Officer Harrison gestured for her to approach. When she drew near, Laura leaned down to look through the open window and saw Detective Miles in the driver's seat. He did not wear a smile today. In fact, he was glaring at her.

"What are you doing here, Mrs. Jennings?" he demanded. "You're supposed to be volunteering for office duty at the campground."

"I know." Laura glanced around quickly. If someone saw her talking to the cops, her cover would be blown for sure. "I couldn't stand it. Norma might need my help."

"Help with what?" Officer Harrison asked. "She looks perfectly capable of eating lunch without assistance."

Laura rolled her eyes. "You know what I mean."

"No, I don't. Ms. Rowland is going to have lunch, period. She's not going to ask any questions. She's not going to do anything except eat a plate of lasagna. You know that."

Yes, Laura knew the plan that had been hatched last night in police headquarters. Though they had enough evidence to pick Gracie up for questioning, everyone agreed that doing so was sure to stir up a media and campground extravaganza. Better to avoid that until they had solid proof. Jeremy was the one who had actually come up with the plan. David, Laura, Katie, and Jeremy were to stay at the campground, with Laura volunteering at the office. Detective Miles and Officer Harrison were to wait until today's lunch was nearly over, and then they would enter Pizanno's through the delivery door in the rear and ask the server to retrieve Gracie's water glass as unobtrusively as possible. They'd decided to wait until the meal was nearly over so as not to cause undue stress to the server, who might give away the scheme with nervous behavior.

Then they would take Gracie's fingerprints from the glass. With luck, the prints would match the ones they'd lifted from the journal and hoped to lift from the poisonous-plant book. Then they would have enough evidence to arrest her.

All morning long, Laura had been unable to concentrate on the paperwork at the office. So she left and told David and the others of her plans. They'd all put forth so much effort on this case, robbing her of a honeymoon. It didn't seem fair that Norma and Terrie got to be there for the grand finale, while she sat behind a desk checking in campers.

She nudged her lower lip out a tiny bit and looked from Detective Miles to Officer Harrison with wide, hopefully innocent-looking, Caribbean-blue eyes. "I just want to be there. I can eat a salad or something like the others. I promise I won't say anything."

Detective Miles heaved a resigned sigh. "See that you don't."

Officer Harrison watched Laura disappear around the corner of the building, a feeling of unease churning deep in the pit of his stomach. That girl was getting too nosy for her own good. Yes, she had helped lead them to the one person he firmly believed was the murderer. But Gracie maliciously murdered her own mother and attempted to plant evidence and suspicion in other directions. Gracie was becoming more and more paranoid. More and more psychotic, Harrison thought. What if she made Laura her next target?

"I don't like it," he said, staring at the edge of the building.

Detective Miles sighed. "I don't like it either. But short of handcuffing her in the backseat, I don't see how we could have stopped her."

Norma and Terrie had already arrived and selected a round table near the big picture window to the left of the front door when Laura entered the restaurant.

"Why, Laura," Norma exclaimed when she stepped inside, "I didn't know you planned to join us today."

Laura forced a smile and tried to act normal. The police had contacted Jeremy to arrange their meeting, after Detective Miles had questioned Norma again yesterday. Norma knew nothing of the importance of today's lunch, and Laura wasn't about to tell Miss Queen Busybody.

"I had such a good time with you guys at the potlucks I decided to come today, too."

Terrie waved to the server and called across the small room. "Can we pull up another chair? There's plenty of room."

At that moment old Stella Greenburg came through the door with Ethel Krantz. They proclaimed themselves delighted over Laura's presence. Just as they were about to be seated, the door opened again.

Gracie Schaffer, wearing an elegant light pink pantsuit with a white eyelet blouse, stepped into the restaurant. Laura's heart skipped a beat as she willed her breathing to remain steady.

"Gracie, sit here," she said, indicating the seat beside her. Her voice came out sharper than she intended. The ladies' heads turned to give her an odd look. "I've been . . . saving it for you," she finished with a lame smile.

"Thank you, Laura. That was sweet of you."

As Gracie hung her handbag over the chair back, she looked nervous. A smile flashed onto her face and disappeared just as quickly. Her eyes darted around the table, stopping when they returned to Laura.

"I thought you were working in the office today."

Laura shrugged. "Cory said he could handle things. I've wanted to try this restaurant before leaving Saint Augustine. What better way than with the friends I've met at Harbor Lights?"

She avoided Gracie's eyes, aware that she looked as if she wanted to snatch Laura by the hair and march her out of the restaurant. The others watched the two of them with varying expressions of curiosity.

Laura picked up a menu and allowed her smile to sweep around the table. "What's good here?"

"The veal Parmesan is to die for," Terrie said, peering at her own menu.

"And their antipasto is the best," added Gracie. "Cory and I have had it a number of times."

"Lasagna for me." Norma slapped her menu closed.

The server approached to take their orders, pen poised over a small notebook.

"We need water," Laura demanded.

Heads swiveled toward her. Had her voice been a little too loud? She felt jumpy, her nerves stretched to the limit. She took a breath. If she didn't calm down, she would blow the whole thing.

"I'm parched," she explained with an apologetic shrug.

The women placed their orders, and the server left. Laura turned in her chair to stare after the woman. She seemed distracted, but not necessarily nervous. Obviously Detective Miles and Officer Harrison hadn't enlisted her help yet.

Within minutes, the waitress returned and set a glass of ice water in front of each of them. They all watched as Laura picked hers up and drank noisily. She eyed Gracie's glass. The smooth surface would hold a fingerprint perfectly. Good.

"I hope that detective didn't upset you again, Norma. I saw him badgering you this morning," Gracie said.

Laura's head jerked toward Gracie. What nerve, setting Norma up to look guilty with that journal and then asking about her in that oh-so-concerned voice. And why wasn't she drinking her water?

"It was just routine stuff," Norma announced. "He wasn't badgering me at all."

"I heard you weren't feeling too good, Norma," Stella said. "Was it the flu or something?"

Laura stopped herself from jumping in. Yeah, it was something all right. Something like tainted coffee.

"It was food poisoning," Laura announced. "Isn't that what you said the doctor in the emergency room told you, Norma?"

Terrie caught her eye and gave a nearly imperceptible shake of her head.

What? Laura was only trying to protect Norma from a vicious killer.

One who still had not touched her water glass. Laura picked up her own glass again. Maybe seeing someone else drink would make Gracie thirsty. Her hand shook with nerves as she held the rim to her lips.

"Well, I'm glad you're feeling better now," Stella said.

"Thank you," Norma said. "The doctor thought it might be food poisoning, but after a few tests he said it was probably some twenty-four-hour thing going around."

Laura drained her glass. Everyone else had at least taken a sip or two, but still Gracie made no move to drink her water. What was the woman, a camel?

"My, Laura," Gracie exclaimed. "You are thirsty."

She turned, her hand partially raised to signal the server to refill Laura's glass. But the server had left the dining room, probably to turn in their orders.

"Here," Gracie said, a gracious smile on her tastefully colored lips, "have mine."

Time seemed to stumble. As if watching a slow-motion replay on television. Laura saw Gracie's arm extend. She opened her mouth to protest, but Gracie's hand grasped the glass, all five fingers touching its smooth sides. She picked it up and set it down in front of Laura.

"I drank a bottle of water in the car on the way here, so I'm not thirsty."

A tornado spun in her mind. Gracie not thirsty? That meant she wouldn't request another glass of water. And when Detective Miles and Harrison asked for her glass, the server wouldn't know to give them the one now in front of Laura.

The one with Gracie's fingerprints on it.

The plan lay before Laura in shreds. She had to do something. Something drastic.

She turned a smile on Gracie. "Thank you."

Judging by the sudden creases between Gracie's eyebrows, Laura failed to make her smile look natural. No time to think about that now. Blood surged in her ears in rhythm to an urgent voice whispering *Hurry, hurry, hurry* in her mind.

Laura made a show of reaching for her own glass, to move it out of the way. In the process, she bumped the full one hard enough to knock it over. Water sloshed across the table like a tidal wave. Norma jumped to her feet, and Terrie and Stella jerked their chairs backward to avoid getting drenched.

"Here," commanded Ethel, taking charge, "give me your napkins."

Grabbing the cloth napkin draped across her lap, Laura

leaped to her feet. Her chair tumbled backward and crashed to the floor.

"I'll get more napkins," she shouted, cringing at the unintended volume of her voice.

But instead of tossing her napkin onto the quickly spreading puddle, she covered the now-empty water glass and snatched it up.

"Uh, and more water."

She whirled and ran in the direction of the kitchen, aware that she had drawn the openmouthed stares of everyone in the restaurant. As she burst through the swinging door that led to the kitchen, she heard Stella say, "My goodness, she's an odd girl, isn't she?"

Equipment and people crowded the small kitchen. Laura ignored their surprised exclamations as she dashed toward the far wall and the door she spied there, carrying the all-important water glass, its evidence safe beneath her napkin.

Outside in the sunshine, she came to a sudden stop, casting her eyes wildly around the back alley. Deserted. Where were Detective Miles and Officer Harrison?

She took off down the alley at a jog. When she reached the corner of the brick building, her eyes were drawn to the detectives' car and two figures in the front seat. Yes, there they sat, their heads turned away from her, waiting for the right time to approach the restaurant.

At that moment a voice froze her blood.

Gracie's voice.

"Laura, where in the world are you going?"

"What does she think she's doing?"

Officer Harrison followed Detective Miles's gaze to the back of the parking lot in time to see Laura screech to a halt on the loose gravel covering the pavement.

"No clue," he answered. "But what's that in her hand?"
Detective Miles's jaw tightened. "Looks like a glass."

Laura whirled. Gracie had followed her through the restaurant's back door. Her purse clutched in manicured fingers, the elegant killer advanced at a fast walk.

"Uh, nowhere," Laura stammered. "I, uh, just needed some air. It was really hot in there."

"No, it wasn't."

Laura took a couple of steps backward as Gracie drew near.

"Stuffy, then," she corrected. "I need to take a walk."

"You're acting strangely, Laura. More than usual. And what are you doing with my glass?"

Laura's mouth dried in an instant. Gracie still stood in the shelter of the building. If she could just get her to take another step or two, Miles and Harrison would be able to see her. She edged backward.

"Glass? What do you mean?"

Officer Harrison heaved a frustrated breath. Didn't that girl understand the concept of a plan?

He reached for the door handle. "I'll get it from her."

"No, wait!" The urgency in Detective Miles's whisper stopped him the second before he opened the door. "She's talking to someone."

Gracie took another step. Laura faced forward, desperately wanting to look in the direction of the detectives' car but terrified to do so. What if Gracie followed her glance and saw the police waiting in the parking lot? What would she do?

"You figured it out, didn't you?"

Laura's heart leaped into her throat. "Figured what out?"

Gracie shook her head slowly, her eyes boring into Laura's.

"I'm guessing everything. My mother, my journal, the oleander, Cory and me. Norma talked, didn't she? She told you about seeing me that day. On the beach. With my mother."

One more step, just one more. Blood roared in Laura's ears as she edged backward once again.

"Get down," Detective Miles muttered.

Officer Harrison mimicked the detective and sank down in the seat. He peeked over the door panel and saw Laura take a backward step. Her body was so tense, she looked as if she might shatter into a million pieces any minute. Her hand trembled violently as it clutched the napkin-draped glass.

A woman moved into view, her eyes fixed on Laura as she took a determined step forward.

His lungs emptied as he watched the killer advance toward Laura.

"You admit you killed your mother?" Her eyes still locked on Gracie's, Laura spoke as loudly as she dared. Was Detective Miles's window down? Was Harrison listening?

"She was never satisfied unless she was screwing up my life. Or someone else's."

"You mean like sending you to boarding school? And divorcing your dad?"

Gracie took another step. "No, not like boarding school or my dad. Like Cory. Me and Cory."

The glass in Laura's hand quivered like a bobble-head hula doll. "You murdered your mother to be with Cory?"

Gracie's laugh came out in a short blast. "You don't understand. My mother didn't understand, either. I tried to talk to her, tried to explain that it was me Cory wanted to be with. Tried to get her to go away."

"And Norma? You tried to set up your best friend."

Gracie shrugged. Her right hand moved slowly toward her left side, where her purse dangled from her shoulder.

What was she doing? Laura's heart threatened to pound through her chest. Did Gracie have a gun in her purse?"

"She's going for a weapon!"

Laura was in danger! Officer Harrison reacted blindly. Pulse racing, he jerked upright in the seat and threw open the door. As he tumbled out of the car, he unsnapped his holster and drew the weapon in one smooth motion. When his feet hit the pavement, he dashed around the rear of the sedan, elbows locked, both hands clutching the grips straight in front of him.

Dimly aware of Detective Miles close on his heels, he ran toward the two women, shouting.

"Police! Move an inch and you're dead!"

Relief wilted Laura's muscles as Officer Harrison dashed forward and thrust himself between her and Gracie.

Stunned, Gracie's hand froze halfway out of her purse holding . . .

A tissue.

"Both hands up, Ms. Schaffer," Detective Miles said. His level tone restored a sense of calm in the situation. "I'll take the purse."

Gracie calmly blotted a bead of sweat from her forehead before complying. As he lifted the purse strap over her raised arm, a sneer twisted her stylishly lipsticked mouth. "I guess the gossipmongers at the campground will have plenty to yap about now."

Laura's knees wobbled as the detective took the handcuffs from Harrison's belt and cuffed Gracie's hands behind her back as he read her the Miranda rights. Only when she had been secured did Officer Harrison lower his gun and whirl to look at Laura.

"You okay?"

"Fine."

Before the detective led the handcuffed Gracie toward his car, he turned his glance on Laura. He took the glass, wrapped in the napkin, from Laura's grip. "Go home. Get some rest. It's over now."

By midafternoon the next day, Laura had almost succeeded in forgetting about all that had transpired since she and David had arrived at Harbor Lights RV Resort.

It was easy to feel cut off and restored, sitting out at the pool with David, the warm afternoon sunlight tempered by balmy breezes. She had briefly debated going back to the motor home to put on a swimsuit and work on her tan, as Katie was doing with striking results. She had decided she didn't want to bother. She was comfortable in her t-shirt and shorts. That was good enough.

She heard the pool entrance gate open, followed shortly thereafter by Jeremy's greeting.

"Watson! Sherlock! I'm glad I found you two here."

Moments later, Jeremy came onto the pool deck and sat in a lounge chair between Laura and Katie. He dragged his cooler closer to his feet. "What can I get you guys to drink?"

"Well, what I'd *like* is a triple margarita," Katie said, "but what I'll ask is—did you bring some of your great sun tea?"

"Tea?" David laughed. "You want tea? Even now that we know for sure that was what Gracie used to slowly kill her mother?"

A lab had finally confirmed their suspicions. Detective Miles had called them early that morning to let them know that the State was charging Gracie with first-degree murder. The police believed that she had deliberately and liberally laced her mother's herbal tea with boiled-down oleander leaves—and that she had tried to poison Norma in the same way.

Both Jeremy and Laura shook their heads as Katie pulled a chair over and sat at the round concrete patio table, moving her hands nervously. "It's times like this," she said, "that I really miss smoking. I would purely love to have a cigarette now. Ten cigarettes. I'm kind of frazzled."

"I could put a little vodka in that tea," Jeremy suggested.

"Well, maybe a little wouldn't hurt. I just don't feel like talking to anybody anymore. Except you guys."

"You would not believe how many campers made it a point to drop by today," David said.

"Some of them have a valid concern," Laura said. "They're worried about the stability of the campground. Many paid up front for months in advance. The newest gossip is that Cory plans on selling the resort and heading back to Georgia."

Katie nodded. "This has all been so overwhelming. I still feel like some wispy little leaf swirling around in a hurricane of rumors."

"Just on the way over here, I must have run into half a dozen people who wanted to know what was going on. I'm just glad it's over." Jeremy handed a glass of iced tea to Katie.

"It's not over yet," David said. "There's still the trial."

"You and Laura are staying for it, aren't you?" Katie asked, sipping her drink.

"Of course," Laura said.

David let out a laugh. "And she said she wasn't enjoying it here."

"Let's make it a group outing," Jeremy said. "The Four Musketeers."

They held up their glasses and clanked them together.

"I for one want to see them toss the book at little Lizzie Borden," Jeremy said.

David nodded. "Bet that's going to be one crowded courthouse."

TWENTY-FIVE

Opening day of testimony in the first-degree murder trial of Gracie Schaffer was a busy one, with seven witnesses called.

But the most significant of those witnesses was Norma Rowland, office assistant manager and queen of the Harbor Lights RV Resort's busybody club. Norma testified that Gracie stated she was planning to get rid of her mother for good one week before Patricia Marsh's demise.

"She told me she hated her mother for always thinking she knew what was best for her life, and that she was planning to get rid of her once and for all," an emotional Norma told the jurors. "I was concerned enough to tell Cory, but he didn't take me serious. He just kind of laughed it off and told me to mind my own business.

"I was afraid and a little freaked out about what Gracie told me, but I also didn't want to lose my job. Then I started thinking that Gracie was just blowing off steam. I didn't think she literally meant what she'd told me."

Norma's testimony didn't stop there. She also said Gracie had gone into detail about how she planned to "get rid of her" by saying, "She had no use for me and I damn sure don't have any for her. I'll poison the bitch and see her burn."

There was an echo of gasps throughout the courtroom.

Norma's testimony was the subject of much dispute lasting several days, as defense attorney Christy Trey, objecting, cited Norma's testimony as hearsay evidence. Judge Michael Turner ruled early Monday morning that, although Norma was testifying as to what she heard, and even though she did have a reputation as a gossipmonger, she was still accurate in what Gracie had stated and what had occurred.

The judge's ruling came after Gracie Schaffer took the stand Friday morning, before the jury was called in, testifying to her side of the conversation with Norma Rowland. Gracie said the only reason she had told Norma she planned to get rid of her mother for good was in hope that Norma would talk her out of it.

Gracie was looking for "advice and counsel" from a friend— from Norma. Gracie testified she was "under a tremendous amount of stress, anxiety, and frustration."

"I wanted to share with Norma some thoughts I was having," Gracie said. "I wanted to share things in confidence. I didn't think she'd go blabbing to Terrie and anyone else who'd listen."

Gracie added, "I did not intend to follow through with actually getting rid of my mother. By poisoning her. Dragging her body out to the beach. Setting her on fire. Those are events that just took place."

State Attorney Jessica Sanders grilled Gracie during cross-examination, and she asked Gracie, "Why would you need to be talked out of a murder that you had no intention of actually committing?"

"I didn't want to murder my mother! I wanted Norma to give me advice, that's all," Gracie said.

"How does Norma telling you not to kill count as advice?" Sanders said. "How is that friendship?"

"I—I . . ."

"Why would you need to go into detail? About your special brewed tea recipe, the one with, I think you said to Norma, 'with just a hint of sweet oleander.' Why go into grisly details about seeing your mother burn to ashes? Why, Ms. Schaffer? If you had not intended to follow through with the premeditated murder of your mother? Are you trying to craft a story around Norma's testimony and the appellate court ruling?"

"No!" Gracie said.

In overruling Christy Trey's objection, Judge Turner said it was a "stretch" to say Gracie's statement to Norma was hearsay evidence. Christy lodged a standing objection to the testimony, but the jury heard it anyway.

While Norma's testimony was certainly the most controversial of the day, the State called six other witnesses Friday, including Cory Schaffer, Terrie Whitmore, Jeremy Myers, David and Laura Jennings, and Detective Bradley Miles.

Jurors also heard Gracie's 911 call, made on Cory's cell phone from the beach crime scene, in which she said, "My mother has been burned to death."

Following the 911 call, jurors heard information about the crime scene from Detective Bradley Miles, the first to respond to the scene; Deputy Harrison, who backed up Detective Miles at the scene; and Lieutenant Steve Backus of St. Johns County Fire Department.

All three men said Gracie was calm and polite at the crime scene and that it was her stepfather, Cory Schaffer, who appeared nervous, agitated, and "out of it." They also testified to the large amount of the victim's remains that were missing from the charred corpse.

After six hours of grueling and emotional testimony, Judge Turner called for a two-hour recess. Gracie was scheduled to take the stand again at four P.M., after that recess.

"It's so obvious she's guilty," Laura said as they headed out of the courtroom. "I don't understand why it's so necessary to keep going over the crime scene details."

"I feel sorry for Cory," David said.

Standing in front of the St. Johns courthouse, Jeremy pointed across the street. "There's a sandwich shop. What do you say? Anyone hungry?"

"After that photo show, I doubt I can eat anything. Maybe soup," Katie said.

They headed across the street to the deli. After they were seated with menus, soup appeared to be the unanimous order.

"It's the system. Everyone gets their turn," Jeremy explained about Gracie's trial and the events that unfolded earlier in the day. "When all is said and done, it's just a matter of who had the most convincing testimony and who did the jurors believe. Sometimes the guilty go free, sometimes the innocent are incarcerated. It's called American justice."

"Yeah, O.J. Simpson knows all about that," David said.

"I think that state's attorney, Tate, is getting to Gracie," Laura said. "She seems to be able to see through Gracie's Pollyanna masquerade right to the Lizzie Borden boarding school psycho she is."

"Can we talk about something else while we eat?" Katie was drained from the day in court. It showed in the droopiness of the outer area of her eyes.

They finished their lunch and headed back to the courthouse. Everyone was seated inside except Cory, who was waiting outside the courtroom on one of the benches, head bowed, elbows on his knees, hands over his face.

David placed a hand on his shoulder. "You okay, Cory? Need anything?"

Cory looked up. "No thanks, David. Guess we better get inside."

Gracie was asked to take the stand as the judge reminded her she was still under oath.

The prosecutor, Madelyn Beltz, stood before Gracie. Dressed in a blue-gray suit, red blouse, black heels, and frosted beige hair that was French-braided, the fifteen-year veteran of the St.

Johns County District Attorney's office stood tall with her hands locked behind her back.

"Gracie Schaffer, did you maliciously plan and execute the murder of Patricia Marsh? Your mother?"

Gracie sat silently staring, her jaw clenched.

"Let me rephrase my question, did you or did you not describe to Norma Rowland exactly how you planned to murder your mother? And did your mother die the exact way you'd described your plan to Norma? Or didn't she?"

Gracie continued to sit still . . . silent. The entire courtroom became eerily quiet. Gracie was nervously tapping her fingertips on the top of her lap.

"Go ahead, Ms. Schaffer, answer the question."

Gracie gave the judge a quick look before staring at prosecutor Madelyn Beltz with wild-looking, glazed eyes. Her jaw was clenched, her teeth clamped together. Then it happened. Gracie snapped.

"Yes! I did it! I killed my mother!" Gracie screamed as she popped up from the witness chair. Hands flailing, body shaking, veins protruding from her neck, she venomously spat out the confession.

The judge wrapped his gavel repeatedly on the oak desk. "Ms. Schaffer, please! Sit down now or you'll be charged with contempt."

Like an obedient child, Gracie sat.

"Go on, Gracie. You were saying?" Madelyn continued.

Still in a raised voice, but not a scream, and still looking like a possessed beast, Gracie said, "I killed her. So what?" Her eyes turned away from the prosecutor and her wild-eyed stare landed smack on Cory's face. "I did it for *you*," she screeched, shaking a pointed finger. "I did it for *us*."

Judge Turner banged his gavel again. "I'm warning you, Ms Schaffer!"

The loud banging of the judge's gavel seemed to quiet the demons inside Gracie. She slouched back and began to talk as if in a hypnotic state. "She deserved it."

"Speak up, Ms. Schaffer," Madelyn said.

"Cory was mine. He loved me. But she was determined to keep him from me, too. Just like she kept my father from me. Just like she took my life from me. Packed me up, tossed me away. The Bible says, 'An eye for an eye.' Well, I took her life like she took mine.

"Cory was going to change all that. He was my only chance for a new life. I finally had someone who loved me. When my mom got sick, it was my chance to take care of her. All I had to do was add a little flavoring to her favorite tea. Oleander. Sweet, sweet oleander." As she went on, the smile on Gracie's face never disappeared.

"A few pieces from a leaf each day. Not too much. I couldn't rush things. All in due time. Sicker. Sicker. Finally, she was gone.

"But not quite!" Gracie let out a little giggle. "I had to get rid of her for good. Make her disappear. Get my ring off her left-hand finger. That was mine, too! Damn thing wouldn't budge and I couldn't worry about it now—later.

"I grabbed her legs and pulled her off the bed. Plop! I dragged her out of the bedroom, down the hall, and out the back door. No one around. Only a hundred and two steps to the beach." For the first time, Gracie looked at Madelyn. "I know. I counted the steps many times." Gracie turned away from Madelyn and went back to staring into space as she went on.

"The beach. The private one. The secluded one. I grabbed the gasoline can I'd stored under the rocks at the entrance of the beach. I let go of her legs and let her drop. I covered her with the fuel." She looked back at Madelyn. "I always loved the smell of gasoline." She turned back away. "I lit the match. *Poof!* Fire everywhere. It smelled like a burnt barbeque. I could still see my mother's face so I said, 'Burn in hell.' Then there was nothing but smoldering bones. The finger. I snapped it off, gathered the ashes around it, and yanked the ring off. My ring. I burned my finger." Gracie raised her right hand and rubbed her thumb and forefinger. "I shoved what was left of her around the beach with my foot.

"She wanted a cruise. Bugged the hell out of poor Cory. She just wanted to take him away from me. Separate us. I shoved some of her ashes into a bottle I also hid behind the rocks. The finger bones just kind of disintegrated as I shoved them into the bottle. I sat down. Took the wax from behind the rocks and sealed the bottle cork tight. I walked to the edge of the water and tossed it out as far as I could. 'Bon voyage, Mama.' Then I went to Cory." She turned her head to the front row of benches where Cory sat.

David leaned into Laura and whispered, "You missed your calling, Detective Laura Jennings."

Everyone had had it. There was silence again. The judge called for a thirty-minute recess.

There would be no need for the jurors to deliberate now on a guilty or not guilty verdict.

Two weeks later, back in court, the judge asked Gracie to stand for the sentencing. As she was bound in hand and feet restraints, her public defender helped her up.

"Gracie Schaffer, for the first-degree intentional homicide of Patricia Marsh, you are sentenced to life in prison, plus an additional forty years for arson and ten years for mutilating a corpse."

No one gasped. No one was surprised.

The judge then added, "An eye for an eye, Ms. Schaffer.

Now, will you please face your victim's survivor, Cory Marsh."

Gracie looked at Cory and smiled.

"Mr. Marsh, is there anything you'd like to say to your wife's killer?"

"Yes, Your Honor, there is," Cory said. He stood. Solemnly, choking back tears, he looked at Gracie. "With seduction, manipulation, and evil, careful planning, you murdered my wife and the woman who did everything in her power to love and protect you. I have only one thing to say to you." Cory placed his right hand across his chest. "You didn't kill all of her, Gracie." He patted his chest gently. "The most beautiful part of my Patricia—her soul—is here. Very much alive in the center of my heart. She will remain there forever. Loved and protected." Cory turned away and walked out of the courtroom.

Gracie was escorted away in leg and arm shackles. She turned her head and shrieked, *"I did it for us, Cory!"*

David and Laura pulled their motor home into the parking lot of St. Augustine beach. Together, hand in hand, they walked to the end of the pier. David looked up at the sound of a seagull screeching above them, then looked down at the bottle in his hand that had mysteriously greeted him and Laura upon their arrival at St. Augustine. Through the trial it had remained bagged and sealed as evidence. Detective Bradley Miles was able to retrieve it for David and Laura after Gracie's sentencing saying, "It's yours. All the evidence we need and have was inside the bottle."

David raised his arm and hurled the bottle far out into the Atlantic. They watched as it bobbed up and down over the waves. The ocean was smooth, the waves coming in with the softest hiss.

"Rest in peace, Patricia Marsh," Laura said.

They turned and headed back to *Passion's Palace*.

"I'll miss Katie and Jeremy," Laura said. "But I don't think I'll miss Saint Augustine."

David smiled at Laura, bent forward and kissed her, then pulled the motor home out of the beach parking lot and onto A1A North. "It's a big country, my love," he said. "And a small world. Who knows? Somewhere down the road we may meet up with Jeremy and Katie again."

ABOUT THE AUTHOR

Award-winning author **JoMarie Grinkiewicz,** who writes under the pen name of April Star, took an unusual route to her writing career. Traveling the roads of America in a travel trailer for sixteen years with her husband, Jerry, she began to write on the road as a means of expressing all her adventures and experiences.

In 1992, shortly after Hurricane Andrew devastated the Homestead, Florida, area, JoMarie and Jerry rolled their travel trailer into a camping resort (which, at the time, appeared to be more of a MASH unit). In an attempt to keep her sanity, JoMarie took a job in the office where she soon discovered INSANITY bred! A year later she became assistant manager and marketing director and in 1996 Jerry joined her in the office with an offer of being campground managers. There they stayed and there is where the REAL stories and characters emerged for what is now a reality—the Wanderlust Mystery Series.

Her debut novel and first title of the series, *Tropical Warnings* (a 2006 release from Five Star Publishing), has gained popularity among mystery fans, RV enthusiasts, and the RV industry.

JoMarie lives in Sebring, Florida, and is again working at an RV resort. She is also an active member of Mystery Writers of America, Romance Writers of America, Sisters in Crime, and the American College of Forensics Examiners International.

About the Author

Stop by and see what reviewers are saying about the Wanderlust Mystery Series at www.authoraprilstar.com.